'What the blue blazes did the boy mean by that?'

Mackenzie tightened his lips. 'That'll be a fine and dandy phrase to teach him, Miss Baxter——'

'Don't twist words with me, *Mr* Mackenzie! You've already told me the boy hears plenty of ripe language from your men. What I want to know is, why did he ask if I'm going to be his new mother? He's already got a mother, hasn't he?'

'It was a child's nonsense, no more. Bairns of that age say all kinds of things——'

'Do they? It's not all nonsense, I'm thinking. "Out of the mouths of babes and sucklings"——'

'I was forgetting you'd be knowing such quotations, you being a professional person.' He might have been trying to flatter her for all she knew, but to Prissy the words were nothing short of insulting.

Sally Blake was born in London, but now lives in Weston-super-Mare. She started writing when her three children went to school and has written many contemporary and historical novels using various pen-names. She loves the research involved in writing historical novels, finding it both exciting and addictive. Conscious of the way that circumstances can change people, she applies this maxim to her fictional characters, providing them with an emotive background in which to grow and develop. *Outback Woman* is Sally Blake's first Masquerade Historical Romance.

OUTBACK WOMAN

JEAN SAUNDERS

Pan Books

First published in Great Britain in 1989 by
Mills and Boon Limited

This edition published 1998 by Pan Books
an imprint of Macmillan Publishers Ltd
25 Eccleston Place, London SW1W 9NF
and Basingstoke

Associated companies throughout the world

ISBN 0 330 37173 8

2 4 6 8 9 7 5 3 1

A CIP catalogue record for this book is available from
the British Library.

Printed by Mackays of Chatham PLC, Chatham, Kent

CHAPTER ONE

RIGHT up until the moment they had finished eating at the small supper party Ma Jenkins had insisted on giving for Priscilla, the other residents in the cheap theatrical lodging-house did their best to persuade to change her mind.

'I still say you don't know what you're letting yourself in for, Prissy,' Ma herself said, sniffing back the emotion that she knew did nothing for her florid face. 'You're a real nice gel, one of the best, and, even if things ain't going well for you now, they've got to be better than going halfway across the world to some heathen land——'

'Australia's not a heathen land, Ma. And everything's proper and above board. The people who interviewed me all insisted that I'll be going to the new land of opportunity.'

Priscilla defended it in the voice that had had more than one group of drunken listeners watery-eyed at her occasional solo singing renditions.

She ignored Ma's mutter that committee folk always said what gullible young girls wanted to hear, and you could never trust what they said anyway, and went on doggedly, 'Besides, I know by now that I'm never going to be a successful singer. Plenty of other girls have got better chances than me, and it's time I faced up to it. What's the use of going on when bookings are getting scarcer every month? And you know very well that being "one of the best" won't pay the rent on my room.'

As Ma Jenkins avoided her eyes, Prissy knew she spoke the truth. And she couldn't stay here on sufferance, however popular she was with Ma and the other boarders. She had too much pride for that.

'You be sure and write to us the minute you set foot on dry land, then,' Ma Jenkins said gruffly. 'We don't want to lose touch with you, or we might think you've vanished over the edge of the earth.'

The rest of the motley group of theatricals who formed the lodgers at 13, Greenway Mews, echoed her words, gallantly overlooking her geographical failings.

'The place won't be the same without your smiling face, ducks, and that's for certain,' Belle, the black-haired magician's assistant, said mournfully.

'And we want you to take this with you for luck,' Ron 'the stupendous rubber-neck' added. 'It's a keepsake, Prissy, something to remember us by. It's from all of us, Ma Jenkins included.'

He thrust the brown paper parcel into her hands, and Prissy unwrapped it with hands that shook a little. She knew only too well the enormity of what she was doing, and perhaps only a girl of her age who was well used to fending for herself would have contemplated such a step. She'd be leaving friends and country behind, everything that was dear and safe and familiar... Some of it *too* familiar, she thought, remembering the unwelcome attentions of the stage-door johnnies, ranging from lords to the showy card-sharps, who thought any girl who went on the stage was fair game for their odious pawing.

She looked down at the bright market-stall plaster model of St Paul's Cathedral the others had put their hard-earned money together to buy for her, and tears stung her eyes. She cleared her throat resolutely. This was no time to be getting maudlin, when everything she owned was packed into two threadbare hold-alls, and this time tomorrow she would be embarking on the greatest journey of a lifetime. A new life...a new world...

'It's lovely, and I'll treasure it always,' she said, the words catching slightly. 'Thank you for thinking of it—all of you.'

'It ain't much, gel.' Ma Jenkins shrugged her ample shoulders. 'And none of us is all that churchified, but when Ron went hunting for summat to give you, it seemed a fitting reminder of your old stamping-ground. We wouldn't like to think you'd forget all about dear old London——'

'I'm never likely to do that! And who knows—I may even come back one day. It's not impossible.'

She spoke with bravado, knowing as she did so that it was the unlikeliest thing in the world. Where would Priscilla Baxter, orphaned and alone in the world, ever find the money to return to England without the government assistance that was sending her to Australia?

She gave a small shiver and Ma Jenkins thrust a glass of brandy into her hand. It wasn't the best. Nothing here was ever the best—except for the warm hearts and generous friendship of these people. Slowly, Prissy looked around at them all, as if to imprint their overblown images on her memory. Some might call them clowns with their blowsy clothes and painted faces and exaggerated mannerisms, but they were the only family she had had for nearly a year and she was going to miss them. She would miss them terribly.

'Give us a song before we all turn in, gel,' Ma Jenkins encouraged her. 'One of me old favourites——'

'Oh, I can't, Ma—not tonight——'

But the street musician with the gaudy neckcloth and soot-blackened moustache was already tuning his old fiddle, and the others were clamouring just as noisily for one of Prissy's songs.

'Nothing sentimental, then,' she said. 'We'd better keep the party jolly, Ma, or I'll end up crying all over the lot of you——'

'And Gawd preserve us from that,' Ma said briskly. 'I ain't put on me best bib and tucker for it to be drowned in tears. How about "The old accordion player with the dimple in 'is chin", then? And we'll all join in.'

Prissy nodded gratefully at this rare moment of understanding from the tough old landlady. Not for anything could she have sung Ma's favourite ditty—'How I'll miss those old familiar faces when I'm far far from home'...

But 'The old accordion player with the dimple in 'is chin' was guaranteed to get them all laughing and joining in, and finishing up the evening on a cheerful note. It was followed by more and more of the same, until Prissy's voice was hoarse, and she had drunk enough of Ma's cheap spirits to make her head spin. Just as well, because it stopped her thinking too much about tomorrow...

'I'm going to bed now,' she said at last. 'If I don't get a good night's sleep I shall never find my way to Gravesend in the morning.'

'Good. Then we can keep you here for ever. Are you sure you don't want any of us to go with you, Prissy? I'll get you lost for sure and nobody will be any the wiser...' Ron slurred.

Prissy shook her head at his nonsense. 'I'd much rather you didn't. I hate goodbyes—I'd rather leave you all sleeping off your thick heads, and go quietly. There's no need for anybody to stir themselves.'

''Cepting me,' Ma said. 'You ain't leaving here without a decent breakfast inside you, my gel, and that's flat.

Gawd knows what muck you'll be served up in Australia. Roast kangaroos and convict food, I dare say.'

'Oh, Ma, I shan't be having anything to do with convicts!' Prissy began to laugh. 'I shall get a respectable position in a respectable household, and when I write and tell you so, you'll all envy me!'

She climbed the stairs to the top of the tall narrow house on legs that felt as if they didn't belong to her, wishing she felt as confident as she sounded and wondering for the hundredth time why she had thought it such a marvellous opportunity when she'd first seen the poster advertising for female emigration to Australia. Still telling herself that it *was* a marvellous idea...it *was*...

Inside her small bedroom, the size of a large cupboard, she leaned against the closed door for a moment, trying to still her rapid heartbeats. Her reflection in the pitted looking-glass gazed back at her, flushed and starry-eyed from the evening's jollities, as if she hadn't a care in the world. She looked young and eager and full of hope at that moment, and she was startled by the irony of it. And also by the thought that of course she looked like that. It was the way she should feel...

Her dark hair was tumbling out of its pins and on to her bare shoulders in one of the gaudier stage frocks she'd worn especially for tonight's party, her blue eyes wide and alive in the piquant face with the determined chin. That chin that had tilted forcefully enough when one or another of the stage-door gropers had thought to make too free with Miss Priscilla Baxter!

And the curving shape of her, that she frequently wished she could keep better hidden from those lascivious eyes...well, all that was behind her now, she thought positively. She had had enough of the demeaning world of play-acting and singing for a pittance, where, unless you were an acknowledged star, you existed rather than lived.

So she was going to Australia to take up whatever post was offered, and to begin a new and industrious life. Thanks to the diligence of her late lamented aunt, who had insisted on teaching her the basics of housewifery and the rudiments of education, Prissy could bake and sew and knew her letters for reading and writing. There must be something for those talents in an energetic young country. It was a challenge, and Prissy was a girl who liked a challenge. She kept repeating as much to herself.

She undressed quickly in the tiny room, shivering in the late chill of the July night. It certainly didn't feel like summer. The draught from the window made her candle-flame waver, throwing dancing shadows on the ceiling as she lay beneath the covers for a few minutes. Once she blew out the candle she would be enveloped in darkness. There was no moon and no stars that night, and London was blanketed in dark clouds.

Perhaps it was better so...and yet she would have preferred it different. However much Australia was claimed by Britain and already partly colonised, it was still on the other side of the world, remote, alien, inaccessible... It would have been sweetly nostalgic on this last night to have stood quietly by the open window, drinking in the scents of the river and the city, some pleasant, some noxious, but all part of home. Part of London and England...

'You're being ridiculous,' Prissy said aloud. 'This is the great adventure, and to have second thoughts now ain't exac'ly showing the pioneering spirit, my gel!'

Unconsciously, she spoke the words in Ma Jenkins's raucous cockney tones, as if the old woman's stout common sense might help to diminish the fear she felt.

She turned restlessly in the bed with its coarse cotton sheets and lumpy mattress. She knew she wouldn't sleep. She was too emotionally drained, too loath as yet to shed her old life and welcome the new. After half an hour of tossing and turning, still unwilling to blow out her candle and lie in darkness, she fumbled in the bag beneath her bed for the well-thumbed poster.

She had taken it from the stage door of the Gilbert Road Alhambra Performers establishment. And at the time when she had finally admitted that the Alhambra was the grandest name for the seediest, most third-rate theatre in the East End, a place that was little more than a front for a bawdy-house, and more than one girl there had been tempted to succumb to that other profession...

Because of the effects of the evening and Ma Jenkins's spirits, the poster was a jumble of black letters that gradually cleared in front of her eyes. She recalled the day she had brought it home to the lodging-house after a particularly miserable night at the Alhambra, with takings appallingly low, and the owner threatening to close down if things didn't perk up soon. It had seemed a good moment to start thinking about alternative positions.

'Listen, Ma, and all of you,' Prissy had said over their supper that evening. 'I want to read out something of interest and see what you think about it. The Committee for Promoting the Emigration of Single Women to Australia is offering passages from Gravesend to Sydney for the sum of five pounds——'

'Five pounds! Sounds like a bleedin' fortune to me, ducks, when they send convicts there for nothin'!' Ma Jenkins had said, scandalised. 'What would anybody want to go to Australia for anyway? A young girl like you would end up in white slavery if you weren't careful.'

'No, I wouldn't. There's a Ladies' Committee waiting to meet the emigrants when they land in Sydney—and see here, Ma. You're free to choose the kind of work you want, and there will be a list of suitable positions ready and waiting. The first thing to do is to write a letter to the Emigration Committee here in London, and to provide a letter of recommendation from a responsible person. I shall go round and ask the Vicar——'

Belle gasped. 'You ain't telling us you mean to go, Prissy? Among all them convicts and roughnecks?'

Prissy looked at her in exasperation. 'Haven't you ever heard of free-settlers, Belle? No, of course you ain't, because you don't know anything about it. Well, I've been making enquiries, see, and Australia's not just filled with convicts, but other decent folk called squatters who've built homesteads there.' She aired her small amount of knowledge. 'Plenty of English people have gone out there of their own free will and made new lives for themselves.'

'And that's what you mean to do, is it, gel?' Ma said keenly. 'Where you going to find the five pounds?'

Prissy felt the heat in her face. 'Don't worry, Ma, I'll see you're not short of your rent money that's owing. There's a special bit here in the poster—see? It says that persons failing to find the required amount will be allowed to go without payment, providing they agree to pay the amount within a reasonable time from their wages in the Colony, and sign their Note of Hand to that effect. It's all taken care of for anybody to see——'

'Seems to me that once they've got you there, they mean to keep you. Supposing you can't find no job?'

Prissy sighed impatiently. Sometimes Ma was worse than a keeper, and, since Prissy was the youngest of her lodgers, Prissy was the one on whom she came down the most protectively.

'The Ladies' Committee will see to that. I told you,' she said triumphantly. 'And look at this footnote—the London Committee reports that on the last Emigration ship to leave Gravesend, most of the females on board obtained good positions within three days of arrival in Sydney. Anyway, where's the harm in writing for details? I mean to find out more, and there's an end to it.'

She hadn't waited for an answer, but swished out of the room with her chin held high. Like a fresh young colt straining to be free of the harness, Ma Jenkins had thought with an irritation born out of fondness for the headstrong young miss.

Prissy remembered that conversation now, with the poster clutched in her hands. It had seemed to her a generous and wonderful thing for the British Government to do, and this year of 1834 should go down in history as a great step forward in keeping the British spirit alive in foreign parts. She had written her letter with great care and waited impatiently for the reply.

When it came, she learned that the required females had to be between fifteen and thirty years of age, and desirous of bettering their condition. She fitted that bill all right! She was nineteen years old and tired of getting nowhere in her present situation. She was young and energetic enough to want new horizons—that might or might not include marriage.

She paused in her reminiscing. Of course her hopes included marriage—as long as it was to the right man. What girl didn't want love and marriage and children? What else was the ultimate goal for a young woman? Whether she would find the culmination of those dreams in a far-off land she didn't yet dare to think. They were dreams that she kept strictly to herself.

But young females were definitely in short supply in the Colonies, and if marriage should be the end result of their emigration, it held an added sliver of excitement to someone as determined and self-confident as Miss Priscilla Baxter, late of the Gilbert Road Alhambra Performers...

She didn't feel in the least self-confident the next day once she'd embarked on the ship bound for Australia, and stood at the rail as it finally sailed away from Gravesend in a mid-July sea mist and slid into a choppy English Channel. She was suddenly very afraid, and if someone had thrown a lifebelt to her at that moment, she was quite sure she would have jumped into the sea with it and struggled back to English shores.

'Terrifying, ain't it?' a quavering female voice said beside her. 'Never mind, love, they say there's nowt to fret over as long as the seasickness don't lay us low. At least there's plenty of us, so we'll just have to do our best to keep up our spirits on the voyage. It'll all be worth it when we get there and find our fortunes.'

Prissy turned to see the scared eyes of a smallish brown-haired girl with a northern accent. She relaxed a little. At least she wasn't alone. She gave a small inward laugh at the thought. Alone! She was never likely to be alone on this ship—filled with screeching females all being herded by the ship's officers into some kind of order.

The girl grinned, bellowing to introduce herself as Kate Thursby from Yorkshire. Prissy knew at once that she had found a friend, and long before they reached Australian waters they had vowed to try to find positions together.

The thought of a cool sea voyage had meant they had worn warm clothes for travelling and packed anything more frivolous that they owned. As the weeks merged into months of seagoing, it became apparent that the warm clothes—and particularly Kate's, made of good Yorkshire cloth from good Yorkshire mills, as she reiterated constantly—were going to be far too cumbersome and sticky for the southern climate.

'I can't imagine why the seasons should be topsy-turvy,' Kate grumbled, shedding layer after layer as the ship sailed steadily south. 'You'd better explain it, Prissy. You've got a far nimbler brain than me.'

'It's not difficult. Australia's in the southern hemisphere, see, so when we have winter in the north, they have summer in the south and the other way around. None of us miss out on anything, we just get warmer weather at different times of the year.'

'But never as warm as this. I've never been so hot, not even on the farm, and that can get right sticky in a fair to middlin' summer,' Kate said, running her finger around the collar of her dress.

She did look uncommonly hot, Prissy thought in some alarm, more so than any of the other women. They were barely halfway through the voyage, and the climate would get progressively hotter. Thoughts of cholera and scurvy ran through Prissy's mind, and she told Kate to sit exactly where she was on the pile of ropes on deck, while she went to find the ship's doctor. By the time he came, Kate announced in a high, shrill voice that her skin felt on fire, and by the evening she was dead.

'A fever,' the doctor said. 'Unfortunately, it does happen on these overcrowded ships, and the girl's people will be informed of the fact as soon as convenient. Meanwhile, she'll be disposed of quietly, and you'll say nothing to alarm the other women, do you hear?' He spoke sharply to Prissy's shocked white face.

'B-but it was not the cholera?' she stuttered.

'It was not,' he said sharply, daring her to suggest otherwise. 'There's nothing you can do for her now and she'll be attended to. Drink this and then go to your bed.'

Prissy swallowed the brandy he thrust at her, feeling its sharp sting all the way down to her stomach, and moved out of the small room like a sleep-walker. She and Kate had formed an instant attachment before leaving English shores, and neither of them had felt the need to consort with the other women. Now she felt more alone than she had ever felt before, even when her elderly aunt had died.

She and Kate had had such plans. They had confided in one another in a way Prissy had never felt able to confide in anyone before. In Kate she had found a true friend. They had intended finding similar positions in good houses. They would eventually find good men to love and marry and their children would grow free and strong in this new land of sunshine. At the futility of such plans, Prissy curled up in her bed corner and wept.

A ship's officer sent for her the next day, and handed her the small bundle of Kate's things.

'Since you and Miss Thursby were friends, perhaps you'd care to dispose of these among the other women. I'm assured there was nothing infectious in her illness, despite the fact that it came on so quickly,' he said un-emotionally. 'I'm sorry.'

Prissy lifted her chin. 'Thank you. I'm sure there are women who will be glad of a few extras.'

She took the bundle with dignity, refusing to cry over the few possessions her friend had owned. For all Kate's insistence on wearing good Yorkshire cloth, a poor farmer's daughter owned precious little, but there were others who owned even less and would be glad of the shawls and woollens, for surely not all of Australia would be as blisteringly hot as the tropical waters through which they were now sailing.

Prissy's meagre theatrical training came in unexpectedly useful as she distributed the clothes and received the guarded thanks of the other women. Somehow she managed to detach herself from the fact that these were Kate's clothes, and that only yesterday a warm, vibrant girl had owned them. Instead, she saw herself as playing the part of a benefactor.

For herself, Prissy kept only the cheap, polished stone pendant Kate had worn around her neck as a special keepsake. It had been Prissy's second brush with death, and one that touched her deeply—if she dared to allow it.

Kate had come to Australia with the same bright hopes as Prissy herself and together they had fancifully seen themselves as pioneers, with the vaguely patriotic notion of forging new links between the old country and the new. Those ideals seemed so infantile now, and made Prissy realise how vulnerable and mortal they all were after all.

Kate's death had the effect of making her close herself off from any hint of friendship from the other women on board, and, if they thought her standoffish and above herself, it hardly mattered any more. If she wore her stage-frocks because they were cool and thin during the warmer days, she no longer cared about the stares of the other women or even the mutterings and hot stares of the ship's crew. She was totally self-contained, and the barrier she seemed to have built around herself cooled much of the crew's ardour.

During the final part of the voyage, the women were told something of the Australian terrain to prepare them for their new homeland. It was very different from anything any of them had envisaged, and some demanded shrilly to be taken straight back to England again, only to be reminded of their obligations, since the majority had been unable to find the five pounds' passage money and were bound by their Note of Hand to earn that sum to pay back before becoming in the least way financially solvent.

Prissy hardly bothered listening to any of the lectures, but began to feel, like the rest of them, the need to stand up for themselves in a land that might demand all of their resources. Slavery it might not be but, from the stern reminders to be dignified and remember their home and church teachings at all times, it felt perilously close to it on those last days of freedom.

The town of Sydney was hot and humid, the enormous natural harbour alive with craft of every description. The sun shone brilliantly in a blue sky; the bustling scene that met their land-starved eyes was stunning in its vastness, peopled with men, women and children of every colour and creed, it seemed to the women.

They crowded on to the decks for their first glimpse of solid ground after being so long at sea, thankful to be rid of the dry bread and high-smelling meat on board that had long been rotten and weevil-laced, and latterly non-existent. Fresh water would be more welcome than wine to their parched throats, and the Catholics among them crossed themselves thankfully as the ropes were finally thrown and caught by those at the water's edge, sending a fine reddish dust flying into the air.

For a moment, Prissy wished she too had the blind faith of the Catholic women. Something to cling to, something to blame when things went badly wrong, something to live for...something with which to understand the meaning of a young girl's death...

'Regretting it already, are we, ducks? Not too many bright lights here, by all accounts, unless you mean to start up some special kind of business of your own with them trashy frocks of yours to attract certain gentlemen,' one of the women sneered.

Prissy's eyes flashed with anger.

'I'm afraid I wouldn't know what kind of business you mean. Perhaps you'd care to explain, since you seem to know about it so well.'

Her companion hooted with laughter.

'That'll learn you, Rosie. Our clever Miss Baxter will always get the better of you when it comes to words.'

Prissy turned away before she got caught up in the torrent of abuse she knew would follow. How she had managed to get on the wrong side of these women she hardly knew. She looked around quickly and saw a small army of what could only be termed God-fearing women approaching the ship.

'My good Gawd, will you just look at these oh-be-joyfuls?' she heard the one called Rosie say, distracted from her taunting.

'Now then, you women, stop your jawing and get your belongings together. The Ladies' Committee will want to get you sorted as soon as possible, and, if you're needing accommodation for the time being, the sooner you get off the ship the better choice you'll have.'

They were herded yet again, jostled together like cattle, but Prissy didn't care. She could suddenly hear Kate's eager voice in her head, as if her friend were there beside her, still part of the great adventure. 'It'll all be worth it when we get there and find our fortunes...'

Stepping on to Australian soil for the first time, Prissy felt momentarily as if she should bend down and scoop up a handful of that red dusty soil and claim it as her own. A handful for her, and a handful for Kate... She knew it was all dramatic nonsense, and probably only a theatrical person would have thought of such a thing.

She didn't actually do it of course, except symbolically in her heart. But the feeling of being at one with this new land was important to her. After all, this was home now. The feeling had the effect of releasing her from the icy chill that seemed to have encased her since Kate's death. For good or bad, for whatever fate had in store for her, this was home... despite the fact that after the months at sea her legs felt decidedly wobbly at being on dry land again.

She noticed another group of people near a makeshift refreshment tent alongside the advancing Ladies' Committee, who were now ushering the two hundred or so women towards an open-sided wooden structure. Some of the second group were dishevelled as if from travelling long distances; others were more distinguished, men in good suits and women in Sunday-best outfits, bonnets hiding their faces from the fierce glare of the sun.

Waiting for the immigrants, Prissy guessed instantly. Waiting to choose the likeliest women to tend their children and clean their homes. The mutterings among the shipboard women said they were all becoming aware of it too—these established Australians were looking over the new arrivals and putting in an early bid for their selection.

Prissy suddenly felt the ignominy of it all. To be picked over in a way reminiscent of Ma Jenkins's prophesied white slavery was demeaning, but within a very short time the women were being sorted and labelled like so many parcels by the ladies of the Committee who were seated importantly at long tables. The women had to line up and give their names and notes of reference to the Ladies' Committee, and after what seemed an endless shuffling wait, it was Prissy's turn at last. She spoke up defiantly.

'According to the information I received in London, ma'am, I understand that we're free to make our own selection of work and can refuse any situation we do not find acceptable.'

The lady she addressed looked askance at this bit of impertinence and pushed her pince-nez farther up her nose.

'That is quite so, miss, but I think you'll find life more than difficult if you refuse the respectable positions we have on our lists. We have experience in this country, and you'd do well to be guided by us.'

She looked the newcomer up and down, noting the spirited and unflinching eyes, and the shimmering, ice-blue stage-frock made of cheap stuff that happened to be the coolest Prissy owned, and drew her own wrong conclusion. 'Of course, there are *less* respectable positions that a young woman can find easily enough for herself——'

Prissy felt her face flame. 'I assure you I am quite respectable, ma'am, and seek honest work.'

'And you're to repay your five pounds, I see,' the lady went on relentlessly, riffling through Prissy's notes. 'I strongly advise you to leave your choice of situation to us, Miss Baxter. The Government does not look kindly on young women who take their generous assisted passage under false pretences. Now, what can you do?'

'Sew and bake and keep a decent house,' Prissy said, eyes flashing and daring the woman to think otherwise.

Out of the corner of her eye, she saw a figure detach itself from the group near the refreshment tent. A tall, aloof man whom she remembered now had stood apart from the rest, his dusty clothes and wide-brimmed hat stamping him as a traveller. He removed the hat as he approached the tables where the Ladies' Committee sat, and, amid the rustle of interest from some of the women in the line behind Prissy, she saw that he was tanned brown by the sun, his eyes a deeper brown to match his unruly coppery-dark hair and the stubble on his chin. His mouth was wide and set tight, as if it hadn't smiled in a long while.

'You have my name on your list, ma'am,' he said tersely. 'Mackenzie, and I've no time for wasting on chit-chat since I've an urgent need to be away from the town. So find me a suitable applicant and have done with it, if you please.'

CHAPTER TWO

BOTH Prissy and the Committee lady looked up in astonishment at this uncouth introduction. Prissy had heard a rolling accent such as his before—it was undoubtedly Scottish—and this man's manner seemed typical of the dour fellows who had occasionally frequented the Alhambra Theatre and had seemed totally unamused by any of the antics on stage. She had labelled them immediately as being without humour. And this—Mackenzie—would seem to verify her assessment.

'You'll please wait your turn, sir——'

Mackenzie brushed the lady's reproof aside.

'Och, woman, I've no time for playing games. For two days I've kicked my heels in this ale-swilling town waiting for the ship to arrive, and I've no intention of sitting idly about while you argue the toss, when my bairn's needing a woman's attention.'

The lady stared at him for a long moment and then ran a plump finger down her list of prospective employers to ascertain the truth of his statement. Prissy had the distinct impression that when Mackenzie wanted something, he got it, despite the protocol that the Ladies' Committee were determined to observe. A shiver of interest and admiration ran through her, despite his arrogance. He was a man who wasn't afraid to speak his mind, and she admired that too.

'I have an application here from a Mrs James Mackenzie from Ballatree Station, New South Wales, needing a young woman in the house to care for a three-year-old child. Would that be your wife's application?'

'Aye, that's the one,' the man said gruffly. 'Do you have someone suitable?'

'Mr Mackenzie,' she said in exasperation, 'the women have only just disembarked. You must understand that it takes a little time to decide on these things——'

'And I've no time to spare on niceties, woman. My wife's application told you well enough that she was ailing and needed help in the house. Anyone who's intelligent enough to sing a bairn to sleep and see to his daily needs will do.'

He stopped abruptly, and Prissy saw his hands clench at his sides for a moment. Ma Jenkins had always said that an entertainer had to be something of a student of human nature and at that moment Prissy understood her meaning exactly, guessing instinctively that for all his brashness here was a man who was sorely troubled.

'I know plenty of songs,' she said without thinking. 'I can sew and bake and do anything that's necessary in a house. I've just said as much. Will I do?'

The other two seemed aware of her for the first time during their little exchange. The lady pursed her lips. The man looked at Prissy as if he didn't really see her at all. It was a novelty to Prissy, used to the lecherous stares of some of the Alhambra's clients.

'If this one's willing, I'll take her,' Mackenzie said at once.

'Now, just a moment, sir——' the lady said indignantly.

'I'm willing,' Prissy said, somewhat startled to hear her own voice saying the words—Miss Priscilla Baxter, stage-struck artiste, who would not normally allow any man to treat her in such an offhand way—but then, nothing about this place or these people, was normal . . .

Yet if anything, what this man offered was the one normal thing about this entire long journey to the other

side of the world. Whatever Ballatree Station was, it implied a home where there was a family. A couple with
a child and a settled life. It was more than she herself
had known for a very long time. Why should she not
accept it?

'Very well. In three or four months' time, you'll be
visited by an official government representative to see
how you're settling in, and to assure him that all is well.
Also, arrangements for the first redemption of the five
pounds' passage money will be put into operation at that
point,' the lady said, clearly washing her hands of this
independent pair. 'If there is any sort of dispute on either
side, recommendations will be made to put you to some
other kind of employment. Before then, of course, Mrs
Mackenzie is quite at liberty to apply for a change of
employee if you are found to be unsuitable.'

'Mrs Mackenzie will not be making any complaints,'
Mackenzie said shortly.

He picked up Prissy's hold-alls as if they weighed
nothing, and asked if she was ready.

She nodded, realising that her hands were damp. In
a relatively short space of time she had arrived in an
alien land and was about to go off to God knew where
with this tall stranger who was already striding well ahead
of her towards a stable housing various horse-drawn ve-
hicles and nags and, if she didn't want to lose all her
belongings, she had better go after him.

She had no time to ponder. She'd made her bed and
must lie on it, she thought, remembering one of Ma's
favourite sayings. Though at least she'd be spared any
such indignity as the words implied. Mackenzie had a
wife and child, and she was fortunate to have been placed
so easily.

Behind her she could hear the cat-calls of some of the
women who had envied or despised her stage-frocks, but

she ignored them all as Mackenzie threw her belongings into the back of a wagon and helped her sit beside him. When he picked up the reins of the horses and clucked them into movement, Prissy lifted her head high and rammed her bonnet more firmly on her head as they drove past the lines of chattering women, spilling out into the sunlight in a flurry of dust. Through the sprawling buildings of the growing town of Sydney with its banks and taverns and rooming-houses, and heading inland for an unknown destination. It was a great adventure, Prissy kept telling herself as she clung to the side of the wagon. The greatest she could ever have imagined. She tried to imprint it all in her mind for her first letter home to Ma Jenkins and her old friends, and to ignore the slightest suggestion of homesickness that might keep her locked in misery.

All the same, the thought drumming through her head to the music of the hoofbeats was that she was barely nineteen years old and had never felt quite so young and alone in her life.

They had been travelling for some long while when Prissy realised the man beside her had been totally silent. The roads, more correctly described as mere dirt tracks by English standards, were dry and arid, and the dust thrown up by the wagon wheels stung her eyes.

In her limited experience, Scotsmen were noted for their lack of conversation save when words were absolutely necessary, and this one was no exception. But, because of her past life and exuberant theatrical companions, Prissy was naturally garrulous. Moreover, the silence was beginning to unnerve her, and finally encouraged her to babble in her usual way in an attempt to converse with him.

'Sir, our association began so quickly that you may not have taken in all my particulars. I come from good old London town, and am Priscilla Baxter, more usually known as Prissy.'

She resisted the temptation to say that most people joked about her nickname, saying a less prissy-looking young woman they couldn't imagine...convinced as she was that this man wouldn't appreciate the joke. She plunged on.

'Will you please tell me more about your home and family, sir? I am intrigued by the thought of caring for a small child. Is it a boy or a girl, and was he or she born here in Australia? You heard me say that I know plenty of songs, and you may care to know that I come from a theatrical background——'

Mackenzie interrupted her flow. 'It makes no difference to me what you did in England, so long as you do your duties in my house, and show care and concern for my son. Robbie has run wild of late and needs a firm hand. I've little time to spare for overseeing the bairn, and I trust you'll not be soft with him, Miss Baxter.'

Prissy stared at him, open-mouthed. She felt a sharp pity for the three-year-old Robbie, who was clearly not shown much of a father's affection. Prissy doubted suddenly whether this man could show affection at all. His profile was hard, handsome in its way, but angular and strong—very strong. He was probably younger than he appeared from his unsmiling exterior. She shivered, wondering if Robbie's wildness came from an unloving home.

But surely not—there was also the mother who was ailing. She bit her tongue to stop herself asking too many probing questions about Mrs James Mackenzie. Clearly the Scotsman considered any questions at all an intrusion on his privacy. Such a trait was going to be difficult for Prissy, who loved asking questions and wanted to know all that there was to know about everything and everybody. Besides, she had a right to know the kind of household of which she was about to be a part.

'I'll do my best to do all that's expected of me, sir. But, please, won't you call me Prissy like everyone else does? It's bad enough being in a foreign country without feeling quite unlike myself with you acting so formal towards me.' She spoke apologetically, hoping to draw some sympathetic response from him.

The man glanced at her, and his face softened slightly for the first time. She was astonished at how different he looked with that half-smile playing about his mouth, though it was gone so quickly she wondered if she had imagined it.

'Aye, that's fair enough comment, providing you'll stop calling me sir in that ridiculous way. I suspect that you don't enjoy being subservient to anyone—am I right?'

She laughed, hearing the sound of it emerge loud and startling after the tension of the day so far.

'Quite right, sir—I mean Mr Mackenzie——'

'Mackenzie will do. It's what my men call me,' he said abruptly.

Prissy looked at him with new interest.

'You employ men, si—Mackenzie? Then what is this station the Committee lady spoke about? I don't understand the term. Are you very rich?'

He laughed then, but with little mirth, his answer telling her nothing.

'If you're seeking a rich husband in Australia, you've come to the wrong place in Ballatree Station, lassie. I know that's what some of you women on the five-pound passage come looking for.'

Prissy sparkled at once. 'Well, I assure you I'm not one of them, *Mr* Mackenzie! I came here to work.'

'Och, tell me some news, lassie! Can you really say that you've never had fond thoughts about finding some dashing young man in Australia to sweep you off your feet? If that's your purpose, you'll find few knights in shining armour where you're going.'

Her instinct to lash out at him was suddenly submerged in remembering Kate. On the long voyage from England there had been many nights, huddled in their cramped sleeping quarters, when they had whispered young girls' secrets to one another, confident that they would stay together and share each other's lives. And yes, for each of them, those dreams had included a man to love, a man who would cherish them, and only with Kate had Prissy ever revealed those dreams.

In her private moments she still mourned Kate acutely. She had found and lost a friend so swiftly it still had the power to frighten her, to realise how vulnerable and fragile she was in what Ma Jenkins would have called the great scheme of things.

When he got no immediate reaction from her, she heard Mackenzie say in his oddly abrupt way, 'Now I've offended you, and I'm sorry. 'Twas not my intention.'

'You haven't offended me,' Prissy said, her voice scratchy. 'I was remembering—a friend.'

'A man, I dare say,' he stated. 'Is he your reason for running away?'

'As it happens it wasn't a man, nor was I running away——'

'Good. Because you'll find you can never run away from yourself, not even to the other side of the world, and I may as well tell you straight off that I can't be doing with tantrums in my house. I've enough of that with Robbie, without another weeping bairn in my charge.'

His ruthless manner made her wonder again about the poor little three-year-old child. Prissy spoke heatedly. 'You are positively the rudest man I've ever met. And if I had anywhere else to go, I'd get out of this wagon right now, and *go* there!'

To her horror, he reined in the horses, and the dust flew up around them in a red mist.

'You're at perfect liberty to do as you please. We'll stop here to water the horses, and you may decide on your future, miss. Providing of course, that you find some other employer willing to take you in. Oh—and you'll be sure to inform the Ladies' Committee of your new arrangements so that you can repay the five pounds' passage to them, of course. As you heard, the authorities don't take kindly to a young woman who takes Government money to come to Australia with no intention of paying it back.'

Prissy gasped, finding the unexpectedly long speech too ludicrous and yet too pointedly true to be amazed by it.

'It was never my intention to back out of my obligations, sir.'

He had leapt down from the wagon and was emptying water from a skin bag into a tin container for the horses, which they drank greedily. He said no more until they were finished, then replaced all the containers in the wagon, and looked at Prissy keenly with those dark eyes as he sat beside her again.

'Good. Then, now that we've got that settled, we'll be on our way. In another hour or so we'll need to find a place to bed down before nightfall.'

She was alerted at once. She realised the terrain had changed considerably since they had begun their journey from the coast. The buildings and houses of the town had long since disappeared, as had the few shacks they had passed as they travelled northwards through the more rugged inland country. All around them were thick shrubby bushes and dense bracken-like tracts, and many tall fragrant trees seeking the sunlight, that were inhabited by screeching, brilliantly hued birds which relieved the monotony of the winding track. Ahead of them was a range of mountains. She licked her dry lips.

'What do you mean by "bed down"? How much farther is it to Ballatree Station?'

'It's a hundred and fifty miles or so from Sydney all told,' he said, ignoring her gasp. 'And, unless we want to kill off the horses, we have to do it in easy stages. Don't fret yourself, lassie. We'll make camp soon, and keep the fire going all night to keep away the wildlife. If you're scared of snakes and redbacks, you can always sleep in the back of the wagon. Higher up in the mountains, there are huts where we'll be warmer than sleeping out of doors. Even in summer, the mountains can be cold at night. Three nights in all should do it, four if one of the horses goes lame, but anywhere is better than sleeping in that Godforsaken town.'

She didn't dare ask what redbacks were, nor force herself to remember that of course it was summer here while it was winter at home. Because the thought of snakes was terrifying enough to push everything else from her mind.

She was furious at her own uncharacteristic stupidity for rushing into this situation without even asking where she was going—and just as furious to know that it wouldn't have meant a thing to her if she had. She had always lived in London, and had vaguely imagined living in another town in a good household where there was endless sunshine in summer and the good old busy town smells would be the same...she was a townie, not a country girl...and she might as well be travelling to the moon, for all that Mackenzie's words meant to her.

She felt his hand suddenly close over her own as her fright transmitted itself to him. For a moment she felt comforted by the feel of it.

'You'll be quite safe, lassie. I'll not let any harm come to you,' he promised.

She was touched by his concern, and then his next words squashed all her finer feelings towards him.

'Besides, I'd not be too keen to make another journey to Sydney to wait for the next immigration boat, and Robbie's in dire need of you. And come midsummer there'll be no time at all for a man to be wasting away the hours on bairns.'

She pulled her hand away from beneath his, with a childish urge to scrub away the warm feeling his skin had left on hers. At least she supposed he had *some* finer feelings for his son, but he had the oddest way of presenting them. He obviously wasn't a man who found discussion easy, and he therefore made even the most caring statements sound forced.

Perhaps it said something for the man that he'd gone all the way to Sydney to find help for his child and his ailing wife, but, right at that moment, founding a Scottish dynasty in this inhospitable country didn't seem such a noteworthy cause to Prissy Baxter. Not compared with the way her thoughts about her future in this man's household began to unnerve her.

Night had begun to throw soft purple shadows over the landscape by the time Mackenzie decided it was time they bedded down for the night. Prissy didn't care for the expression. It sounded all too intimate and Bohemian.

She should be used to such free and easy expressions with her theatrical background ... but back in England such freedom of speech was usually said in the camaraderie of folk who understood all about the lure of the stage, of the sound of applause ringing in the ears, of the feeling of being *somebody* for a little while, whether you were playing a different part each night in a summer season or on stage for an hour at a time in a long run and hoping to be discovered.

Perhaps she could pretend she was playing a part now, Prissy decided, and all the terrors of the forthcoming night were only make-believe, no more than props ...

Mackenzie jumped down from the wagon and led the horses off the track until he found a suitable clearing. By now, Prissy was too scared to make any comment, clinging to her thought that this was not happening in reality, and silently watching as he pushed away the undergrowth with a stout stick. She tried not to notice the small scuttling movements in the thickets, nor the protesting cries of birds suddenly flapping their wings and disappearing into a velvet night sky.

'We'll make camp here,' he said. 'For supper there's bread and meat in the wagon, and we'll heat enough water to make tea once I've got the fire going.'

He was completely resourceful, Prissy discovered. There were coarse blankets and everything needed for several nights' survival in the wilds contained in the wagon. There was a bag of feed for the horses, and containers of water. Without being told, she guessed that they would need to be frugal with the water. There'd be no chance of a refreshing splash to waken herself up in the morning. And anyway, first of all they had to get through the night.

She waited in the wagon as Mackenzie got a fire going, clearing every bit of brush and bracken well away from the small glow. It reassured her. Surely no wild animals or slithering unmentionables would cross that barren circle of ground with the fire burning brightly in the centre? When she said as much, Mackenzie said shortly that the necessity of keeping the fire under control was mainly because of the danger of starting a bush fire, bringing yet another hazard to her mind.

She was beginning to be totally disorientated now. The slight delirium brought on by months at sea and still not finding her land-legs yet was another problem she had no intention of informing him about. He shook out his blanket and laid it carefully on the ground, and suggested she did the same.

'You said I could sleep in the wagon——' she began.

'Suit yourself, though the blankets will be more comfortable to sit on while we eat. If you're wondering if I have thoughts of molesting you, lassie, you can rest easy.'

'I was thinking no such thing,' Prissy said, feeling somewhat foolish at his explanation. 'I trust that you'll remember you're a married man, and I'm sure your wife must have complete faith in your honour to send you to Sydney alone to bring back help.'

She saw how his eyes gleamed in the firelight, and something that could have been a twist of pain came over his face, already shadowed by the contrast of light and dark.

'I don't forget my duties,' he said harshly.

Prissy spoke timidly as he poured water carefully from the skin bag into a tin kettle and pushed it down among the glowing wood embers. A thin trail of water on its surface hissed and steamed and was gone.

'Have I offended you now? I was merely complimenting you and your wife on your obvious trust in one another. Is she at home alone except for the boy?'

He sat on his haunches, staring into the fire. He was a big man, undiminished by the action.

'Ballatree Station is isolated,' he said. 'Our nearest neighbours are twenty miles away to the south, but we aren't entirely alone. We have our stockman, his wife who does some of the cooking, the regular stockhands and the ringers who come seasonally, and then there are the bushies.'

Prissy felt that sense of unreality steal over her again. He spoke in a language not dissimilar to her own, and one that she had recognised at once, yet, however long he had been in Australia, he had already become part of it, claimed it and owned it.

She spread out her blanket and sat down opposite him, watching his face through the dancing firelight, and warmed her hands before the fire, cold without knowing why.

'Don't you think you'd better tell me exactly what Ballatree Station is, and what you do there? You owe me that much, Mackenzie. I don't want your wife to think me a complete ninny when she meets me!'

Again that long, deep silence that she couldn't understand, yet which told her instantly there was much more to know about this man than his mere way of life.

'You won't meet my wife—exactly. She's no—she's there all right, but she won't be having anything to do with you. It won't be quite the way you'd expect.'

Prissy jumped up at once, her heart pounding.

'What game are you playing, Mackenzie?'

Whatever he might have answered was halted by the most extraordinary and nerve-stretching sound Prissy had ever heard. It came out of the night, that had suddenly and swiftly become quite black outside the circle of firelight and the myriad stars above.

It was a sound of clanking and rattling and dragging, weird and unearthly, and reminded Prissy in those first terrifying moments of the stories of grave-robbers and she cursed the vivid imagination that went with her late profession. Grave-robbing scenes were a favourite drama of some of Ma Jenkins's semi-professionals, acted out with relish, to leave hearts quaking and put teeth on edge.

Mackenzie was on his feet at once, as sharp as a blade, and Prissy clutched at him, uncaring that he was employer and she employee. At that moment he was just a man—much-needed as hunter and protector. He shook her hands away, needing to be alert.

'What in God's name is it?' she gasped.

'Calm yourself, lassie. Whatever 'tis, 'tis human, and can be dealt with.'

Prissy was aware of three things at the same time. One was the fact that Mackenzie had a rifle in his hand, which she presumed had been ready beneath his blanket. Two was the realisation that along with the clanking and dragging there was the sound of a voice hallooing out of the darkness. And three, that it had felt undoubtedly pleasant to be held for those few seconds against the coarse cloth shirt covering James Mackenzie's chest.

'Say who you are and come close where I can see you,' Mackenzie snapped.

'The name's Badger, late of the smoke, and I'd be mighty glad of a warm and a lie by your fire, mate. No need to feed me, for I've victuals enough for all if you're wanting some,' said a voice, so unbelievably cockney that Prissy could have wept with relief.

The man stepped into the circle of light, leading a nag no less bedraggled than himself. He was short of stature, so that his tattered greatcoat reached to his feet, hung about with pots and pans, as was the horse, proclaiming him to be a travelling salesman. Above the comic garb was a creased and leathery face, surrounded by a shock of greying hair and matching beard. The smile on his face at seeing them was gap-toothed and warm.

'Tain't often I meet with such congenial travelling companions, ducks,' he spoke directly to Prissy. 'You and your man are a sight for sore eyes and no mistake.'

She felt embarrassed at this assumption that she and Mackenzie belonged together. She saw his hold on the rifle slacken slightly, but he did not relinquish it.

'What's your business, man?' Mackenzie said brusquely.

'Ain't it obvious?' Badger spread his hands expansively, and the pans about his person clanked anew. Prissy felt slightly hysterical at the sight of this unexpected gargoyle of a man. Surely every pan with which he decorated himself must be scratched and dented by the time any good housewife thought about buying them...? 'Now if your good lady wants a spanking new set of pans for the kitchen, I can do 'er a special price——'

'We're not buying anything,' Mackenzie said. 'You're welcome to share our fire for a wee while, but we've no water to spare.'

'I've plenty of me own,' Badger said cheerfully. 'You're from north of the border, ain't you, mate? The English border, that is.'

'The Scottish border, yes,' Mackenzie said, in what was for him a rare moment of humour.

Badger laughed raucously, settling himself down on the ground and divesting himself of the greatcoat, complete with pans. Beneath it he wore a checked weskit and trousers, and looked even more of a sketch. For a second, Prissy wished she could gather him up and transport him whole to Ma Jenkins's theatrical lodging-house. What a scream the inmates there would have at seeing him, better than all their studied attempts at portraying such a man!

'Sorry, mate—missis. I was forgetting how touchy you Scottishers could be.'

'I'm not Scottish,' Prissy said at once. 'I'm from London, same as you.'

Badger looked at her with delight.

'Is that so? Well, ma'am, this calls for a celebration, don't it? Will you share a drop of rum with me? Fresh off the boat and donated to me by a friendly sailor in return for a set of eating irons.'

'I don't know about that...' Prissy said doubtfully, not wanting to offend the man, but not particularly keen to take a drink either.

'We want no spirits here,' Mackenzie said forcefully. 'We're opposed to the use of it and would prefer you to be on your way as soon as you've warmed yourself.'

Prissy looked at him with astonishment. She was more amused than offended by the newcomer, but Mackenzie was eyeing him now with outright animosity.

Surely he wasn't of a religious disposition that forbade strong drink? She'd heard of some of these narrow sects that forbade almost everything. She wouldn't have suspected Mackenzie of being one of them—and, if he and his family were so inclined, it would contrast sharply with everything in Prissy's warm and generous nature that would embrace the whole world as friends... and would make her wonder if she had made a serious error in throwing in her lot with him.

'You could at least let Badger have some tea,' she said indignantly.

'We've no water to spare for extras and I'd thank you to remember it, woman.'

She noted how he called her woman instead of lassie. As if he owned her—or wanted to give the impression to this stranger that he did.

'I'll supply my own water, ducks,' the man said easily. 'And a cup of tea would be very welcome. But if your man wants you to himself—and I don't blame him,' he added with a wink, feasting on the way her stage-frock clung to her rounded shape, 'then I'll be on me way soon enough.'

Prissy saw how Mackenzie's rifle was still a part of him. He sat easily enough, but she could sense the raw tension in him, and it was Prissy who poured the tea into one of Badger's own tin mugs for him, and who accepted the bag of water in exchange. The three of them lapsed into silence while Badger drank noisily, and then heaved himself up to go. He shrugged his arms back into his greatcoat and said he hoped to meet up with them again sometime.

As he reached the edge of the clearing, pulling at his nag's reins, Mackenzie called to him. Badger turned, and as Prissy watched with outraged eyes she saw Mackenzie slowly pull the stopper from the skin bag and let the water pour on to the ground where it was quickly swallowed up in the dust.

'Are you quite mad...?' she gasped, and then stopped as she heard the sound of Badger's rasping laughter.

'All right, matey, but there'll be plenty more on the road between here and Sydney. There's always takers who can't resist a spot of good navy rum or an extra skinful of water.' There was an edge to his voice, despite the jocularity, and he disappeared into the night as quickly as he had come.

Prissy whirled on Mackenzie. 'Why did you do that? How could you have been so rude to the man? Couldn't we have done with the water even if we didn't want the rum?'

'And found ourselves drugged for the night while that scavenger robbed us blind?'

Prissy stared at him, taking in the words. Mackenzie put his hands on her shoulders as she stood stiff with indignation.

'I've been in this country longer than you have, lassie, and you learn to smell the bad 'uns. Trust me, and I'll get us both to Ballatree safe and sound.'

'How did you know?' she stammered.

'Call it instinct. Just as I knew you'd be right for me,' he said as he turned away. 'Settle for the night, now. We've a long way still to go.'

Her thoughts whirling with all that he knew and she didn't, and all that she would obviously need to know about the strange, vast new country, she followed his lead without any more argument. She wrapped herself in her blanket and stayed close to the fire, abandoning any thought of moving from his side and sleeping inside the wagon. She thought she would never sleep in this strange environment, with the fire crackling and the silence of the night broken by animal sounds she couldn't identify.

But finally she slept from sheer exhaustion, and the last thought sliding through her mind was the extraordinary one that Mackenzie had spoken as though he'd actually chosen her. She hadn't even thought he'd noticed her. Out of all those women pouring off the immigration boat, he had *chosen* her? She couldn't fathom it, and gave up trying. But, despite everything, there was a certain exhilaration now in being here, safe in this man's care.

CHAPTER THREE

'DON'T move a muscle,' Mackenzie said softly.

Prissy was instantly awake, numb with terror as the huge shadowy thing stood over her. She caught the glint of two fierce eyes in the dying firelight, and a small beaked head atop a thin serpent-like neck . . . she bit her lips hard to stop herself from crying out as the neck seemed to sway over her for what seemed an eternity, then suddenly it lumbered speedily away into the darkness, leaving her damp with fright, limbs shaking, teeth chattering.

'Here, drink this.' Mackenzie thrust a cup towards her, and she tasted raw spirit, fiery and bitter. He wasn't averse to one of the sins of the flesh after all, then. The incongruous thought flashed through her mind, dragging a sliver of humour to the rescue.

'What the hell and damnation was that?' Prissy burst out, the old vernacular coming to the fore in the husk of sound that was her voice.

And praise be to glory, but there was surely a hint of a smile in Mackenzie's answer now.

'It was an emu, lassie, what they call a flightless bird. He's harmless as long as you keep your distance, but he can give you a nasty bite if you scare him. It's the protective instinct. Most wild things react in the same way; leave them be, and they'll not harm you.'

'*I* wouldn't scare *him*?' she croaked.

'Aye, well, mebbe he was unused to seeing a bonnie lassie in a skimpy blue dress out in the bush.'

41

So he had noticed after all. Prissy had been quite sure she'd been no more than a female in a whole line of chattering magpies who'd happened to be in the right place at the right time when Mackenzie had come forward to make his move and demanded help for his bairn.

Gawd almighty, she thought, deliberately filling her head with Ma Jenkins's favourite expression. Why the blue blazes was she thinking of the babe as a *bairn*? She was beginning to think in *his* terms now, which said a lot for the man, because there had never been one yet who could dominate her thinking.

'It's one of the costumes I used to wear on the stage. I'm sorry you don't approve!' she said inanely, as if such a conversation were an everyday thing when she was sitting out here with a stranger in the Australian bush and had just had the fright of her life.

She sat up straight and wrapped her arms around her knees, her dark hair hanging limp on her shoulders, much of its gloss tarnished by the dust of the journey. Sleep seemed to be a thing of the past now. But a pearly dawn was already lightening the remnants of the night sky, and the haze of insects hovering above the dying fire had scattered.

'I never said so. But it would explain why you know a lot of songs.' He spoke as abruptly as ever, as if he too thought normal conversation were more desirable than Miss Prissy Baxter.

'Well, I wasn't all that good,' she acknowledged, mildly surprised that she wasn't applauding herself the way she usually did. Somehow in this clean air of the early morning, before the heat of the day had turned the dew on the vegetation to steam, it seemed a time for honesty. 'I'd never have seen my name in lights.'

'Is that what you wanted?' Mackenzie said, as if such a thing was beyond him. Prissy felt defensive then, for herself, for all those clownish, loving friends who had peopled her life in what seemed like another age.

'What's wrong with it? It's an honest living. You sell your talents, not yourself, Mr Mackenzie!'

'I never meant to imply anything else. You are the most irritating lassie to come my way. Do you always fly off your broomstick when anybody questions you?'

She gave a cheerful grin. 'Usually. It's one of my failings. But I wasn't lying when I said I knew some songs. Do you want to hear one?'

Mackenzie lay back on his blanket, his hands laced behind his head. They should be making breakfast, moving on, covering more miles to Ballatree...but somehow here, isolated in their small circle, he felt and shared the lure of a different world with this lassie with the stars still lingering in her blue eyes, no matter how much she denied them. Besides, it put off the moment of returning home...

'Aye, sing me a song.'

She began softly, unconsciously singing of love that had died and would be no more, the words plaintive in the small voice that popular taste decreed would never reach the heights, but that reached deeper into Mackenzie's heart and soul than he desired.

'That's enough,' he said harshly when she'd only half finished the song. He prodded the fire into life again, sending sparks flying and making Prissy cough. 'We'll make tea and eat some flat cake, and then be on our way.'

Prissy stared. 'Didn't you like my singing?'

'It'll do fine for Robbie, and that's what I'll be paying you for. You'll be keeping that hasty tongue of yours a wee bit in check, I trust—and I don't mean your language, the bairn hears plenty from the ticket-of-leavers. But one bairn in the house is enough to be going on with.'

Prissy's high-flying temper was up in a minute.

'If you don't want me to stay, I can soon look around for something else. We both have to suit one another, Mr Mackenzie.'

She stared unblinkingly into his brown eyes and he stared as relentlessly into hers. She knew she was breathing heavily, and that the soft swell of her breasts was visible in the low neck of the stage-frock, which she now knew was quite wrong in this outlandish place, and could have dashed her chances of a real job in a respectable home. He breathed heavily too, as if impatient with this chit of a girl who seemed to nettle him at every opportunity, and Prissy wondered if, after all, she had damned herself. He was infuriatingly right. She did have a hasty tongue.

For long minutes, it was as if there were only the two of them in the entire world, clashing, assessing, and finally accepting what they saw.

'I think you'll do very well for me,' Mackenzie said abruptly.

'That's all right, then.' Prissy bore no malice and spoke with satisfaction, knowing this was all the praise she'd get from this austere man. 'So where's this flat cake we're eating for breakfast? I'm starving, even if it don't sound too appetising to me, begging your pardon if your wife baked it and I'm being rude again.'

He stood up, with his blanket still slung around his shoulders like a cape, and moved across to the wagon. Water and feed for the horses was his first priority, then a cloth-wrapped bundle of food from a basket for themselves. The fire burned more brightly now and he pushed the kettle squarely on to it. Prissy eyed the uninteresting-looking cake in the cloth, though compared with some of the fare on the ship it was a regular feast, she reminded herself.

'My wife didn't bake it. Iona did.'

'Oh. Who's Iona?'

'She's my stockman's wife. I told you about her.'

She was constantly exasperated by him. He was a man of few words all right, and seemed to think that one remark about something was sufficient to tell her all there was to know. She tried to keep her patience.

'What's your stockman called, then?'

'Davy. Davy Golightly.'

Prissy burst out laughing. It sounded to her like some farcical name dreamed up for a character in a third-rate play. She saw that Mackenzie wasn't laughing and tried to smother her mirth.

'Somebody should have prepared me for this place.' She straightened her face, trying to be serious. 'There should be some kind of register back home of the odd characters and the lurking dangers to be encountered in Australia. There was a Superintendent and his wife on board the ship who were supposed to be taking care of us and answering questions, but nobody bothered to ask them much, and they weren't exactly forthcoming to the likes of a coupla hundred females——'

'Have you finished?' Mackenzie said, as she prattled on. 'Davy Golightly's my best man, and I'll thank you not to ridicule him.'

'I never would! Not to his face, anyway. It's just his name—it's so—so——' She pealed off again, and was stopped by Mackenzie's freezing voice.

'It's the nearest English equivalent of his Aborigine name, lassie, and he's as proud of it as you or me of our own, and I'll thank you not to forget it.'

This stopped her at once. 'You mean he's black?'

Mackenzie spoke drily. 'They usually are.'

'And his wife—Iona. She's black too?'

'Does it bother you?'

She hadn't even had time to consider it. She'd never met any black people, but she knew they existed. In Africa, and places like that. At home, actors blackened their faces and performed antics supposedly like them in plays or farces. She'd also heard some vague non-sense about only white people needing to apply for Gov-ernment-assisted passage. Young women, single or widowed. Those were the only conditions. She'd had no idea what she would meet when she got here. But why should it bother her? It obviously didn't bother James Mackenzie and his wife and child and, since she was now in their employ, she'd trust in their judgement. She gave a shrug.

'They're the same as us under the skin, ain't they?'

Mackenzie smiled properly, just as the dazzling first rays of the morning sun splintered the trees behind him. Prissy caught her breath.

He was tall and strong, yet fined down from an out-doors existence without an ounce of spare flesh on him. And just for a second, with his blanket slung casually around his shoulders, and that aura of light behind him, he looked almost—Biblical. She dashed the fanciful thought away, thinking she must be going a bit dotty in the head.

'As I said, you'll do for me, lassie.'

She blinked, not quite knowing what she'd said that was so right, but hearing a different quality in his richly burred voice. She couldn't quite identify it, but it had the effect of making her feel warm inside all the same.

'By the way, you'll do whatever you need to do over there in the bushes, but I'll clear the ground first with a scrub broom.'

The warm feeling vanished. He was talking basic necessities now, and the thought of anything lurking in the undergrowth when she needed to squat was enough to chase away any exuberant thoughts that this high old adventure was obviously destined to be her rightful role in life...

The day began in a sultry way and quickly assumed blistering proportions. Once they were away from the humid shelter of the bush and approaching the shimmering blue-hazed mountains, there was little shade to be found anywhere. The horses plodded on, hour after hour, well used to the conditions, as was the man. Prissy most definitely was not.

She complained bitterly—about the heat and the flies, and the constant dust spinning away from the horses' hoofs and the wagon wheels, filling her throat and her lungs until she couldn't breathe...couldn't speak... Mackenzie finally reined in the horses near a scattered group of eucalyptus trees as she coughed and spluttered. The silver-grey leaves whispered and crackled as a slight breeze lifted and moved them.

'Lassie, the day you stop speaking will be a day to remember,' he said keenly. 'Save your breath, and your throat will mebbe not protest so much.'

She glared at him. Her skin had been prickling for a long while from the heat, and he seemed totally unconcerned. He was already tanned to a healthy bronze and apparently took no discomfort from the sun, but her arms and face would be disgustingly red and blotchy if she was exposed to it for much longer.

'When are we going to stop?' she demanded to know. 'I ache all over from the jolting.'

'We've stopped. There's a waterhole down the steep bank just yonder where we'll rest for a short while before we start the climb through the mountain pass. It will get a bit rugged farther on——'

'You surprise me,' Prissy said sarcastically.

Her head throbbed and she began to wish she had never taken on this position. Why could she not have waited, instead of rushing headlong into something the way she always did? Why could she not have insisted that the Ladies' Committee find her a suitable post in Sydney town, where there would have been music and life and gaiety and everything she was used to, albeit in a place where summer passed for winter and vice-versa?

'Give me your hand,' Mackenzie said, and before she could argue he had grasped it and helped her down from the wagon.

For a second she was held close to his chest again. She could feel his heartbeats. She could smell the rough fabric of his shirt mixed with his personal scent that was not unattractive. She was so close she could see the texture of his skin, weathered and rough, and totally unlike the smooth skins of the actors who rubbed creams into their faces every night to remove the stage make-up and took such good care of themselves.

She had a sudden urge to touch that face, to feel the texture beneath her fingers and to caress that tight, unsmiling mouth with her fingertips, just to gauge his reaction. What would it be? Horror? Anger? Or something else...? He let her go, and Prissy flexed her back, marvelling as always at the way a man's body could react to a woman's without him even being aware of it.

In her line of business, she had been taught to know the signs when it was necessary to keep a man at bay. She knew why a man's eyes darkened and why he felt the need to run a finger around the nape of his neck. She knew how to recognise when the pulsebeats in his throat quickened.

Though why Mackenzie's reactions should have been stirred by her at that moment, she couldn't imagine. She hadn't moved towards him, and had kept her features bland. He made no secret of the fact that she irritated him—and he was married with a bairn. That put him strictly out of bounds in her code and, she guessed, in his. It was no more than a physical reaction that had nothing to do with emotions, of which he seemed sadly lacking, Prissy decided. It was all the better so. They wanted none of those complications.

'We're not alone,' Mackenzie observed, pointing towards the waterhole while leading the horses behind them and as they made their way over the uneven ground.

Prissy followed his gaze and saw a small group of what looked like dogs drinking greedily at the waterhole.

'What are they?' she asked.

'Dingoes,' he said briefly. 'They'll have their fill and be on their way. We'll stay back out of sight and wait.'

She didn't need to ask then if the doglike creatures were dangerous. Everything in this country seemed to be dangerous. The blue water reflecting the cloudless sky above looked so tempting, and long before the animals had finished drinking Prissy was almost desperate to sink beneath its inviting softness and wash away the dust and grime of the journey so far.

She turned to say as much to Mackenzie, when a rifle shot blasted the air and reverberated around the small hollow below. The shock of it made her heart leap, and one of the dingoes dropped instantly, his head blown to bits. Prissy turned away, sickened, as two riders stormed towards the waterhole, bellowing and firing wildly, until the rest of the pack scattered in terror.

'Bloody fools,' Mackenzie said savagely. 'They only had to bide their time. Now the water will be polluted.'

Horrified, Prissy realised that he expressed no pity for the dead animal, only anger for the fact that the water would be polluted...and then, as he grasped her near to swooning body and spoke sharply into her ears, she saw the sense of it. They needed the water, and so did their horses, and so would any other travellers who came this way...in the outback the need for survival was more important than worrying about the fate of one dead dingo.

'The men are leaving,' she whispered. 'Why did they kill it if they didn't want the water?'

'Sport,' Mackenzie said. 'Some men kill for the love of it. If it's not the dingoes, it'll be the kangaroos or the crocs. They wear their skins like trophies.'

She shaded her eyes from the sun with her hand, pulling the inadequate bonnet farther down over her face.

'And you? Would you kill animals for sport?'

She wanted him to say no. She wanted to go on respecting him.

'You'd better decide that for yourself. Come on, I think if we go to the far side of the waterhole we'll be all right. Those fellows won't be back. They'll be chasing the rest of the pack.'

They picked their way carefully around the waterhole, and Prissy avoided looking at the dead mass of the dingo. Mackenzie was right. On the far side, the water was still cool and unruffled, and the horses drank their fill, while she splashed herself luxuriously, revelling in the sensation. Mackenzie bent down and buried his head beneath the glittering water for a few minutes, to come up shaking himself like an untamed thoroughbred. His hair clung damply to his head in coppery strands that would dry quickly in the heat of the day. Prissy couldn't resist doing the same, letting the sun dry the long strands of her hair as she fingered out the tangles and twisted it into a knot on top of her head.

When they were ready to leave, he filled several waterbags to put in the cool of the wagon. The sun was high in the sky now, almost directly overhead, and he suggested that Prissy sat well back inside the wagon for the most shade. They would be approaching the lower slopes of the mountains, and by nightfall they would reach the pass, where there was a hut for travellers' convenience.

It was too hot for talking. Prissy found that she needed to conserve all her energy for existing on the long wearisome journey overland. At times she began to feel lightheaded, and several times Mackenzie stopped the horses and insisted she drank a few mouthfuls of water and ate more of the flat cake or took some cold meat. It became an effort to make her lips move as she chewed obediently, and often during the endless hours she wondered about the truth of the Sydney Committee lady's words.

Would anyone ever travel this long distance to check on one over-confident young woman on her way to some Godforsaken place called Ballatree Station? Prissy doubted it very much. She had probably been abandoned already, particularly after the way she had so brazenly accepted a stranger's offer of work...

She awoke from a half-sleep to hear Mackenzie say, 'We're here.'

'At Ballatree Station?' she said muzzily.

'No, lassie. At the mountain shelter. We'll take a hot meal here and then you won't feel so bad.'

Why should he talk about a hot meal, when she was burning up with the heat? Even as she thought it, Prissy realised that it was no longer the case. She was shivering in the thin frock, and it was no longer light. How long she had slept she couldn't imagine, but the day had gone, and they were into another night.

This one was very different to the last, she saw at once as she climbed down from the wagon on stiff legs. All around her, above and below and beyond, as far as she could see in the purple dusk, were the mountains, majestic and awesome and silent, empty of vegetation except on the lower, darker slopes, from where they rose to great soaring peaks of a magnitude Prissy had never seen before.

If she had never believed in eternity, she could believe in it now, in this place, in this silence where nature had ravaged where it would. The thought came unbidden to her mind, sending her usual chirpy thoughts scattering to the winds.

'Bring the blankets. We'll get inside the hut and get a fire started, then see to the animals and ourselves,' Mackenzie ordered, as if such magnificence was of little importance to him compared with the need for warmth and sustenance. She pulled the blankets from the wagon, pulling one of them around her to keep out the chill, and followed him.

'Wait,' he cautioned at the door. He went inside ahead of her, the rifle in his hand. He stood perfectly still, letting his eyes and ears become accustomed to the dimness inside, lit only by a pale moon overhead.

Prissy swallowed. Presumably, everywhere they went there would be this need for caution. The need to watch and listen and poke and prod and kill...

'All right. The place seems unoccupied,' Mackenzie said, not lessening her fears in the least. She tried to talk normally, to show some interest, to stop herself shivering for reasons other than cold.

'How did this place get here? Who built it?'

'It was built by convict labour, when the first settlers wanted to cross the mountains to see what lay beyond,' Mackenzie said. 'We've a lot to thank them for.'

Prissy stared as he lit a candle. The small flare of light lit the dingy hut with its crude fireplace in one corner and nothing else. It was merely a shelter from the outside elements, no more.

'You'd thank convicts?' she said scathingly.

Mackenzie looked at her. For a minute the suspicion showed in her eyes and he shook his head.

'No, lassie, you needn't think you're coming to a convict's home. I'm a free settler, a squatter, and built my place with my own hands. But you wouldn't condemn a man after being transported for the smallest of crimes and serving out his sentence, would you? A lassie with your generous nature?'

'If that's meant to be a compliment, I'm not sure how to take it,' she snapped.

'Take it as it's meant,' he said, which told her exactly nothing.

'You don't have them working for you now, do you?' Prissy said, still with her English doctrines of the wickedness of criminals fixed in her mind.

'Only the ticket-of-leavers. I told you.'

He got a fire going with the ease of one well used to surviving in the wilds when he had to. Prissy snuggled into the blanket around her shoulders. Again there was that assumption that she understood everything he said without explanation. But this was a different language, after all, and this was a different world.

'Are you going to tell me what they are or do I have to guess?'

Mackenzie looked up from the fire. The flames had quickly caught on the dry wood and danced around his face. At that moment, Prissy thought he looked like a fire god, a heathen devil. She was tired beyond any tiredness she had known before, her imagination ready to play weird tricks with her.

'Convicts who've served their time and got their pardon, their ticket-of-leave,' he said shortly. 'Now, let's get settled. You look as if you could do with some hot mutton stew. Help me unload the provisions.'

She moved as if in a dream. By the time the smell of hot, none-too-fresh mutton stew was drifting into her nostrils from the tin can over the fire, she began to think she must be in the grip of an hallucination, and none of this was really happening. She was not really going to live on what was presumably some sort of farm, with blacks and ex-convicts, and a Scotsman who was the epitome of all those dour Scotsmen ever portrayed on the stage.

If it was all true, then she must have taken leave of her senses to leave all that she knew best. Without re-alising that she did so, she gave a small sob deep in her throat, and Mackenzie heard it.

Prissy felt the unexpected touch of his hand on her head. 'Don't fret, lassie. You're my responsibility now, and I've promised to let no harm come to you.'

He spoke gruffly, as if unwilling to let any sentiment show, but for Prissy it was a warm, intimate moment all the same. She nodded, not wanting to lose the sweet sensation by one of her idiotic replies, and got on with her allotted tasks. Later, she ate the mutton stew with some relish, realising how enormously hungry she was. She drank the steaming tea and rolled herself into her blanket like a veteran of such privations, trying uncom-plainingly to find the least bone-racking space on the hard floor and deriving a kind of comfort in knowing that Mackenzie would protect her, come what may.

*   *   *

Morning came all too soon, and after a sparse breakfast they were on their way again. It seemed as if they had been travelling for ever. The aches and pains in Prissy's body all seemed to merge into one great entity now, so that she couldn't have told where one bruise ended and another began. Sometimes she almost thought she glimpsed a sign of admiration in Mackenzie's eyes for the way she faced each new experience, but he never praised her and she guessed that it wasn't his way. How did his wife ever come to marry such a man? Prissy wondered suddenly.

'How long have you been in Australia?' she asked, trying to ignore the way the horses sometimes stumbled through the mountain passes and the wagon wheels rattled alarmingly on the uneven track.

'Seven years,' Mackenzie said briefly. 'We've done well by most standards. We've a ready market for our wool, and there's never a shortage of shearers every summer.'

He might have been speaking in a foreign tongue to a town-bred girl used to the smoke of foggy London. He caught her look.

'*Sheep*, lassie. Ballatree is a sheep station. Did you not realise that?'

'Oh, naturally,' Prissy said, exasperated. 'I had it all spelled out to me in letters a mile high before I left London that I'd be living at a sheep farm——'

'Station. We call it a station here.'

'Why?'

He gave a long sigh. 'Mebbe because we're so isolated, and each place is a welcome resting place for travellers. Who knows where words come from? It seems to suit the land and that's all that counts.'

He suited it too, Prissy could see that. He fitted it like a glove.

'So your son—Robbie—was born here?'

'Aye.'

She heard the softness in his voice for a moment, and knew at once that the child was dear to him. A new Australian, she supposed, when all the rest of them were the aliens. It was a piquant thought. She was about to say more when he stopped her, the softness gone.

'No more questions, Prissy. You'll see the lie of the land soon enough, and we're on the last part of the journey now.'

He'd actually used her name, Prissy thought, and it was such a surprise that she decided to be content with his remark. They spent two more nights in the open that were reminiscent of the first, but at least then they were beyond the mountains at last and down into the plains once more.

If plains they could be called, this rough, uneven, snake-infested country where you had to be wary where you put your feet and even more wary when you squatted for nature's sake and every bush hid a threat of something perilous that could kill with one bite. And there was always the dust and the heat and the flies...

But there were beauties, too, that Mackenzie pointed out to her. There were great brilliant butterflies that hovered magnificently in the trees. Birds of such startling colours and characteristic cries, as Prissy had never seen before. And by contrast, the delicate pink and grey of the galahs, and little darting lizards scuttling for shelter under rocks at the wagon's approach, that looked almost primeval, but which Mackenzie said were harmless.

There were the luscious wild red groundfruits that Mackenzie told her were quite edible, and which quenched the thirst so delightfully and stained their mouths red like clowns' mouths and made them laugh involuntarily at one another. And Prissy thought how different this man could be if only he would laugh more.

There were the occasional dust-whorls from other travellers on horseback or in wagons, though none near enough to tell if they were friends or foes. Mostly they were in a strange world of their own, the two of them, seemingly going on to the centre of the earth together, alternately dazzled by sunlight and relieved to be inside the dark, welcome shade of the bush, whatever the hazards.

And then, after four days and nights, they came out of the bush over a small rise, and there was only dazzling sunlight overhead, in a blue sky that seemed to stretch into infinity. And below, in the distance, but near enough to identify, were long, low buildings bunched around a solid-looking one-storey house with trees shading its veranda. There was a vast area of cleared land that had been fenced, and there was grass growing on the dark soil, if more parched-looking than the verdant English green that Prissy remembered. And there were great clusters of dirty white animals, weaving and running together as if they were pulled on strings, their mournful bleatings mingling with the everyday sounds of yapping dogs, all reaching out over the emptiness surrounding the homestead in a welcoming cacophony of noise.

'Civilisation!' Prissy gasped.

'You could call it that,' Mackenzie said. 'We call it Ballatree Station.'

'Oh, good Gawd Almighty! You didn't prepare me for a blessed palace, did you?' Prissy said, expansive in her relief at seeing that the end of the journey wasn't just a miserable shack. 'I think you've been having me on all this time, Mr Mackenzie.'

She grinned at him in delight, and then saw something in his face that almost stopped the excitement. It was a raw pain, a secret, private look laced with guilt. It was gone in an instant, but intuition told Prissy she was half right, anyway.

It wasn't just that, compared with herself, Mackenzie was definitely short on words and there was still plenty he could have told her in advance about her new home. It was more than that, and she sensed with certainty that there was something momentous he hadn't yet told her.

CHAPTER FOUR

THE distance between the foothills and the house was still deceptively far, but the nearer they got to Ballatree Station the more impressed Prissy became. The sight of the sprawling buildings that had seemingly sprung up out of thin air might have struck some people dumb. Nervousness simply made Prissy more of a chatterbox.

'You never told me it was going to be a perishing palace! It's enough to give anybody stage-fright! Why haven't you said anything about it all this time? You could have warned me what I was coming to.'

She spoke accusingly, as the white buildings assumed ever larger proportions as the wagon took them down from the lower slopes, to the vast bush-covered plain below. Behind and above them, the more barren rocks of the mountains gleamed in the brilliance of the morning sunshine, like polished pewter against a cloudless sky. But Prissy was more concerned now with the prospect of approaching civilisation than the wonders of nature.

Mackenzie actually laughed. 'I thought you told me you were a Londoner!'

'And what's that supposed to mean?' She couldn't keep the resentment out of her voice. Now that they were nearly here, she was acutely nervous of what lay ahead.

Was there going to be a small army of Aborigines, who would speak a language she didn't understand? And men called bushies and ticket-of-leavers who did strange jobs she'd never heard of, and masses of sheep bleating all day and all night . . . and a wife who must be eccentric at the very least if Mackenzie's veiled hints were to be

59

given credit...a child who needed some handling...and there was also the nagging thought that, apart from Mackenzie's wife, Prissy was likely to be the only other white woman at Ballatree Station. And just who could tell what kind of problems that was going to stir up!

'Ballatree Station's hardly a palace, lassie. Didn't you ever see the royal palace in London?' Mackenzie was saying. 'Even I have seen that and I come from the other end of the country.'

He stopped abruptly, but his words were enough to stir up new interest in Prissy. She frowned as she studied him from beneath the sun bonnet she wore constantly now to shield her complexion from the fierce daylight.

'Have you been to London, then? You never told me that. What did you think of it? Isn't it simply the best place in the whole world?'

She spoke enthusiastically, her self-confidence momentarily restored. She realised she liked the thought of him having been to London. It made a small link between them, knowing they had seen the same places, smelled the same good old London smells...making her feel less alone and homesick...

'I'm surprised you ever left it if you feel so strongly about it,' he said drily.

'I could say the same about you and your Scottish background, come to that. You've never lost your strong accent, in—what was it? Seven years? Not that I mind it, though. I like to hear a bit of an accent in folk, otherwise we'd all end up sounding the same, wouldn't we?' Realising she was gabbling on, and that he was her employer, after all, she added hastily, 'Anyway, you were going to tell me how many times you've been to London.'

'Was I?' he countered, and then shrugged. 'Och well, it was just the once. My wife and I stayed there for two nights before we took the emigration ship to Australia. She wanted to see the bright lights, so we had a carriage ride around the town. We saw the palace and the Tower and all those places folk are meant to find so wonderful.'

'Don't tell me you weren't impressed by them?' Prissy was amazed and outraged at the flatness in his tone. How could *anyone* not like London? Defensive pride of her birthplace made her sharp.

'I prefer open spaces,' Mackenzie said. 'It's why I'm here, where a man can breathe.'

She was exasperated by his terse replies. 'Breathe in dust and flies, you mean,' she said, automatically brushing a small cloud of them away from her face with a grimace. 'I bet your wife liked London. Did you take her to see the horses in the parks? And did you ever go to the theatre while you were there? I was only twelve years old and still had a family of my own seven years ago, so I wasn't play-acting then, or you might have seen me in a show. That would have been a laugh, now, wouldn't it——?'

'Do you ever stop asking questions?' Mackenzie snapped, and Prissy suddenly realised he was angry.

'Not when there's something I want to know,' she said, tilting her determined chin. 'Why shouldn't I be interested in you? I'm going to live with you, aren't I? In the same house, I mean,' she corrected herself quickly. 'Seems only natural that I should want to know what it's going to be like. You haven't even bothered to tell me much about your wife yet. What does she look like? Dark? Fair? Tall? Short? Fat? Thin?'

He reined in the horses with such a jerk that Prissy almost lost her balance in the wagon. She shot backwards and then forwards again, grasping desperately at Mackenzie's sleeve to stop being hurled out of the seat and landing ignominiously in a tangle of bush.

'What did you do that for?' she yelled. 'Are you trying to kill me before I even get to Ballatree Station?'

He was breathing very heavily. She was still holding on to his arm, and she could feel the tension in it. His jaw was rigid, his eyes dark with that strange private anguish she was positive lay hidden there. She had a sudden deep suspicion.

'You do have a wife, I take it? What's her name?' She shot the question at him. If he floundered over it . . .

'Flora,' he said harshly. 'Flora Blaney Mackenzie, late of Aberdeen. And the bairn's called Robbie Angus Mackenzie. My own full name is James Joyner Mackenzie, and I'm thirty-four years old and have all my own teeth. Now, is there anything else you'd like to know or can we proceed?'

Prissy felt a wild desire to laugh. It was so ludicrous to be sitting here in the middle of nowhere, introducing themselves as if they were the best of society.

Especially since Mackenzie's words had reminded her so vividly of two of Ma Jenkins's lodgers acting the part of a pantomime horse last Christmas, with one of them shrieking out the words 'And I've got all my own teeth too', while he flashed the enormous false chompers at the audience . . .

'Have I said something to amuse you?' she heard the man say, and guessed that her face had betrayed her. Her cheeriness vanished.

'Oh, for pity's sake, Mackenzie, don't you ever unbend?' she snapped. 'If I told you what I found so funny, you'd probably carry on sitting there poker-faced. I never met such a humourless man. It's true what they say about the Scots——'

'Try me.'

'What?' She stopped in full flood.

'What did I say that was so funny?' he went on relentlessly, determined not to move on until she did. And it was so damnably hot to be sitting here motionless, without a breath of wind to stir up the dust or the branches of the trees, and Prissy was beginning to wilt.

'It was just that remark about having all your own teeth, and I was remembering two of my old mates. Ron Phipps and Willy the Wily dressed up as a pantomime horse and Willy had to say the very same line...'

A gust of nostalgia swept over her so fast it took her completely by surprise. One minute she was resentfully relating the tale to Mackenzie, and the next she was blubbing against his shoulder without even knowing quite how she got there. And to her utter amazement she realised he was laughing. Not at *her* exactly, but at the daft story she'd just told him.

'Lassie, are you telling me you had a friend called Willy the Wily?' he said. 'And you had the gall to call Davy Golightly's name odd?'

She could hear the smile in his voice, and when she looked up at him, her eyes still full, she thought she detected a look of understanding on his face, as if he sensed after all just how vulnerable and alone she really felt, twelve thousand miles from home and where so far she knew no one but himself. She felt her own mouth curve into a half-smile.

'We had some dafter ones than that,' she said, the memories not quite so heart-tugging when they were shared. 'Ron was known as the stupendous rubber-neck, and then there was Daffy, the girl with three eyes——'

'Now you're the one who's being daft——'

'No, honestly! 'Course, the third eye wasn't a real eye. It was a huge mole in the middle of her forehead that she used to paint with stage make-up to make it look like another eye. When she waggled her head about under the lights it looked really weird.'

They were having a perfectly ordinary conversation, Prissy thought. If this could be called an ordinary conversation... but at least they weren't being as guarded as they sometimes were with each other. Not that *she* was ever guarded. She had no secrets, and she was always willing to share her thoughts with anybody willing to listen...

As if Mackenzie himself had decided that this bit of socialising had lasted long enough, he removed her from his shoulder where she'd been pressed comfortably close, and jerked the horses' reins again. They jogged along in silence for a few minutes, and it was almost possible to imagine they were just any two people enjoying an afternoon ride on a lovely sunny day...

Somewhere ahead of them there was the faint sound of voices shouting to one another, and with an odd feeling, almost of regret, Prissy knew that these four days with a stranger were coming to an end.

They'd been more than interesting, she admitted, and certainly something to fill her letters home with when she wrote to Ma Jenkins and the rest of the theatricals. The awful sea journey that had finally come to an end; finding and losing her friend Kate with such devastating swiftness; the pompousness of the Ladies' Committee in Sydney; the strange and hazardous journey to Ballatree Station and meeting the treacherous Badger along the way... and James Joyner Mackenzie.

She realised he had heard the shouting, too. For him, it was obviously familiar, part of the business of the working day. Their own brief rapport had gone, and she saw that closed look come over his face again, just as if it was a mask he chose to wear against any invasion of his privacy.

It was a shame, Prissy thought. He could be quite nice when he wasn't angry with her. She wondered if he was angry with everybody. She wondered how he behaved with his son. He'd certainly softened when he mentioned him. Robbie Angus Mackenzie...what a mouthful for a small boy...and she wondered how he behaved towards his wife. In public and in the privacy of their bedroom...

She was already hot, but she felt her face get hotter at the thought. It was the kind of thought no young, single woman should have about a married couple. But, at Ma Jenkins's, Prissy's world had been more Bohemian than most, and such discussions had been deliciously wicked and frank among the inmates. She might be quite innocent of men, but she had a sure theoretical knowledge of what marriage entailed between a man and a woman in love——

'What's wrong?' Mackenzie said.

She flinched, aware of her own surging thoughts, and she felt the comforting touch of his hand on hers before he put it back to the reins. He spoke again.

'I'm sorry if I startled you. You looked so pensive, I wondered if you were regretting coming here already. You're not, I hope?'

Prissy tried to answer lightly. 'I haven't decided yet. It all depends on whether your wife and son like me. They're the important ones in all this, aren't they?'

She glanced at him, and briefly their glances held. She caught her breath, wishing she could read his mind. His eyes were dark beneath the wide-brimmed hat, his mouth taut. For a second she wanted to run her fingers around that harshness and bring the smile back to his face. She liked his smile. She liked his voice when it lost its gruffness and warmed to the rich Scottish burr she found so fascinating. And she didn't need telling that it was the daftest thing any young, single girl could do to start liking a married employer too much!

'Just as long as you remember that,' he said, all the harshness back. 'I'm concerned for the bairn, and I'll trust you not to be gazing up at the stockhands with that wide-eyed look when you should be attending to his needs.'

Prissy's finer feelings towards the man were gone in an instant.

'I assure you I shan't be looking at anybody with a wide-eyed look if you're an example of what the men here are like,' she snapped. 'And I'm sorry if that offends you, Mr Mackenzie, but I've already told you I'm not looking for a husband. I'm here to work. That's what you'll pay me for, and you won't be disappointed.'

'You're not averse to men, are you?'

She laughed out loud at the very idea. 'Of course not! What woman in her right mind would say such a thing? But neither am I taking the first Tom, Dick or Harry who asks me to marry him just to get the soft life. I've got principles.'

'You certainly wouldn't get the soft life married to an Australian outbacker,' he commented.

'It's a good job I've no intention of marrying one, then!' she replied pertly.

One of the horses stumbled over a rut and the wagon lurched. Prissy clung on tight to the boards, not wanting to be pushed unwittingly into Mackenzie's arms again, in case he thought she had done it on purpose. All this talk of marrying was unsettling. Unless, of course, *he* was regretting hiring her, and it was his way of hinting that if she got hitched he'd be done with her...

As soon as the thought came into her head, she dismissed it. He didn't talk in riddles. If he wanted to say a thing, he'd say it plainly, the same as herself. In that, they were alike, she thought in surprise. And her sixth sense told her positively that there was still something he didn't *want* to say to her yet.

The long, low house and adjoining buildings could be called attractive, Prissy conceded. The whiteness of the walls reflected the glare of the sun rather too much for her eyes that were so tired from travelling, but the blue-painted shutters at the sides of every window matched the colour of the front door and gave the whole place a slightly frivolous look.

She wondered if his wife had insisted on giving a cheerful look to the place, in this barren wilderness she'd come to. It must have been nerve-racking to come to this new country after the township of Aberdeen. Prissy knew nothing about the land-lie of Scotland, but anything must seem civilised compared with this, especially how it was seven years ago. Mackenzie had presumably built all this with his own hands. She warmed to the woman and admired both her and her man greatly.

'Was the blue paint your wife's idea?' she asked conversationally, as Mackenzie seemed to have sunk into a morose silence again.

'It was not,' he said, to her surprise. 'It was Davy's.'

'Davy Golightly?' Prissy tried again to bring a smile to his face, but he merely nodded.

'Aye, 'tis part of his tribe's belief. His ancestors lived wild in the bush, though nowadays they live in huts and organised villages. They're superstitious about the colour blue, being that of the sky and the sea. Painting the doors and shutters blue is supposed to bring good luck to the house. It was a small thing to do to keep my stockman happy.'

'But you don't believe it,' Prissy said intuitively.

'We make our own luck, good or bad, and I've no faith in charms and the like. The sky turns black every night and where's your luck then?'

'I never heard such a miserable thing,' Prissy was un- accountably distressed by this statement. 'It may be black every night, but the next morning it's blue again, isn't it? The sun goes away at night, but it comes back again to warm up the earth when daylight comes again.'

'Don't try to impress me with your homespun phil- osophies, lassie. You don't understand this country yet. When you do, you'll forget all about luck and realise that only hard work pays dividends.'

'You need a bit of time for play too,' she muttered, suddenly sorry for the wife who'd followed him out here with love and hope, and wondered just how much Flora Blaney Mackenzie saw of her man now.

She turned away from him, reassessing the place she was to call home from now on, the home Flora would have come to so eagerly. There wasn't much in the way of a garden in front of the homestead. A staked wooden fence surrounded the immediate property, and seemed to Prissy to stretch a long way. Near to the house there was a patch of cleared land where a few straggling roses thirsted for water among some hardy shrubs in the blis- tering heat of the sun. There were some shady trees near the house, and beneath them was the one homely touch, a child's swing.

There was no sign of people yet. The men whose voices they had heard were evidently away from the buildings now, and it surprised Prissy that there was no wife and child rushing out to welcome Mackenzie home. He must have been away for more than a week. If she was his wife, she'd have been rushing into her man's arms...

The blue front door opened. Against the dimness of the interior, Prissy saw a very dark face with squashed features, in particular a wide flat nose. The face had a ridged sloping forehead, and Prissy realised she was looking at a very ugly young woman of short stature, incongruously wiping her floury hands on an apron. With slight hysteria Prissy thought that this person with the polished ebony skin should really be barefooted and carrying a spear alongside her menfolk instead of wearing perfectly normal apparel...

Then a small boy came running out from behind her skirts and brought normality back. He was dark-haired and dark-eyed, and so much a mirror image of James Mackenzie that nobody could mistake them for anything but father and son.

Robbie was shouting and whooping as he flung himself towards Mackenzie, who was down from the wagon in an instant and swinging his son round and round in the first expression of pure joy Prissy had seen in him.

'Pa, Pa, don't go 'way again. Iona says you'll promise if I ask it. Did you bring me presents?'

Mackenzie laughed, his eyes warm with love for the child. 'Yes, I brought you something, but you'll have to wait a while until I find it. And why should I go away again, you ninny? You know full well I only went to fetch someone to look after you. This is Prissy. Say hello to her now, there's a good wee laddie.'

The boy's excitement visibly lessened a little, although his arms were still tightly around his father's neck. He glared towards Prissy. She smiled encouragingly, suddenly aware that she really didn't know how to handle small boys at all, and this one didn't look exactly pleased to see her. After a few seconds' scrutiny, when Mackenzie repeated his instruction for Robbie to say hello he buried his face in his father's neck and muttered something unintelligible.

'Come on now, Robbie, I canna hear a single word,' Mackenzie said, and Prissy could see at once that, though he loved his son, he was short on patience.

He put Robbie down on the ground and knelt down beside him, holding the boy away from him. 'If you've something to say, then say it properly and don't mumble.'

For a second the boy continued to glare mutinously from his father to Prissy and back again. He finally took a deep breath and shrieked out the words.

'Is she my new mother?'

Prissy gasped. The Aborigine woman came forward at once and took the boy from Mackenzie as he put him firmly down on the ground. She sounded apologetic.

'The boy, he overtired, Mackenzie. He been waiting for you long time, and he want his afternoon sleep. Come on now, Robbie. You see Pa later.'

He was still protesting noisily, kicking against her skirts as she hurried him inside. Prissy felt her heart thud against her ribs. Mackenzie turned away without comment to start taking her hold-alls out of the back of the wagon and didn't even attempt to help her down. She clambered down stiffly, feeling as if every muscle was stretched to its limit, and thinking longingly of to-night when she would sleep in a real bed with real sheets... but that could wait. There were more important things to sort out. She marched towards Mackenzie, hands on hips, uncaring if it was ladylike or not.

'What the blue blazes did the boy mean by that?'

Mackenzie tightened his lips. 'That'll be a fine and dandy phrase to teach him, Miss Baxter——'

'Don't twist words with me, *Mr* Mackenzie! You've already told me the boy hears plenty of ripe language from your men. What I want to know is, why did he ask if I'm going to be his new mother? He's already got a mother, hasn't he?'

'It was a child's nonsense, no more. Bairns of that age say all kinds of things——'

'Do they? It's not all nonsense, I'm thinking. "Out of the mouths of babes and sucklings"——'

'I was forgetting you'd be knowing such quotations, you being a professional person.' He might have been trying to flatter her for all she knew, but to Prissy the words were nothing short of insulting.

'My profession was respectable and honourable and I'd have you know it——'

'That's as may be. Do you think I'd have hired you for my son's welfare if I didn't think you fitted that description full well?'

'Just why *did* you hire me?' she challenged him.

It would be good to think he'd thought her eminently suitable, a cheerful companion for his son, a confidante for his wife...

'You happened to be first in the line when I approached the biddy in the big hat at Sydney harbour. You said you'd be willing to come and that was that. I didn't ask for the moon, and besides, you knew well enough what was written on my application form,' he snapped, wounding her more with every word. 'Mrs James Mackenzie was merely requesting the services of a young woman for help in the house and with the bairn——'

'So where is she?' Prissy snapped back.

For a moment she thought he was going to have an apoplectic fit. The veins on his forehead and in his neck seemed to stand out like cords, and it was obvious that he was holding himself in check with an enormous effort. He suddenly dumped her hold-alls on the ground and grabbed her hand. She had no option but to follow him, her feet skimming over the dusty ground as he strode ahead, pulling her after him, well away from the main building of the house towards a small thicket around the back.

She suddenly felt frightened. That Mackenzie had a hasty temper she was all too aware—it matched her own. That he could be unpredictable was another trait that she usually didn't find at all alarming in a person, it often added a piquancy to their character... but to be man-handled by this silent stranger before she'd even set foot inside his house was something different... She didn't even *know* him, however much four days thrown in his company had made her believe she did.. He was still an enigma to her, a self-contained man who didn't want to be known or understood or loved...

'Will you please stop?' she gasped. 'Mackenzie, you're hurting me, and whatever I've said to offend you, I'm sorry.'

He didn't pause and she was almost running to keep up with his long legs. The heat of the day was beginning to make her feel faint. She could hardly think straight any more. Tears smarted her eyes as she wondered just what kind of barbaric country she had come to, where a man could treat a woman so brutally, and the great adventure was turning into a nightmare...

'You wanted to know the whereabouts of my wife,' she heard Mackenzie say harshly. 'Well, there's your answer, lassie.'

Prissy caught her breath on a sob, opening her eyes without realising how tightly closed they had been in those last few minutes. She blinked furiously a few times, hating herself for feeling so weak and out of control. The only sounds were the constant noise of the cicadas in the thicket of trees, Mackenzie's laboured breathing, and her own, ragged and gasping.

Then she saw where he pointed, and shock rippled through her, because she had never expected anything like this. She had never even guessed...

There was a rectangular mound of earth enclosed by wrought-iron railings, presumably to keep out any marauding animals. At the head of the mound was a rough-hewn piece of stone on which some simple words had been scratched. None of it looked old or weathered.

'Flora Blaney Mackenzie. 1806—1834.'

Just that. Nothing more. No sentiments, no flowery verses, no emotional words of farewell. The starkness of it made it seem all the more terrible. For once, Prissy couldn't find any words to say.

'I'm sorry,' Mackenzie said finally, when they had both stood motionless for what seemed an age.

She flinched, not wanting to look at him, yet knowing that she must. His face had that set, hard look on it again, but now she knew there was good reason for it. He wasn't a man who cared to show his feelings, but that didn't mean they weren't still there, deep down.

'Why should you be sorry? It wasn't your fault, was it?' She bit her lip. The words hadn't come out the way she had intended, and it was a tactless, ghastly thing to say. The man was obviously still suffering after losing his wife.

And if he wasn't... her vivid imagination took over. If he wasn't then, for all she knew, he might have poisoned Flora or strangled her or...

She was shivering, despite the heat of the day. In here, within the thicket, it was steamy and claustrophobic, and they were well out of sight of the house. She felt Mackenzie's hands on her shoulders and gave a little cry. He didn't seem to notice it.

'I'm sorry because I should have told you before. I just never seemed able to manage it. A man should be able to get used to these things. We have to accept that dying's a part of living, and to make the best of it.'

Prissy became aware that he was angry. She mumbled platitudes, clumsily trying to offer him comfort.

'I should just think you did find it hard to say. A man needs time to mourn these things. No man's strong enough to dismiss the years he's spent with his wife so easily——'

'I'd thank you not to analyse me,' Mackenzie said shortly. 'And six months is long enough to get used to the way of things——'

She stared up at him. 'Six months?' she echoed.

Somehow she'd assumed it was very recent. Her thoughts whirled, her own anger bubbling up inside her.

'Then your application form was sent to Sydney under false pretences. It wasn't your wife who sent it at all. I saw the date on it, and it was only a month ago...'

She backed away from the burial place. It wasn't decent to be standing here wrangling with the man when the remains of Mackenzie's wife were enclosed inside those wrought-iron railings like a silent sentinel. It wasn't seemly to start surmising exactly what Mackenzie had had in mind when he applied for a helper for his wife and child...his *deceased* wife...

She turned and ran, but there was nowhere to go, and he caught up with her easily. Now his hands were brutal on her arms as he held her captive.

'All right, so it was a small but necessary deception. Do you think those narrow-minded Committee folk would have agreed to send a young woman into the outback if they knew she was going to be the only white woman for miles? I had no devious motive in mind. I need help for my bairn, as you can see for yourself.'

Unwittingly, with every word he made her see the appalling situation she had got herself into. She was always too impulsive, rushing into things without giving them any proper thought, trusting to intuition. And now she was the only white woman for miles around... Prissy ran her tongue around her dry lips, and tasted the dust on them. It wasn't even English dust. It was alien, full of dangers she couldn't even contemplate yet.

She pushed the thought away before she went completely mad. She was already light-headed, lacking proper sleep, needing food, and desperate for something to soothe her parched throat. Needing time to take stock and decide what she had to do next.

Her thoughts switched abruptly, because the memory of young Robbie Mackenzie's words were no longer a child's nonsense. She could hear them again in her head, said in that shrill, aggressive little voice.

'Is she my new mother?'

He must have heard the words somewhere, put two and two together, and had already built up a strong resentment against Prissy. She could hear Ma Jenkins's voice too, warning her that she might be going into a life of white slavery, and remembered the chirpy Prissy who had laughed off such warnings.

She didn't feel like laughing now. She spoke as contemptuously as she could to the man who was holding her, praying that her voice wouldn't quiver as much as her legs did. She valued honesty above all things, and was hardly able to contain her fury at his deception. All the same, it was a fury mixed with fear.

'And what about you? What do *you* need, Mackenzie?'

CHAPTER FIVE

HE STARED down at her without speaking. Because of his height, the brim of his hat shielded his eyes and she could only see the lower part of his face. His well-shaped mouth above that stern jaw was one that any woman would find attractive, but Prissy was in no mood to consider such things right now, and was annoyed that the thought should have entered her head at all.

'It's every man's right to have a home and family. The bairn needs a woman's care.' He avoided giving a more personal answer to her question without really telling her anything, and he spoke without emotion.

Prissy fumed. It was an irritatingly non-committal reply, yet in a way it made him seem a little more human and gave her back a vestige of pride. At least she was capable of caring for a child. A while back, she'd really been ready to believe he'd cheated her, bringing her to this wilderness land and about to force her into a farce of a marriage.

And none of it would have seemed to be against her will, she realised. She'd agreed to come. More than that, she'd *offered* herself, but not in the way he might think, and it was time she put him exactly right on that.

'Please understand that I'm not here as a marriage bargain, Mr Mackenzie,' she said coldly. 'I came here to work and nothing more. Is that understood?'

'Naturally I expect you to work for your living, since you're not here on sufferance.' He ignored the words completely this time, and she could detect a hint of sarcasm in his voice.

She answered in the airy, infuriating manner that Ma Jenkins had always called her madam voice.

'I haven't decided whether I'll stay or not yet.'

The minute she'd said it she knew it was a mistake. She saw the twist of a smile on his handsome mouth.

'You don't actually have any choice.'

'Why don't I? You said the next homestead was no more than twenty miles away, and I could surely get somebody to take me there——'

'None of my men would take you anywhere I didn't want you to go, lassie. And you're forgetting something else,' he said with infuriating calm.

She snapped at him, 'What am I forgetting?'

'The papers you've signed. You belong to me now for as long as we suit one another. Or mebbe in this case it should be for as long as we can put up with one another.'

Prissy gasped. What he was suggesting might not be officially called white slavery, but it might as well have been for the bonds he applied.

'And you're forgetting that some representatives from the Ladies' Committee will be calling to see if I've settled in in three or four months' time, and I might well have a few things to say to them when they do!'

Her triumph quickly faded when he gave a short laugh. 'Och, aye, I'll agree that we've a definite three or four months to get to know whether we'll suit. And in that time you'll mebbe be seeing things differently. You'll know if you like the land, and if the land likes you.'

She refused to admit how the phrase charmed her creative mind. Instead, she realised how she had committed herself, trapped by her own cleverness.

But he was right, of course, and there had never really been any choice. Not since she'd signed the papers and thought herself no end of a swell in getting a post so easily and quickly after stepping off the emigration boat. She felt her shoulders sag, the false pride fizzling away.

Mackenzie spoke briskly. 'We'll be getting back to the house now, Prissy. We all need to adjust to the new way of things. Besides, you're tired now, and things will look better after a good night's sleep.'

He managed to convey the ludicrous impression that this was no more than an ordinary walk they'd been taking at the end of an ordinary day.

She walked beside him all the way back to the house. It was farther than she'd realised, since they'd practically run to the thicket in a fury, and as she walked, she was aware of homesickness and tiredness sweeping over her in waves. She longed for England and home.

She longed to be clasped in the bosom of her theatrical family, listening to all their nonsense and eating one of Ma Jenkins's undistinguished meat pies for supper. She wished Kate were here, sweet, pretty Kate with whom she could have laughed over this predicament and taken the sting out of it all.

She was awash with misery as she and Mackenzie plodded over the uneven ground. She remembered with a new aching misery that she hadn't even been able to raise the five pounds' passage money to come to Australia, so she was tied hand and foot to the new country and, for the time being at least, to this man.

But by the time they neared the white building with the blue front door again, Prissy had made a definite resolve. She might be tied to Australia for the foreseeable future, but she'd be damned if she'd remain tied to James Mackenzie for one minute longer than necessary.

Inside the house it was blissfully cooler than outside, although Prissy soon realised that it was little more than

an illusion, and within minutes she was feeling the
crawling heat on her skin again. The child had been put
to bed for an hour or so, since it was the hottest part of
the day, without a breath of wind to stir the trees or
allow humans to breathe.

The stockman's wife came out from the kitchen to
greet them again, and was introduced to Prissy properly.
For the first time in her life, Prissy felt her hand clasped
by a hand that wasn't merely made black with grease-
paint for a performance, and met the wide grin of a
mouth that seemed over-filled with teeth. Iona was
younger than Prissy had imagined, perhaps only a few
years older than Prissy herself. She could never be called
handsome, but the warmth and friendliness in the amply
proportioned little figure made up for all that.

'Welcome, lady,' Iona said, and Mackenzie gave a
small snort.

'There's no need to be so blessed formal. Her name's
Prissy, and you can use it as well as the rest of us. Make
us some cold tea for now, there's a good lass, and if
there's some bread and meat going we'll be glad of it.'

It was incongruous to Prissy to hear the black woman
addressed as a good lass, but she evidently adored
Mackenzie and was happy to do his bidding, however
brusque his words.

'You want see kitchen?' Iona invited Prissy, and between two women Prissy knew that this was immediate
acceptance. And she sensed at once that the Aborigine
woman had no feelings of resentment or jealousy towards her, which was something of a relief after all the
recent traumas. If lack of jealousy was an Aboriginal
trait, then she was all for it. She needed a friend, and
it didn't matter a jot to her what colour friends came
in.

'I'd love to see it later, but can I see my bedroom first?' she pleaded. 'I feel so grubby, and I'd dearly like a bowl of water to wash away the dust.'

'I see to it,' Iona said at once. 'You take to room,' she addressed Mackenzie. 'I bring water.'

Prissy hid a smile at the sudden realisation that Iona was giving him orders, and he was already picking up her hold-alls and moving towards a long passage.

She followed him until he opened the door of a room and put her things inside. She couldn't resist an exclamation of pleased surprise. It wasn't the poshest of rooms, but it had everything she could want. The bed was covered with a bright patchwork quilt, clearly visible through the gauze of a mosquito net that Prissy assumed was necessary equipment.

There was a dressing-table and a cupboard for her frocks, and a night-stand for her convenience. Several rag rugs covered the wooden floor boards that had been stained to a rich mahogany, and there were thin curtains at the window. The walls were covered with dark wallpaper on which bluebirds flew gaily among bright pink cabbage roses.

'It's a lovely room,' she said honestly. 'It's far better than the one I had at my old place in London.'

Mackenzie dumped her belongings on the floor.

'You mean something actually pleases your ladyship?'

She felt her face go even hotter.

'I told you Ballatree Station looked like a palace and I meant it. I certainly wasn't expecting to find something like this out in the wilds. And...and I'll do my best with the boy, Mackenzie, really I will.'

She was suddenly embarrassed, knowing how she had argued and fought with him during the last four days, never knowing the truth of his situation. And prepared, for the moment, to be generous and forgive him his faults.

'That you will, lassie, or I'll be sending in complaints to your Ladies' Committee,' he said keenly.

'Complaints?'

She blinked, not expecting this after she'd as good as held out an olive branch.

'Both sides have to suit,' he went on. 'You may not suit me yet, nor Robbie neither. Did you think you were the only one concerned in all this? I'd heard that London folk think they own the earth, but even if that wasn't like a red rag to a hot-blooded Scotsman, they don't own this particular part of the earth, lassie. In Australia everyone's equal.'

Sometimes he could be as garrulous as the next one, especially when he got on his high horse, she thought.

'Except that some are bosses and some are not——'

'Aye, and that's about the truth of it. You'll do well to remember it. Now then, when Iona's brought your washing water, do what you need to do and come and have some food. You'll soon revive your spirits, I've no doubt.'

His last words were said with more of a dry acceptance than encouragement. And then he was gone, leaving Prissy staring at the open door. He really was the most exasperating, irritating, and, yes, *interesting* man she had ever met... She paused, admitting that it was definitely so. Life was never dull when James Joyner Mackenzie was around, but it had only just occurred to her.

Some people might think him extremely dull with that dour expression and aggressive manner that he could don so easily. But there was another side to him. One that she had only glimpsed so far. This home that he had built for his wife and son showed love and devotion.

Prissy had already seen rare moments of tenderness in him, and there was no doubting his love for his son. And the man himself . . . that smile that could transform his long face so dramatically . . . and the way his voice could soften and become richer, almost seductive, when he chose to make it so . . .

She shivered, wondering why such daft thoughts should come into her head right now. She was so appallingly tired, and the sight of that bed was so inviting . . . she lifted the mosquito net and pressed the mattress a few times. It was soft and bouncy, and it surely wouldn't matter if she just lay down for a few blissful minutes, just until Iona brought her the jug of water . . .

Images floated in and out of her head behind her closed eyelids. Great cabbage-head pink roses in full fragrant bloom in an English summer, with an ugly-beautiful black face in the middle of them. The chink of china and the warm pungent scent of oil-lamps . . . a handsome man whose face she couldn't see properly leaning towards her and murmuring words that she couldn't follow.

But the timbre of his voice lingered in her head. It was one that could make her toes curl the way they'd used to in the old days, when a performance at the Alhambra had gone really well and instinct told her that this was something good . . . there was a small person held high in a larger person's arms and that deep voice again was telling him he had to behave . . . and all of them floating in and out of her senses so that she didn't know whether she was awake or asleep, fully conscious or merely dreaming . . .

Slowly, Prissy turned her head towards the window. The panes of glass were dark with night now, and she could see a myriad of stars through them. Australian stars, the thought slid vaguely into her head, and on the other side of the world where night was day, the morning might be only just beginning...no wonder her head felt turned upside-down. *She* was turned upside-down!

Someone had lit the oil-lamp on her dressing table, and its warm yellow glow lit the room and threw soft shadows around it. She was still so hot...she saw the jug of water in the bowl on the night-stand and she wondered if she was still half-dreaming.

She blinked a couple of times as if to clear her head. The full realisation of where she was came sharply into focus at last. She wasn't at home, in England, and the roses in her dreams had been only those on the patterned wallpaper. The black face was Iona's, the others belonged to Mackenzie and his son, presumably come to inspect her and see that she was still breathing...checking up on their new acquisition for Ballatree Station.

Abruptly, Prissy sat up and hugged her knees. She felt so dishevelled, still wearing the dusty stage-frock that seemed so out of place, but was the only thing to stop her melting clean away. Her long hair in which she'd always taken such pride was straggly and unkempt as it fell over her shoulders, and suddenly the weak tears wouldn't stop. She buried her face in her knees and wondered just what the indigo blue blazes she was doing here.

'Feeling better now?' Mackenzie's voice said.

Prissy's head flew up at once, the tears still on her cheeks. She dashed them away at once. She didn't believe in keeping emotion in if it needed to come out, but she didn't intend letting this man think she'd gone all lily-livered either. It didn't occur to her that there was anything out of place in his appearance in her bedroom whenever he chose. She was just a child to him, another source of annoyance like his son could obviously be at times. She spoke jerkily.

'I'm all right. I didn't mean to fall asleep like that. I'm sorry. I'll get up right away.'

He strode across the room and put his hand on her forehead. His hand was cool on her skin and for a moment she was aware that she'd like to keep it there. He removed it with a nod of satisfaction.

'Yes, you're all right. There's no fever, just exhaustion. It's just as well. We're so far from anywhere that by the time a doctor gets here a fever's usually run its course and done one of two things.'

She didn't need to ask what they were. The patient either got better on her own, or did the other thing. She was tempted to ask if that was what had happened to Flora Mackenzie, but she didn't dare. Particularly as his next words reminded her that Prissy would be more of a nuisance to him if she died than if she constantly irritated him like a burr beneath his skin.

'Besides, I couldn't be doing with all the extra trouble just now, with shearing just around the corner. The Ladies' Committee would be wanting to know all the ins and outs, I dare say, and I'd have to waste time in starting all over again to find a nursemaid for Robbie.'

Prissy could hardly believe she was hearing him aright. How could anyone be so insensitive? He wasn't concerned about her well being at all, just about himself and his blasted sheep and his own affairs . . . before she could even get her tongue around her outraged reply, he had seen the sparkle come back to her eyes, and she realised that he was grinning.

'That's better. The last thing I want for Robbie is a gloomy companion. Now you look more like the Prissy Baxter with plenty of spunk that I first saw. For a minute I thought we were in for a flood. Not that we couldn't do with it, mind. The creek's threatening to dry up and a bit of rain would do our sore eyes a power of good, to say nothing of a good summer grazing to put healthier wool on the sheeps' backs.'

She hardly noticed what he said, she just felt relief at seeing him smile again. She might not feel comfortable here, yet, but he was her only lifeline in this alien place.

'So you don't really want to get rid of me already?' she burst out inconsequentially.

'Did I ever say that I did? Taking a four-day trip to Sydney and then hanging about for the boat to arrive and settle the business, and then another four-day trip back here, wasn't my idea of heaven, lassie.'

He had the most charming way of dousing a compliment, but she was getting more used to him now. She could even learn to overlook the insults, whether they were intended or not, and concentrate on the bits of his conversation that interested her most.

'What is, then? Your idea of heaven, I mean.'

She dared to ask it, assuming that she was the business he'd had to settle, and suddenly realising she was quite enjoying the incongruity of sitting here in a bedroom in a strange new country, exchanging interesting trivia with a man she hardly knew.

And yet she did know him. In a way, she already knew the heart and soul of him, the parts that mattered. She knew he was capable of loving and caring, of surviving and conquering and building for the future. He was everything a woman could want in a man.

'Heaven?' Mackenzie broke into her startled thoughts. 'You tell me the answer to that if you can, lassie. Nobody ever knows what heaven is until they find it. It's one of life's great unsolved mysteries, and so will Iona's stew be if we don't eat it soon. Five minutes from now and it'll be cleared away from the eating-room, right?'

'Yes, sir,' she said smartly, resisting the urge to salute and wipe that smile from Mackenzie's face.

After he left her room she sat quite still for a few more seconds, just revelling in the fact that they had actually behaved like two normal people for once, without sparring with one another. It was a pleasant change. It probably wouldn't last, but it was something to savour while it did.

Prissy got up quickly, and splashed the cold water around her face and neck, glorying in its sensuous touch on her heated skin. She would never take such luxuries for granted again, she vowed. She changed her frock quickly for a cleaner one. It was hopelessly creased from the journey, but still cool and fresh, the cream-coloured cambric emphasising the way her skin had gradually become tanned to a soft golden hue.

She looked at herself in the dressing-table mirror with some surprise. She had changed. She was a different girl from the one who had taken such care of her skin in the way theatrical folk did, but it suited her. The outdoor life had brought a new kind of sparkle to her eyes, too. She brushed out the tangles in her hair and began to feel almost human again.

Before she left the bedroom, she struggled ineptly with the window catch to let in the evening air, until she finally realised foolishly that it opened inwards. It was still as hot as Hades, but at least it would freshen up the air in the room, she decided, and closed the door behind her to follow the tempting aroma of hot meat stew.

Mackenzie was deep in discussion with his head stockman when Prissy found the aptly named eating-room. The house was built on one level, with all the rooms going off one central passage, so it was easy enough to follow the trail. The eating-room was sparsely but serviceably furnished with a huge table and a set of chairs, and a large sideboard and server. The table was already set with four places on a white damask cloth and Iona was just carrying in a steaming tureen of stew.

Even while Prissy was wondering how they could bear to eat it in this climate, it was making her mouth water. She was extraordinarily hungry by now. She hadn't eaten anything since taking a frugal meal with Mackenzie at about midday as they left the foothills of the mountain ranges, and already that seemed like days ago.

She looked with some interest at the head stockman. She guessed that Davy Golightly was probably about Mackenzie's age, although Prissy found it hard to gauge properly, because to her the smooth, polished dark skin of the Aboriginal people, ridged only by that distinctive sloping forehead, somehow seemed ageless. Davy was somewhat taller and thinner than his wife, but there the surface difference ended.

Prissy's instant impression of the two Aborigines was that the dark skins were the same, and so were the wide toothy smiles and squat flaring noses. Davy's black hair was as wild and curly as his wife's and only a mite shorter. It was clearly the habit for the two of them to eat with Mackenzie. With the two of them here, at least this house resembled something of a home. Even more so with herself making up a quartet...

She was glad when Mackenzie broke into her thoughts just then.

'Come and meet Davy Golightly, lassie, whom I've already told you about. The rest of the men live in the bunkhouse and do their own cooking, and you'll be seeing them round and about the place in due course, but Davy and Iona live in the main house and we all muck in together.'

'I'm happy to meet you, Davy,' Prissy said.

She spoke freely and naturally. This strange gathering didn't seem as odd to her as it might to some other young ladies fresh out of England. She was quite used to a mishmash of folks mucking in together, as Mackenzie called it, and if these new ones were of a different skin-tone to herself, it only added to the Bohemian flavour she loved. They were all the same under the skin, she'd told Mackenzie, and she meant it.

'Davy happy meet you too. Davy like white ladies,' he announced, at which Mackenzie laughed out loud.

'You'd best be careful how you say such things, laddie, or our Miss Prissy will be getting the wrong idea.'

'No, I won't,' she grinned back. 'I think it was a lovely thing to say, and I understand perfectly.'

Davy's smile grew even wider, and Prissy felt that at least these people were the kind who didn't see hidden undercurrents behind everything she said. Davy Golightly was open and honest, and she instantly warmed towards him. And to Iona too, who beamed as if Prissy's compliment to her husband embraced herself as well.

'You like mutton stew?' Iona asked now, spooning out a great helping of meat and vegetables on to Prissy's dish.

'I certainly do,' she said with relish, and endeared herself forever to the other girl by finishing every bit and only pushing back her dish after she'd had three helpings.

'I'm glad to see you're a woman with a healthy appetite and not one of these who only pick at their food,' Mackenzie said drily, when she realised what a pig she'd made of herself.

'I'll slow down from now on,' she grinned, feeling the sash of her frock beginning to pinch tight. 'I don't want to end up too fat to get into my clothes.'

Davy had his own ideas about that.

'Men like fat women to get arms around,' he commented, demonstrating with exaggerated arm movements that amused Iona greatly and caused Mackenzie to tell Prissy that their tribe considered it a great asset for their women to be well covered.

'Well, I'm never going to insult you by refusing your lovely meals, Iona,' she said quickly, knowing she had a lot to learn if she was to live side by side with these big-hearted people.

She drank copious amounts of water that first evening, partly because she was still so parched and partly just because it was there and it was so lovely to drink as much as she liked. After the main meal Iona brought a basket of fresh mixed fruits to the table, washed down with the strong black coffee that they all seemed to like, and to which Prissy hoped she would become accustomed in time.

She found it hard to control her yawning. She was still unutterably tired, and the buzz of conversation was beginning to merge into unintelligible gibberish in her brain. Some of it was clearly in Davy's native tongue, she realised, and guessed that this was a novel way for Mackenzie to effectively shut her out of business matters that didn't concern her.

'Does anyone mind if I go to bed?' she broke in, thinking this the height of bad manners. 'I'm very tired and I need to be fresh to meet Robbie properly. I'll see everything in the morning.'

The two men grinned at one another.

'Everything will take more than a morning, lassie, but 'twill be a good start. Aye, goodnight then, and sleep well.'

She got up slowly, her joints having stiffened now that they had actually stopped travelling and the ground wasn't constantly moving beneath her. It still felt as though it did, though, and she walked carefully back to her room and opened the door.

The next minute, she gave a great shriek as a cloud of living things swarmed towards her, attacking her face and neck and bare arms, while she spat furiously as they threatened to fill her mouth. She stamped her feet as if that would rid her of the things, and in seconds Mackenzie and the others came running. As soon as they saw her, they pulled her bedroom door shut behind them, enclosing all four of them in her room as Prissy fought furiously to scrub at her arms and neck.

'You idiotic woman. Did you have no more sense than to leave the window open without closing the shutters?'

Mackenzie strode across and banged the window shut. 'You've got all the insects in creation swarming about the place now, attracted by your lamp.' Before she could say anything, he had cupped the glass and blown out the lamp, leaving a pungent smell of oil in the room.

'The smell might help rid the room of some of them and, Davy, fetch the swatter and we'll do the best we can.'

Prissy stood in acute misery as the men did what they could. She heard the wail of a child's cry and heard Mackenzie curse quietly before Iona scuttled off to soothe Robbie, woken by her scream.

It didn't take all that long for the men to be satisfied they had done all they could.

'At least you had the sense to leave the mosquito net covering over the bed, so there'll be no insects inside it,' Mackenzie said brusquely. Prissy was thankful there wasn't enough light in the room for him to see her guilty face. The net wasn't covering the bed through any thought of caution on her part. She'd just assumed the bed had to be made up that way, and had thrown the cover back before she went to the eating-room.

'Is all right now,' Davy said more kindly. 'You know next time.'

She certainly would. Did Mackenzie think she was clairvoyant, knowing all there was to know in this awful place without being told? She was about to make some scathing remark when his next words chilled her.

'Just be thankful there was nothing more deadly than insects in the room. We've had a good search round, and there's nothing else to worry about.'

She didn't even dare ask what he meant...

'Thank you,' she said in a small voice, resisting with a great effort the urge to scratch and scratch at her bitten skin until the men were out of the room.

Davy disappeared, leaving Mackenzie to give the room a final check, and ensure that the shutters were firmly closed before he opened the window again. So *that* was why it opened inwards, Prissy thought weakly. As he lit her lamp she looked fearfully about the room, but the dust cloud of insects had gone.

'I'm really sorry for all the fuss I caused,' she said. 'It won't happen again.'

For a second Mackenzie looked at her steadily, and before she could guess what was happening he had put his hands on her shoulders and kissed her lightly on the forehead.

'You weren't to know. I'm as much to blame for not warning you. Get some sleep now, lassie, and things will look brighter in the morning. You're home now.'

When he had gone, her eyes pricked with tears at the unexpectedness of his words. She undressed quickly and slid into bed inside the mosquito net, pushing aside the quilt and just covering herself with a cotton sheet because of the heat. Her skin itched abominably, and it was a long while before the irritation let her sleep, but she was comforted and still disbelieving that Mackenzie had kissed her.

It could hardly have been called a lover's kiss, but the touch of his mouth against her skin had been the first real gesture that he saw her as something more than a nuisance or a nursemaid. And she wouldn't even begin to wonder why it meant so much to her.

CHAPTER SIX

PRISSY was only aware that it was morning when she awoke with the feeling of something heavy on her legs. She was almost too afraid to look, in case it was something awful . . . but she was more afraid not to know. She opened her eyes a chink and saw Mackenzie's son sitting cross-legged on her feet and staring at her unblinkingly.

'Hello, Robbie!'

She was more relieved than anything else, knowing that she wasn't about to encounter some horror of the night, nor some outlandish animal or hobgoblin, but a living, breathing, perfectly normal little boy.

'I don't like you,' Robbie said mutinously. His lower lip stuck out, making him resemble so exactly a miniature version of his father in a bad temper that Prissy almost laughed out loud. But that would be the very worst thing she could do, she thought hastily.

'You don't know me yet, so how do you know you don't like me? You've got to get to know somebody first, before you know if you like them or not,' she said reasonably.

Whatever he thought about that, he obviously had something else on his mind.

'I don't want a new mother. I want Iona.'

He began to wail loudly, and Prissy decided the only way to deal with this was to treat him as an intelligent human being and not mollycoddle him, which was something he clearly didn't want from *her*.

'I'm not your new mother, you silly little boy,' she said crossly. 'I'm your nursemaid, and nothing else. I'm not anybody's mother.'

He stopped wailing, and Prissy had the distinct impression that he could turn the waterworks on and off whenever he chose. He was completely spoiled, she thought, but it was no wonder, poor little dab, losing his mother when he was only three years old. If it was six months ago, he probably wouldn't even remember her clearly any more, and Iona would have become his chief attachment. No wonder he didn't want anybody else.

'What's a nursemaid?' Robbie said, still sullen.

Prissy sat up in the bed, pulling her feet from under him, surprised to find they'd gone a bit numb. She wondered just how long he'd been sitting there.

'It's somebody who plays with you and sings to you and takes you for walks and things like that,' she said. 'You like playing games, don't you?'

He stared at her unblinkingly. He had the oddest way of doing that, and she remembered that Davy and Iona also had unblinking stares. He'd been in their company too long, Prissy thought. However well-meaning they were, the boy needed care from his own kind. Mackenzie was right in that—and no doubt he was far too busy himself to pay much attention to his own child. Indignation overcame everything else at that moment.

'Sometimes Pa lets me play with horses,' he was full of importance now, 'and I go with Iona to the creek for water. I like that. I ride on the cans.'

'Yes, well, we'll have to see about that,' Prissy muttered, thinking it all sounded highly dangerous. 'Anyway, go away now and let me get dressed, and then we'll have some breakfast. Is your daddy—is your pa up?'

'He went out with Davy. They come back for breakfast,' Robbie said.

Prissy supposed the days started early for the men, even though she had no idea what a sheep farmer did all day. Sheep just wandered about and ate grass, didn't they? Guiltily, she guessed there had to be more to it than that, and shooed the boy out of her room while she washed, and then donned a serviceable cotton frock. This was the first day of her new life, she reminded herself. She now had a status—nursemaid to Master Robbie Mackenzie and difficult or not, she intended to make the best of it.

By the time she was ready she could hear the men's voices again, and this time she went unerringly to the kitchen where Iona was stirring an iron potful of porridge.

'You like?' Iona asked.

'It smells good,' Prissy said, though she'd never really been fond of the stuff. She recalled being told that it was the Scots' staple diet, so she supposed she'd have to get used to it.

'You take boy to table, please,' Iona went on in the clipped patois Prissy found so quaint.

It was as if in learning to speak the English tongue they'd decided to discard the use of any superfluous words where one or two would do just as well. A bit like James Mackenzie did, except that he was perfectly articulate and cultured enough—in his own way...

'How did you sleep after all the fuss?' he greeted her that morning.

'Very well, thank you,' she said coolly, refusing to bristle. 'That's one mistake I shan't be making again, I can promise you.'

'Good,' he grinned. 'Oh, and there's probably some cream about somewhere if your skin itches too much. Sometimes the heat of the day brings it up again.'

He could have told her that last night, she thought in annoyance. Some soothing cream might have sent the inflammation down quicker. Unless he thought a night of itching would be a suitable penance for her misdemeanour.

Then she forgot her uncharitable thought and watched, open-mouthed, as he sprinkled salt on to the dish of porridge Iona served him, and didn't use even a dash of milk to moisten it further.

'That's salt!' she exclaimed. 'It'll taste horrible!'

'Not so horrible as your English way of making it like slop,' he said calmly. 'This is the proper Scottish way.'

It was on the tip of Prissy's tongue to say that this wasn't Scotland but, then, it wasn't England either, and everybody had to adjust to new ways. But taking salt on her porridge wasn't one of them. She poured milk over her own portion and then a liberal helping of sugar. Immediately she tasted it, she pulled a face.

'This milk tastes awful! What's in it?'

'It's the only milk you'll get, so you may as well get used to it.' Mackenzie had an edge to his voice now. 'It's goat's milk, and while we're on the subject, you might remember not to be too heavy handed with the sugar. We're not due to fetch our next supplies for three weeks.'

'Goat's milk!' The thought of it was enough to make Prissy feel ill. Goats were nasty smelly creatures with old men's beards. She'd only ever seen them in a clumsy amateur circus act when they'd got out of hand and clambered over the barrier to eat whatever grass they could get hold of.

She pushed her dish away, and Mackenzie pushed it back towards her.

'Will you please not act more childishly than the bairn? You're here to set an example, not to encourage him into disobedience.'

She saw that Robbie too had pushed his dish away, copying her. She didn't blame him. The milk tasted horrid, strong and unpleasant. She saw Mackenzie's jaw harden as Robbie told him shrilly he hated his porridge. Battling with herself, Prissy finally spoke to him encouragingly.

'We'll both eat it all up, then I'll take you out on the swing. Look, if you put a bit more sugar on it, it tastes very nice!'

She dared Mackenzie to argue with her as she sprinkled a little more sugar in a fine spray over the stodge, and did the same for Robbie. To be fair, it did make it a bit more palatable, and she supposed she'd get used to it in time. By all accounts, she'd have to.

'The swing will have to wait until later,' Mackenzie said, when they'd all finished breakfast. 'I've taken time off this morning to show you something of the place, so you'll be familiar with it.'

'Can I come?' Robbie said at once.

'Yes, laddie. We'll go in the wagon.'

Prissy groaned. She was eager to see all of Ballatree Station, but the thought of sitting in that jolting wagon again was enough to make her wilt.

'Must we? Can't we just walk around the place?'

Mackenzie smiled faintly. 'Aye, we could, if I had two days and more to spare, but I don't.'

'Surely it wouldn't take that long?' Prissy said in disbelief. It sounded like bragging to her.

Mackenzie looked at her thoughtfully. 'You have no idea, have you? Did you no prepare yourself for what you'd find in Australia, lassie?'

'Of course I did. I prepared myself for a house in a town where there'd be modern comforts and decent civilised company, where I could be a—a lady's maid or something——'

'Well then, you should have thought farther than the end of your nose,' he said shortly. 'And you shouldn't have taken the first offer that came your way if it wasn't what you had in mind. I'm sorry I can't oblige you by giving you fine seams to sew and outings at the theatre to occupy your time, but 'twas you who said you wanted to take the job here. I recall it quite clearly.'

He just would, Prissy thought bitterly. It was obviously going to be thrown back at her at every opportunity.

'Are you fighting?' Robbie asked with interest.

They both looked at him. Davy and Iona might not have been in the room at all. There were only the three of them, Prissy, Mackenzie and the child.

'No, we are not,' Mackenzie said. 'We're merely discussing things, and there's a difference. Hurry up and finish your food now, and we'll get started. I haven't got all day to spare on this.'

He sounded so impatient, Prissy was surprised he could spare any time at all. He was obviously of the opinion that children should be seen and not heard, and preferably not seen too much either. She knew he had a business to run, and that must be of prime importance in making a living out of this inhospitable country, but people's feelings counted too. Mackenzie seemed to have forgotten that.

Or else he had loved his wife too much for him to let any other feelings come into his life. If that was the case, she was doubly sorry for the child, because it meant he had lost both mother and father.

Some time, when the time was right, she meant to tell him so. He couldn't send her packing, because there was nowhere for her to go. In a way, he was as much tied to her as she was to him, and she was only just realising it. It was a thought that both comforted and annoyed her.

Before they left the house she went to fetch her sunbonnet. The sun was already climbing high into the cloudless blue sky she assumed was normal. In a rainy, cold and wind-swept England such sunshine would be blissful.

Here on the other side of the world, in this dusty fly-hazed country, it was almost blasphemous to think wistfully of a shower of rain to cool the hot earth and bring the welcome scent of damp leaves to the nostrils, but she did. She thought of it with a sudden desperate longing...

'Ready?' Mackenzie said, his wide-brimmed hat rammed down on his head again. Robbie too, wore a hat that covered his head and shielded his shoulders from the fierce heat, though he'd be well used to it now, of course. He was literally a born Australian.

'As ready as I'll ever be,' Prissy muttered, seeing that the wagon was already outside the door awaiting them. Mackenzie lifted up the boy and sat him between them, and clicked the reins to get the horses moving away from the house and almost immediately on to the plain. They looked like any little family going for a day's outing, Prissy thought fleetingly, and then clung on for her life as the wagon wheels hit a stone.

'Sorry about that——' Mackenzie began.

'There's Hans and Fred,' Robbie suddenly shrieked, snatching off his hat and waving madly to two riders approaching them in a swirl of dust. They each wore wide-brimmed hats similar to Mackenzie's own, and their attire was informal and workaday. Tearing along at the horses' hoofs were two excited dogs. The men reined in their horses expertly, seemingly unaware that the dust made Prissy choke, the dogs barking with furious pleasure at seeing Mackenzie. He shouted at them to be still and they obeyed immediately.

'G'day, boss—ma'am,' one of the men said in a guttural accent, touching his fingers to the brim of his hat as he acknowledged Prissy. 'Fred and me have been noting the signs, and I'd say there's the likelihood of a storm brewing. Could be a week or more before it hits, but mebbe we should think about getting the beasts settled into closer contact.'

'Aye, I was thinking as much myself. There should be plenty of time, but see to it, Hans. Pass the word on to the rest of the men,' Mackenzie said, and Prissy wondered if mention of a storm was meant to be a private joke. The sky was as clear as she had ever seen it, but before she could decide the truth of it for herself, Mackenzie was speaking to her.

'You'll be seeing plenty of these two, Prissy. They're my boundary riders, and keep the fences in good order and the sheep from straying into the bush, where we'd probably never see them again. Hans came here from Germany at the same time I arrived in this country and has been with me ever since, and Fred's from your own hometown.'

'Are you from good old London then, miss?'

The one called Fred spoke up at once. Prissy hadn't failed to notice the look of admiration in the man's eyes. If that was like balm to her senses, even more so was his voice, raw cockney if she'd ever heard it.

'Yes, she is.' Mackenzie answered for her. 'She's come to be a nursemaid to Robbie, and I'll thank you both to remember that and pass on the information to the rest.'

Prissy preferred to speak for herself, and wasn't letting Fred go that easily. She beamed at him.

'Well, I must say it does me good to meet somebody from home and listen to a voice I can understand properly! I've been here less than a week, and it feels as if I've been travelling for ever, what with the long sea journey and all. What part of London are you from, Fred?'

'East End, ducks. Can't you tell?' he grinned.

Mackenzie was brisk. 'Look, let's leave all this chit-chat for another time, shall we? I don't want to keep the boy out too long for him to get overtired, nor be away from my own work any longer than necessary.'

'Right enough, boss,' Fred said at once. 'I'll be seeing you later, miss, and then maybe we can have a good old chin-wag about the smoke. You're a fair sight for sore eyes out here, though, ain't she, Hans?'

The German muttered his assent, less talkative than the other but perfectly agreeable, and they rode off again, the dogs yapping at their heels. As the wagon started moving, Prissy turned to Mackenzie, her eyes still shining.

'Why didn't you tell me you had a Londoner working for you? You must have known I'd be interested!'

He shrugged. 'I didn't think it was that important, and anyway, I'd forgotten until that moment. Fred's been here more than a year, and we get all sorts.'

She ignored any implication that might be read into that remark.

'I suppose you've been here so long that everybody else seems like a foreigner to you now. But didn't you think it might have made me feel a bit less homesick to know Fred was a Londoner too?'

He glanced at her, suddenly thoughtful. 'It never occurred to me that you'd be feeling that way. Right from the start you seemed such a self-assured young woman I'd forgotten how young you are. Nineteen, isn't it? You're no but a bairn yourself.'

He almost made it sound as if the thought concerned him, but she bridled at his words.

'It's natural to feel a bit lost when you go to a new place for the first time, especially one so far away. I thought you'd have sense enough to know that. And for your information, it'll be my birthday on the fifth of next month, and then I'll be twenty years old. I've been fending for myself for a long while now, and I know how to take care of myself. I'm not a child, Mackenzie.'

She looked at him defiantly, just in case he was anticipating any trouble between herself and his men. Their glances locked for a moment, and then she saw how his gaze shifted. It hovered on the pulses beating in her throat and then moved lower, to where the soft swell of her breasts dipped into a curving waist and womanly hips.

She knew instantly that he was seeing her in a different way at that moment. Even in the dusty glitter of her stage-frocks he hadn't looked at her like that before, not in the special, intimate way a man looked at a woman he was becoming aware of, Prissy thought, and it made her draw in her breath.

He turned abruptly back to the reins and urged the horses forward.

'No, lassie. A child you are not.'

Robbie's attention had been caught by one of her words.

'Are we having a birthday cake? Did I have candles on a cake once, Pa?' He frowned, as if he couldn't quite remember.

Prissy answered quickly. 'You probably did, but grown-up people don't have birthday cakes, love.'

Mackenzie saw his disappointed face and spoke just as quickly. 'Why don't they? If Prissy wants a birthday cake, she can have one. We'll get Iona to bake her one, shall we, Robbie?'

Prissy stared in exasperation at this unpredictable man who was quite ready to do this for his son, and yet begrudged the necessary time he had to spend away from his sheep farm to hire a nursemaid for the boy.

If he'd taken more care about it, he might have found someone more suitable—somebody older and more sensible. Instead he was stuck with Prissy Baxter. Then suddenly, and for no particular reason, she realised she didn't mind quite so much that for the time being they were both stuck with each other.

A couple of hours later, she was more than ready to believe that the extent of Mackenzie's property covered thousands of acres. She felt as if they'd personally traversed every one of them. Mackenzie told her they had only explored the tip of the property. The homestead had been long out of sight, and the enormous numbers of sheep, called mobs, straggled away in every direction. After Hans and Fred had ridden away, there had been no other sign of life except for occasional distant riders who waved their hats towards the wagon and then were gone about their business. And the extraordinary animals called kangaroos that leapt into their horizon for some moments and then disappeared as quickly into the bush.

'How on earth do you know which are your sheep, and how do you get them rounded up for shearing?' She was quite pleased to know she'd remembered the correct parlance.

Mackenzie laughed. 'There's no likelihood of sheep rustling because there's no other sheep station for miles around, and I pay my men good wages to keep a watchful eye on the stock. We've got solid fencing all around the property that's constantly being renewed, and as for round-up time, well, you'll get to know all about that in about six weeks, and then we'll get down to the shearing. We get all the help we need at that time, men who come back year after year, and plenty of drifters willing to do the menial tasks for a day's pay and a bite of supper.'

For Mackenzie, it was quite a speech, Prissy thought, and he became amazingly animated when talking about his work. It was becoming obvious to her that he was a man more comfortable with animals than people.

'Can I help with the sheep too, Pa?' Robbie said eagerly. Mackenzie ruffled his dark hair.

'Not this time, laddie. You'll have to wait until you're a bit bigger, but you can help Iona with the shearing suppers, and take some of the stuff outside for the men. You'll like that, won't you?'

'Can I help too?' Prissy said.

'Och, that'll be expected,' Mackenzie said drily. 'Nobody sits around idly when it's shearing time. It's hellishly tiring, but when it's all over and if we've had a good season, it'll all be worth it, and there might be a bonus in it for the fripperies young lassies like. You did say you could sew, I believe.'

So he remembered that too.

'Yes, I can. I used to sew some of my stage-frocks,' she said, unable to stop a small sigh of regret for those heady days. Looking back on them, they seemed so much more exciting than they actually were, especially the times when the customers didn't pay to come and see the shows. Times when the managers were obliged to close after a few weeks, or pay the performers such a pittance they could barely exist on it.

'You'll find a few bolts of stuff and sewing materials at Ballatree Station if you've a mind to do such things. The bairn will be needing new shirts soon, so it would be useful if you could turn your hand to it.'

Mackenzie spoke unwillingly, and Prissy didn't need telling that these things had belonged to his wife. She resisted the temptation to ask something more about her now that she knew some of it already. Besides, the child was seated between them, and it didn't seem to be the time.

'I'd like that,' she said instead. 'I could always do a bit of mending for you as well.' She hadn't missed the fact that there was a tear in his shirt and a button missing, things that a wife usually attended to.

'Aye, I'd thank you for that. Iona's not one for tidying a man,' was all that he said to her suggestion, but she felt satisfied enough that he hadn't dismissed it.

By the time they returned within sight of the homestead, Prissy had had enough of riding around in the wagon. Her muscles were protesting again, but there were still a few things Mackenzie wanted to point out to her before they went inside for the midday meal.

'You'll see that the homestead is built near to the creek,' he commented. 'It runs all around three sides of the buildings, and you'll do any washing you need to do there. The bush is kept cleared away from the edge, and the water's good enough for drinking. Iona brings the small cart here every day with the cans to collect water for the day's supply. We've never had a long enough drought yet to dry up the creek completely, but we're still careful with it, all the same.'

'So that's what Robbie meant when he said he sits on the cans,' she said.

'Aye. I'm telling you what's what, since you'll be helping Iona with some of the work.'

Prissy hadn't bargained on this.

'What else do you suggest I do? Milk the goats?' she asked sarcastically.

'If you have the mind to do it, aye,' he said to her horror, his eyes unblinking.

'I don't! I was teasing.'

'You'll no object to collecting the eggs from the hens, I take it? They won't bite if you don't disturb them off the nests——'

'I thought I came here to be a helper, not a farm worker,' she said indignantly, and chewed her lip, because things would have been all so different if Flora Mackenzie had still been alive. Presumably then, Prissy would have been in sole charge of the child and the wife would have done these chores that she presumably enjoyed doing. But now there was no wife, and Prissy guessed that the black woman would be more than willing to share the housewifery tasks.

'We all have to do jobs we don't like,' Mackenzie said, his voice remote.

'Are we going to see the horses, Pa?' Robbie had been still for long enough and began jumping up and down in the wagon as it slowed.

'All right, though most of them will be away with the men.' He looked at Prissy. 'Have you ever ridden a horse?'

'I have not! And I don't intend to——'

'I can ride,' Robbie chanted. 'I'm cleverer than Prissy!'

'You're not going to let the bairn beat you, are you?' Mackenzie said softly, and she stared at him, aware of his challenge. 'Davy can teach you——'

'Why can't *you* teach me?' she said, amazed at her own words. She wasn't happy around animals of any sort, and horses were so big, with those enormous teeth, and a way of snorting and kicking their powerful hoofs...

'Done,' said Mackenzie, while Robbie whooped again, and Prissy wondered weakly just how she'd got herself into this at all.

They left the wagon at the stables in charge of the young boy who took care of them, and Prissy wrinkled her nose at the horsey smells that wafted out. There were only two horses in the paddock now, a docile grey mare and a small pony that Robbie told her belonged to him.

'He was a present after—well, to keep him occupied,' Mackenzie said briefly. 'I'll just show you the bunk-house for the men and the shearing sheds, and then we'll go and have some food. And you'll probably be interested to see our bit of cultivated garden at the back of the house. Robbie can show you that later.'

Robbie was already showing signs of tiring of this new game of showing a newcomer around.

'She said she'd push me on the swing,' he said sulkily.

'And so I will——'

'Don't call her *she*,' Mackenzie said sharply. 'She has a name, and you'll use it.'

'*You* don't,' he shouted. 'You call her lassie all the time.'

'Then from now on, you and I and everyone else will call her Prissy,' Mackenzie said stonily.

She might as well not have been there at all, Prissy thought in amazement. Mackenzie had this knack of shutting out everyone but the person he most wanted to talk to. He'd done it at breakfast, and he was doing it now. And she didn't want to be shut out of his horizon. She wanted to be part of his life. She had to be, now that she was here.

'Excuse me,' she said loudly. 'I am here, you know. This conversation does concern me.'

The man and boy looked at her with the same expression of surprise. Robbie Mackenzie was going to be the spit of his daddy, Prissy thought. A sheepman, obsessed with his own concerns, and the rest of the world could go to blazes.

'I know that,' Mackenzie said. 'It's you that I'm thinking about—Prissy.' He remembered just in time, and she felt her face relax in a grin, because unknowingly the boy had done something she'd wanted ever since she met the man.

She'd wanted to hear her name on his lips, in that deep rich voice she was beginning to know so well. She'd thought the term lassie was a charming one, until she realised it gave her no real identity of her own. It was the same way Fred had called her ducks as Londoners always did. It meant nothing. With Fred, it didn't matter. With James Mackenzie, it did. As far as he was concerned, she had to feel like a person who was needed, if only for the benefit of his son.

In the afternoon, Mackenzie had left the homestead and Robbie was taking his afternoon rest. He hadn't wanted to go, and Prissy had had quite a tussle with him to get him into bed. She had only succeeded by singing him a little ditty, and promising that she would do so every afternoon and night-time before he went to sleep.

It was one of the things Mackenzie had wanted of her, and it was little enough to keep the child happy. She was alternately irritated by him and suffused with sadness for him to have lost his mother at so young an age.

She left him sleeping peacefully and went on a small tour of the house by herself. Iona was down at the creek, scrubbing the weekly washing, and Prissy realised it was the first time she had been alone since coming to Australia. Sociable though she was, she enjoyed having time to herself, and she wandered through the house, opening doors and just looking, in genuine interest and curiosity.

She discerned which were Iona and Davy's quarters by the haphazard bedroom and sitting-room, and she went out of them quickly. There was a room full of odds and ends, including the bolts of fabric Mackenzie had mentioned, which Prissy could make good use of, and a bedroom that must surely be his.

It was a man's room that had once had a woman in it. The uncanny presence of Flora Mackenzie was almost tangible. Prissy stood quite still in the doorway, almost apologetic at intruding, and feeling angry at herself because there was nobody there at all. It was just a room...

She backed out of it and found her way to a large sitting-room. She hadn't had time to find it until now, and it was the most pleasant room of all. There was a large window, framed by heavy curtains, and rugs on the floor.

Comfortable chairs were grouped around the fireplace, and there was a pianoforte in the corner that made Prissy's eyes light up. She ran her fingers over the keys, and guessed from their tinny notes that nobody had played them for a very long time. More than six months, she was prepared to wager...

Something drew her gaze then to the oil painting above the mantelpiece. She studied it for a long time. It was that of a pretty, dark-haired young woman tenderly holding a baby in her arms, and Prissy didn't need three guesses to know the identity of the sitters.

She heard a door open and shut and was about to flee, not wanting Mackenzie to find her here when she was feeling quite peculiar and depressed, when Iona came into the room. Prissy breathed out in relief.

'Thank goodness it's only you! I was looking at the portrait. It's Mackenzie's wife, isn't it?'

The dark woman nodded, her normally cheerful face filled with sorrow.

'Such lovely lady,' she said sorrowfully. 'So sad for Mackenzie——'

Prissy had to know. 'How did she die, Iona?'

'Down by creek. Great big fella come creeping——'

'A *man* killed her?'

Iona shook her head, waving her hand expressively from side to side and then pouncing with her fingers.

'Snake. Big, big fella.'

Suddenly Prissy didn't want to know any more. All the perils of this new country were magnified a hundredfold if the pretty wife of James Mackenzie had taken an innocent walk by the creek and been bitten by a snake.

She'd be very sure to keep her window shut tight every night from now on. Last night it had been only insects trying to eat her alive, but she'd rather be fried by the heat that risk any other kind of creepy crawly thing getting into her room——

'Big fella long gone.' Iona was shaking her arm. 'Mackenzie shoot him dead. I make tea for you now,' she said proudly. 'English lady like tea.'

Her hand was still on Prissy's arm as she followed Iona numbly to the kitchen, unable to rid herself of the thought that, as a novice in this so-called land of opportunity, she was no more than one of Mackenzie's lambs, going to the slaughter.

CHAPTER SEVEN

ROBBIE'S acceptance of his new nursemaid was still very wary a week later, by which time Mackenzie decided to give Prissy her first riding lesson. By then she had got to know her way around Ballatree Station, was on friendly terms with most of the stockmen and was getting used to Iona's sudden disappearing acts, when Prissy would be left to serve up dinner, or even cook it.

It didn't bother her too much as long as the other woman wasn't away for too long.

'You'll get used to the odd ways of the Aborigine people,' Mackenzie informed her. 'They don't like to be confined to houses for too long and can feel threatened by them. Sometimes you'll find that Iona is merely closeted up in her room to be by herself, and at other times she goes off into the bush, with or without Davy.'

'But surely that's terribly dangerous?' Prissy was appalled at the thought of all those lurking perils.

'Not when generations of your ancestors have lived in the bush, and all their instincts are inherent in you.'

'In other words, it's more unnatural for them to live the kind of life we do.'

'Exactly. And we have to respect their ways if we're to live harmoniously together.'

She realised that Mackenzie accepted people for what they were, and it was a trait she admired in him.

'Aren't you worried that one day Davy Golightly will just go off and leave you, and take Iona with him?' she asked.

111

'Davy's too loyal a stockman for that.' Mackenzie shrugged. 'It's always possible they may leave, in fact they occasionally do, but they always come back.'

'I admire your trust. I'm not sure that I'd have as much faith as you,' Prissy said.

'Some time you've got to learn to trust people, lassie. I thought you'd found that out on the road to Ballatree Station. After all, you went away with a complete stranger.'

'You didn't trust Badger though, did you?' she asked suddenly, preferring to get away from the uncomfortable thought that she certainly had gone, willy-nilly, into the unknown with a perfect stranger. If Ma Jenkins had known of it, she'd have been horrified. In fact, even now, Ma Jenkins and the rest of the theatricals were probably wondering what had become of her, since the one scrappy letter she had written before she left the ship at Sydney, and she resolved to make letter-writing a priority task.

'If I'd trusted that vagabond, you'd probably be dead by now,' Mackenzie was saying. 'No, I'm not daft enough to trust blindly, but I believe in my own instinct, same as the Abos.'

'Do you trust me?' She wasn't sure why she was prolonging this line of discussion but she wanted to hear him say it—and it put off the moment when she'd have to get up on the horse.

'If I didn't, you wouldn't have charge of my bairn. And now that you've done your fishing and got the compliment you wanted, we'll get ready for the first lesson. You've managed to put it off for long enough.'

Robbie was impatient to see her get on with it too, and it galled her to see the way he clamoured to watch the lesson, since she was quite sure she was going to make a fool of herself.

'I'm doing this under protest, and I look like a clown,' she complained.

Mackenzie had insisted that the only way to rid herself of fear was to face it head-on. But apart from her natural apprehension she felt utterly foolish and unfeminine, as he'd instructed her to wear an old pair of the smallest work trousers that could be found, one of her thinnest blouses and a man's slouch hat rammed on her head to keep the fiercest rays of the sun from her neck. Robbie told her she looked like a skinny bushman, which didn't endear him to her.

'You look fine,' Mackenzie grinned when he saw her. 'Almost an outback woman.'

She glared at him. 'Is that supposed to be a compliment?'

'Why shouldn't it be? Do you think yourself so much better than any other women in these surroundings?'

'What other women?' She ignored the steely voice. 'The only one I've seen so far is Iona.' She caught his look and tilted her chin. 'And no, I don't think myself superior to Iona, so don't go putting words in my mouth that aren't there! Are you telling me there are other women around here that I haven't seen yet?'

He ignored the question and told her to hurry up, since he had work to do and couldn't spare all day on her lesson.

All the same, Prissy suddenly realised how much she was missing the companionship of other women. Iona was friendly enough, but she knew nothing of England and English ways. Another woman to talk to about things they both knew and loved would be like being in the company of Prissy's old friends again. She missed them badly, but she'd be damned if she'd let this man know how much. And she missed Kate too…her throat caught as she thought how wonderful it would have been if she and Kate could have found employment together...

Robbie was told to wait outside in the paddock while she and Mackenzie went into the dim musty interior of the stables, and her head went down as she was unexpectedly engulfed in sudden misery at the memory of Kate.

She felt Mackenzie's hands on her shoulders and she looked up at him, startled. Behind her, the mare whinnied at their presence, nuzzling her nose against Prissy's back. Taken by surprise, she gave a small cry and wilted against Mackenzie's chest. Before she could guess what was happening, she felt herself pulled more tightly into him, and his mouth covered hers in a rough kiss. It lasted no more than seconds, yet to Prissy it seemed as if the seconds were held captive, frozen in time.

'I shouldn't have done that and I'm sorry,' Mackenzie's voice spoke close to her head, clearing her mind as she struggled away from him. 'But you looked so sad, lassie, and I don't like to see you that way.'

Prissy forced a quick smile to a mouth that seemed to be burning all of a sudden. A mouth that had just been tempted to respond madly to that unexpected kiss...far more madly than either she or Mackenzie could have anticipated. The realisation shook her.

'I'm not sad, just wondering how the blue blazes I let myself be talked into getting anywhere near a horse. And please don't bother your head about one little kiss. In theatrical circles we kiss folk all the time, and we all know it means nothing.'

She spoke airily and with a totally false note of sophistication that deceived Mackenzie completely. His eyes narrowed, his mouth tightening as he led the mare out of the stall and walked ahead of Prissy into the glaring sunlight outside. And she wondered just why she had spoken so brazenly, when it was nothing at all like she was feeling. Nor was she one to give her kisses lightly, as she had implied.

But then, she *hadn't* given that kiss to James Mackenzie. He had taken it, and the imprint of his mouth on hers was still there. And Prissy knew in an instant that she wanted to feel it there again, not roughly, or out of sympathy, but with all the passion of a man for a woman. The knowledge all but stunned her.

And then she had no more time for thinking or dreaming, because Mackenzie was instructing her none too gently to get her foot into the stirrup and haul herself on to the wretched animal's back, and she needed to give all her concentration to staying astride the beast, rather than to matters of the heart.

Prissy discovered that the brewing storm the boundary riders had predicted had nothing to do with the thunder, lightning and lashing rain of an inclement England. The storm arrived three days later, whirling in from the bush in great thunderous spirals of red dust that stung the eyes and got into mouths and lungs and nostrils, and took away the ability to speak and hear and even think.

After three days of instruction into horsemanship, which she privately thought she was never going to master, Prissy ached in every bone. Neither did it help to have young Robbie gloating at every mistake she made.

'Can't we stop now?' she constantly begged Mackenzie. 'I wasn't cut out to sit on a horse——'

'Neither was I, but you'll discover that in the outback riding's an asset that shouldn't be underestimated, and it's best that you learn as soon as possible. Come on, don't let the bairn beat you, lassie!'

Mackenzie was a relentless tutor, knowing just the right words to say to put her on her mettle. And, rather than admit defeat, she gritted her teeth and floundered back and forth across the paddock on the mare's back.

When the storm finally broke, Prissy could almost think of it as a reprieve, since it stopped all outdoor activity except for the stockmen's work. They still braved the wind and dust to ensure that the stock was kept safe, and Mackenzie worked as hard as his men. Inside the house, every door and window was kept firmly closed, and it was difficult to see anything through the windows, clouded as they were by a film of dust. It was frightening and claustrophobic, and it lasted for seventy-two hours without ceasing.

By the end of it, the noise of the wind had become wearisome and monotonous, and Prissy was filled by a sense of panic and disorientation, wondering if she was ever going to get out of this terrible place, where the oppressive heat of the house and the irritability of its inmates were beginning to have an effect on everyone.

Iona spent many hours in her own room, humming in a strange chanting way that Prissy found unnerving. Robbie quite simply got crosser and more frustrated as the hours went by, and Prissy was hard pressed to keep him entertained. Only when his father came home for a few hours at a time did he really recover from his boredom and throw himself into James's arms. And Prissy found herself envying the easy way the man and the boy related to one another when everyone else seemed to be so much on edge.

'The worst of it's over now,' Mackenzie said quietly to Prissy above the boy's head. 'Has he been all right?'

'He's been fine.' She decided that fibbing was easier than worrying him with the times she could have slapped the child for his bad temper. Mackenzie looked tired to the bone and it wasn't fair to burden him further with her own problems. 'We've sung rhymes and I've taught him a new song about London town. We've played guessing games, and he's told me all about the time he found the baby kangaroo and fed it with milk on a spoon until it went back to find its mother—do storms like this happen very often?'

Finally she said what was uppermost in her mind, running her tongue around her parched lips. She found it difficult to talk properly, since the dust had still permeated every crack in the house, despite the precautions, and she felt as though she had breathed, tasted and eaten dust for ever.

'Not so often around here,' he assured her. 'Droughts are very common, of course, but these dust-storms are usually of short duration and then move on. We won't be due for another for months, maybe not all summer. Fortunately the creek was full, and Davy's brought up more water, so you've no need to be stingy with it, lassie.'

'She's Prissy,' Robbie mumbled against his father's chest. 'You said we've got to call her Prissy.'

She saw Mackenzie smile gently and stroke the boy's coppery head.

'So I did, my wee one. Well, you go off and have a nap now and I'll come and read to you in a little while, and meanwhile mebbe Prissy will make me a hot cup of tea.'

'Of course I will,' she said, surprised to admit how deeply the sight of the man stroking the boy's head affected her. He could be such a dour, uncompromising man, yet she knew instinctively that there was a wealth of love inside him. Prissy guessed that most of his emotions were still kept firmly in check because of his wife's death, but she was equally sure that Mackenzie was a man with a great capacity for loving.

Robbie obeyed his father at once and went off to his room. Prissy went out to the kitchen quickly, and pushed the iron kettle more firmly over the cooking range. The water was half boiled already and wouldn't need much longer. As she straightened up, she turned to find Mackenzie watching her.

'You're a good lass, Prissy. You'll make a good wife and mother one of these days, despite what some might have thought from your fancy clobber. My bairn's not averse to you, even though you might think otherwise from his little tantrums,' he said abruptly.

She was astonished at the rare compliment, sure that there was nothing hinted in what he said. With any other man, there might have been, of course. She hid her feeling of pleasure beneath her usual banter and spoke teasingly.

'Why, if I didn't know you better, Mackenzie, I'd say that was the most half-hearted proposal of marriage I ever heard!'

She expected him to laugh back, and to say something to the effect that he'd see hell freeze before he asked such a flibbertigibbet as Prissy Baxter to marry him! Instead, she suddenly realised that he looked perfectly serious, and her heart skipped a beat for a minute. Surely he *hadn't* been making some clumsy attempt at a proposal!

'Would it be such an outlandish thing to consider? The bairn needs a mother, and there are times when a man must put aside all other feelings to think of his children. The boy could grow attached to you soon enough and he's in need of some stability...'

He became aware of her outraged face. Prissy clasped her hands together for two reasons. One, because they were shaking so much at her own secret longings and, two, because if she didn't, she was perfectly sure she would hit him. Her voice was high and indignant.

'Are you showing your true colours at last, Mr Mackenzie? Is this what you really brought me here for, under the pretence of needing a mother's help for your son?' she demanded.

'It is not! I had no such intentions when I hired you, and you must believe that,' he said angrily.

'Why should I believe anything you say?' she blazed. 'You weren't so honest about your wife, were you? You let me come here, believing there was a Mrs Mackenzie in charge of the household, and that I'd have simple duties to attend to. I certainly wouldn't have come if I'd thought you wanted me to be your *wife*.'

She spoke the word as if it was the most loathsome thing she could imagine. He strode forward and grabbed her to him, shaking her hard. She wasn't frightened by him, nor the sudden force of his feelings, whatever they were. She was half thankful that he had feelings, after all. It wasn't natural for a man to be so remote from everything that he might have been a block of wood. And James Mackenzie at this moment was anything but a block of wood...

She was held tight against his chest, and she was held captive again within his powerful arms. And, furious though she was at this sudden showing of brute strength, shivers of excitement were beginning to surge through her veins. She could feel every sinew of his body against hers, and, whatever his noble reasons for wanting a new wife to provide a mother for his son, his own needs betrayed him and told Prissy there were other considerations too.

One of his hands slid up behind her head and held her fast so that she couldn't move. Then she felt the pressure of his mouth on hers, and this was a kiss that didn't stop after a few seconds. It went on and on, drawing out a response in Prissy that left her weak and wanting more. And when they drew apart Mackenzie was breathing as heavily as she.

'Think about it, lassie. Naturally I'll expect the usual wifely duties, but you'll have security and a home and want for nothing, and it's understood that your passage money will be paid over to the Ladies' Committee at once.'

However she might have reacted to his proposal, to say nothing of the effects of his kiss, it was all wiped out in a second at this last remark.

'Do you think you can *buy* me?' she spluttered in a red rage. 'I'm not one of your sheep to be bought and paid for and expected to perform certain duties whenever you say the word! I've got more respect for myself, Mr Mackenzie, and I'd have thought you had more respect for your wife than to besmirch her name by being so satisfied with second-best! Have you forgotten her already?'

Tears suddenly scalded her eyes, knowing how definitely she *would* be second-best, and knowing with certainty just how much she would want to be first in the heart of this man, *if* she ever agreed to marry him!

'I've no wish to discuss my wife with you,' she heard him say coldly, and she realised that he had reverted at once to that other self that allowed no emotion to intervene in his life. 'I've made you an offer and you've made it plain what you think of it. The offer's still there. It's against my better judgement, and it's purely for Robbie's sake, and I'd ask you to think carefully about it.'

'I've already thought about it, and I'm insulted by it,' she bellowed at him. Behind his head she saw an astonished black face as Iona came into the kitchen, startled

out of her habitual afternoon reverie by all the rumpus.
Prissy glared at Mackenzie.

'Didn't you say something about reading to your son,
or is that something else you're going to forget?'

He turned on his heel and left the two women, and
the singing of the kettle gave Prissy something to do with
her trembling hands. She bit her lip as the boiling water
slopped over and scalded her.

'Damn thing,' she said, tears smarting her eyes.

Iona took the kettle calmly out of her hands. 'No sense
to be crying over boss. White woman from supply depot
cry over him and he still don't marry her.'

Prissy stopped crying at once.

'What white woman? Are you telling me there are
other white women around here? What supply depot?
And what do you mean—he still don't marry her?'

The Aborigine woman laughed, stirring the brew they
called sweet tea, which Prissy had discovered was made
from a liquorice-flavoured creeper found in the bush,
and pouring Prissy a cup of the stuff. It was refreshing
enough, if not quite like the tea she'd drunk at home,
but there were more intriguing things to think about at
that moment.

And besides, it took her mind off the momentous dis-
covery that she was falling in love with James
Mackenzie. It was quite mad. She hadn't known him
long enough to fall in love, but such considerations of
the head were of little consequence when the heart said
differently.

'The one at White Junction,' Iona said blandly.

'Well, where's that, for pity's sake?' She was impatient, wishing the woman wouldn't just sit there with
that faraway look in her eyes, so homely and com-
placent, while Prissy wanted to know everything in an

instant. But that wasn't Iona's way, and Prissy tried hard to contain her frustration.

Iona waved vaguely. 'Long way. Where we buy flour and feedstuff.'

Prissy tried to count to ten and failed.

'Tell me. Would it be about twenty miles to the south, by any chance? And is it where our nearest neighbours live?' She vaguely remembered Mackenzie saying as much on the journey here. Already it seemed so long ago, as if she had been here for ever.

Iona nodded. 'White Junction the place where boss buy supplies. Nice young lady live there.'

'What nice young lady?' Prissy said crossly. If there was another young woman living in the vicinity she wanted to know about it. They could be friends . . . even as the thought crossed her mind, she knew that friendship with a young woman who was vying for James Mackenzie's affections was an impossibility. She must be going crazy, she thought faintly. Touched by the heat . . .

Iona ticked off three large black fingers, reciting parrot-fashion.

'Mr Sam Hatherall, Mrs Adele Hatherall, Miss Edna Hatherall.'

'And who are they?'

Iona looked at her as if she was a stupid child, incapable of understanding. Prissy resisted the urge to stamp her foot. She tried another tactic, asking different questions this time.

'Iona, does Mr Sam Hatherall own the supply place? Is Mrs Adele Hatherall his wife? And is Miss Edna Hatherall his daughter? And—are they English?'

The black face broke into a slightly surprised smile. 'That what I been saying this long time!'

So at last she had it straight. There was an entire family living at this White Junction place, and, if Prissy interpreted the rest of it correctly, Miss Edna Hatherall had had her sights set on James Mackenzie—and got nowhere.

Mackenzie came back to the kitchen and demanded his cup of tea, since reading to Robbie had made him even more parched. Prissy eyed him dispassionately. He was tall and broad-shouldered, and he carried himself well. He was tanned, with a rugged outdoor look, and he was still young enough to be considered a virile husband by any doting mama who wanted to marry off her daughter.

The fact that he had been widowed so tragically only added a haunting appeal to those shadowed brown eyes, that any self-respecting woman would want to see light up with love for her and her alone. Prissy swallowed suddenly. Yes, he would be quite a catch out here, where eligible men could be counted on the fingers of one hand.

Stockmen were a fine and healthy breed, but a land-owner, with a huge spread of land and countless sheep for slaughtering and shearing and his own homestead, was a far better prospect for any girl. No wonder a man like James Mackenzie viewed any girl stepping straight off the emigration boat with some suspicion.

No wonder he assumed every one of them wanted marriage and the easy life...well, some of them had more pride than to take the first offer, Prissy thought keenly, especially when it was said with the offhand insult of merely wanting a mother for his bairn...the usual wifely duties included...

She felt her cheeks burn as she realised that she had been staring at Mackenzie's face for some minutes, and that he was now very aware of it.

'Well, lassie? Do you approve of what you see, or do I have a smut on my nose?' he said drily.

She was thrown into confusion for a minute. What would he say, if he knew that at that very moment she had been letting her imagination roam to unknown places? Assuming that the *usual wifely duties* would include sharing his bed—and all that that entailed.

Prissy's air of worldliness extended no further than a basic knowledge of what would be required of a wife, but her own instincts told her unerringly that with the right man, as long as love was there, the experience would be wonderful, almost mystical...and, no matter how hard she denied it, in her heart she knew that James Mackenzie was the right man for her—the only man in all the world.

She lifted her head and spoke accusingly, taking refuge in anger. 'Why didn't you think to tell me there was an English family living at this place called White Junction? Didn't you think I'd be interested to know that? You bring me all this way, to the back of nowhere, and don't even bother to tell me there's another English girl living not twenty miles away——'

'I said our nearest neighbours lived some twenty miles away——'

'You never said who they were, did you? You never thought I might have been keen to make contact with this—this Edna Hatherall...'

She was aware that Iona had melted away again. Perhaps Aborigines didn't argue as much as white people, Prissy thought wildly. Perhaps she thought Mackenzie had brought a madwoman to live among them. But she stood her ground, hands on hips in one of the thin stage-frocks she'd been forced to wear again, because of the cloying heat inside the house during the dust-storm. It was the most incongruous attire for the outback, but she was beginning to think that conventions hardly mattered any more.

'Why should you want to meet Edna Hatherall? You and she would have nothing at all in common——'

'How do you know that? We're both women, aren't we?' And by all accounts, each with a certain feeling for one James Mackenzie.

She heard him sigh. 'Prissy, Edna's very highly strung, and I hardly think you and she would get along. Mrs Hatherall's of a very religious nature, and they don't converse easily with strangers.'

'They're in the wrong business, then, aren't they? Don't they have to meet people if they own a supply depot?'

'Oh, Sam's sociable enough. It's just his womenfolk who are a bit narrow-minded.'

He stopped abruptly, and Prissy stared, seeing everything in a flash.

'You think I'm not good enough for them, don't you? You think because I'm a theatrical I'm one of your flighty pieces of baggage——'

'You know that's not true,' he said angrily. 'I'd never have asked you to come to Ballatree Station if I'd thought that. I'd certainly never have asked you——'

'To *marry* you? Well, you didn't exactly *ask* me, did you? You put a proposition to me which I found frankly insulting. I'm paid to do a job here—at least, I will be once my passage money's repaid,' she amended quickly, 'but you wanted to relieve yourself of paying me anything. I'd heard that Scotsmen were mean, and all you were offering was unpaid nursemaid-cum-housekeeper-cum anything else your lordship had in mind!' She was so wound up now she said the first reckless thing that came into her head.

He grabbed her wrist hard. 'Dear God, Prissy, you have the canniest way of reducing a man's actions to the most base of all. Is that what you really think? That I just wanted to get out of paying you to keep you here indefinitely?'

It sounded so foolish and unlikely that she had the grace to blush. She moved away from him and shook her head.

'No, of course I didn't really think that. It was a daft thing to say,' she muttered. 'But I won't be bought. No man puts the price of a home on my head just to put a wedding-ring on my finger.'

She turned away blindly. She could hardly blurt out that it wasn't merely security she would want from a man. It was love... and as long as love was there, she would go anywhere, suffer anything...

'I'm sorry. I've insulted you and it was not my intention, lassie,' she heard Mackenzie say quietly. 'And of course you must meet the Hatheralls. I'd be neglecting my duty as your employer if I didn't introduce you to our neighbours. I'm going to White Junction next week to pick up supplies and you can come with me.'

'Oh, well, all right...'

Mackenzie gave a crooked smile. 'Getting cold feet already at the thought? You'll do fine, Prissy.'

He went outside to greet the men and to call them in for some tea and flat cake, and, since she was the only one there to provide it, Prissy busied herself with the influx of stockmen in the suddenly overflowing kitchen.

She laughed and joked with the men and enjoyed their teasing, and all the time she was seething inside because there were times when Mackenzie seemed to read her thoughts so well.

Yes, of course she was getting cold feet at the thought of meeting these Hatheralls at White Junction! The father sounded all right, but the holier-than-thou Mrs Adele Hatherall promised to be a formidable lady, and the highly strung Edna, with her apparent ardent wish to marry the owner of Ballatree Station, was definitely not the type of friend Prissy Baxter might have sought!

By the time the day arrived, Prissy had recovered herself a little, and saw this visit as something of a challenge. She was not an actress for nothing and if these Hatheralls expected to see a prim spinster lady she'd darned well give them one.

Mackenzie took one look at her when she went into the dining-room that morning and burst out laughing, taking in the high-buttoned brown frock and demure hairstyle, the flowing dark locks scraped back into an unbecoming knot on top of her head.

'What the dickens have you done to yourself, lassie? Is it a school marm I'm taking with me to White Junction?'

Her blue eyes flashed at this reception.

'I thought you'd want me to show these people that you didn't hire a Hottentot to look after your son. I thought you'd be pleased that I didn't show you up...' To her horror, she felt her eyes sting, and she blinked them fiercely.

Mackenzie got up and came around the table to place his hands gently on her shoulders. He had done a similar action before, and every time it seemed to Prissy that the warmth of those long sensitive fingers burned right through her flesh, filling her with a kind of tingling energy she couldn't explain.

'Prissy,' his voice was gentle too, so gentle it made her shiver, 'I never wanted you to be anything other than yourself. Surely you knew that? I've never censured you for what you were or what you are. So go and change out of that ridiculous garment and loosen your hair, for God's sake, or I'll begin to think I'm escorting a missionary around.'

'Is that so bad?' It sounded slightly blasphemous to hear him speak so, but he merely laughed and slapped her playfully on the backside as if she were as much a child as Robbie.

'Not at all, except that it's not what I want of you, girl.'

Their glances held in locked surprise for a moment, as each contemplated these words. In some idiotic way, the fact that he'd called her girl instead of lassie indicated to Prissy that he acknowledged her as an Englishwoman at last, and not just an extension of his property.

As for Mackenzie, he realized in a flash that he didn't want to see this free and lovely spirit confined in conventional trappings that stifled her personality. He wanted her to be herself, glorious and unrestrained. He turned abruptly away.

'Go on now, and wear something more in keeping with yourself, and say goodbye to Robbie, or we'll never hear the end of it.'

'Isn't he coming with us? He was full of it yesterday.' She had assumed that Iona was getting him dressed, since neither of them was present at the breakfast table.

'He's coming down with a cold and the jolting would be too much for him. It's best that he sleeps it off.'

'But he'll be so disappointed!' Guiltily, Prissy had considered the boy's presence as a buffer between her and these unknown Hatheralls.

Even more guiltily now, she felt a shaft of acute pleasure, knowing that she and Mackenzie were going to be alone for the entire day—except for the inconvenience of the visit to White Junction.

'He'll get over it,' Mackenzie said, in that dry voice. 'I've promised him I'll bring him back a gift from the supply depot, and that's enough to bring a smile to his face. Hatheralls keep a supply of children's amusements.'

'I shall bring him back something as well,' Prissy declared. 'I'll go and tell him so right away.'

It sounded almost like an ordinary day, she thought fleetingly. A man and his wife going to the city and bringing back toys for their child...

Except that this was no excursion to a civilised English city, but an expedition to the wilds of the Australian outback. And she was not James Mackenzie's wife.

CHAPTER EIGHT

PRISSY discovered that, as well as being a supply depot, White Junction also handled any mail that passed to and from England. Once a month, Sam Hatherall travelled down to Sydney and saw any packages or letters from the outlying districts on to the next boat leaving for home, and picked up any mail to go to outlying homesteads. The recipients collected them from White Junction the next time they called for supplies. It was a long-winded arrangement, but the only one that sufficed. And now that she knew of it, Prissy wrote a lengthy letter to Ma Jenkins and all the inmates of her former home.

'It's nothing like I imagined it would be,' she wrote. 'The country is much bigger and hard to describe. It's like a desert in places and a jungle in others. It's always hot and there are flies everywhere, and the mosquitoes really bite. But the sunshine makes up for all that.' She added that bit hastily, in case they should think she was bemoaning her lot.

'I'm settled in with a nice family who live on a sheep station, and I take care of their little boy, so I can still practise my singing as he likes to be sung to sleep at night.' She carefully avoided mentioning the fact that there was no wife in the family. It was far better to let Ma Jenkins believe everything was as it should be.

'Once the awful sea journey was over, I was so glad to be on dry land again I'd have settled for a job far less agreeable than the one I have now, so I consider myself lucky. You're not to worry about me, and perhaps you could write to me some time and tell me how everybody is.'

It was the nearest she could get to saying how badly she missed them all, and that just writing this letter was filling her with the most awful bout of homesickness. She blew her nose hard and finished on a cheery note.

'It's my birthday soon and Mr Mackenzie's little boy is insisting on having a cake made for me. What a scream, eh, Ma? Me, with a birthday cake at my age! An old lady of twenty! Anyway, there's no more news for now, so I'll sign off, from your affectionate Prissy.'

She sealed it in an envelope and tucked it in her bag to take with her to the supply depot, trying not to be depressed at the thought that it might be many months before Ma Jenkins received the letter, and just as many months before Prissy got a reply, if she ever did.

White Junction was a collection of slatted wooden buildings that seemed to Prissy to suddenly appear in the middle of nowhere. There were half a dozen assorted buildings, but apart from the Hatherall family there were only several assistants and handymen and a few Aborigine men and women workers living there. Prissy was beginning to realise that in the outback, nothing could be compared with anything she had previously known, but this was a kind of civilisation, at least.

After twenty miles of travelling in the heat of the Australian sun, any sign of life was welcome and, even though she and Mackenzie had started out early, it was midday by the time they reached their destination. By then, Prissy was feeling decidedly hot and sticky and thankful that Mackenzie had insisted that she change out of the brown high-necked frock, which would have been choking her by now.

Instead, she wore one of her prettiest frocks in palest lemon, in a soft silk fabric that was only faintly shimmering, and certainly not flashy enough to send Mrs Adele Hatherall into a swoon. It had a matching parasol and bonnet, and although this might not be a trip into the grand metropolis Prissy defiantly wore it all. Her hair was unpinned from its tight knot, and fashioned in a more becoming style, loose around her neck.

From the porch of the homestead building, the two Hatherall women shielded their eyes from the sun to see who was approaching from the north. Then a smiling Sam Hatherall was bustling out of his general store, with its dusty smells of flour and corn, and bolts of fabric and bric-a-brac imported all the way from England, and was greeting Mackenzie cheerily as he jumped down from the wagon, holding out his hand to help his companion alight.

Prissy's naturally healthy complexion was enhanced by the warmth of the sun, and by what she saw as a somewhat awkward situation, knowing what she did about the Hatherall daughter from Iona's careless chatter. The women approached them, and alongside Prissy Miss Edna Hatherall looked decidedly waxy and undernourished, and appallingly aristocratic. She reminded Prissy of some of the smart young ladies who had come visiting the Alhambra theatre. Slumming, was what they called it.

The two young women eyed each other cautiously as Mackenzie made the introductions, and when the other girl made no move towards her Prissy held out a hand generously.

'It's very nice to meet you, Miss Hatherall. I didn't know until recently that there were any other people living so near. Perhaps you can come and visit me some time and we can talk about England...'

She stopped in nervous embarrassment, wondering what on earth had made her say such a daft thing, as if she were some gracious lady, inviting this arrogant young woman to her own home, instead of being the hired help at Ballatree Station. She felt Edna Hatherall touch the tips of her fingers to Prissy's and remove them quickly.

'I'm afraid I never go visiting. The heat doesn't agree with me.'

Prissy was tempted to ask what the blue blazes she was doing in Australia, then, if the heat didn't agree with her. But Mrs Adele Hatherall's manners were clearly better than her daughter's, and she smiled at Prissy in a friendly enough way.

'We'd heard that dear James had found a suitable person to look after poor little Robbie, and I hope you're not finding the task too impossible, Miss Baxter.'

'Not at all, I——'

'You're very young.' The woman's eyes took in every bit of Prissy's appearance, and in an instant Prissy knew that the brown high-buttoned calico would have been the more correct garment to wear.

'I'm almost twenty, ma'am.'

'Indeed. A very young age to leave your home and family and to venture to the other side of the world unescorted, surely?'

'I have no family. I was brought up by an aunt who sadly died some years ago. I've been independent for a long time now.' She didn't quite know why she'd chosen that particular word, but she saw Mrs Hatherall's eyebrows raise slightly at this outspoken young woman, and then the lady turned her attention to Mackenzie.

'And where is little Robbie today, James? You know how Edna loves to play with him.'

Her duty done to the stranger, she ignored Prissy completely from then on and spoke gushingly to

Mackenzie, her comment causing Prissy to guess sagely
that from her sour expression Miss Edna Hatherall
wouldn't have the faintest idea of how to entertain a
child.

'He has a summer cold and I thought it wiser not to
bring him,' Mackenzie said briefly.

'What a shame. Still, you and . . . Miss Baxter . . . will
take a bite to eat with us, won't you? We were only saying
the other day how much we were looking forward to
seeing you again. You stay away too long, James. There's
really no need to make mere monthly calls to collect supplies. You know how we always enjoy your visits.'

'I do have a sheep station to run,' he said drily.

'Yes, of course.'

She spoke as if such a task were of no consequence,
and Prissy decided that both mother and daughter were
completely empty-headed, while the man, Sam
Hatherall, was the complete opposite and made her feel
more welcome than either of his womenfolk.

She suddenly remembered something and spoke up
quickly. 'Mr Hatherall, I have a letter to send to
England. I understand I can leave it here,' she said,
drawing the long envelope out of her bag.

'You've been educated, then?' Mrs Hatherall said, not
bothering to hide her surprise.

Prissy answered archly, concealing the fact that she
was seething with rage underneath. 'Oh, yes, ma'am. I
can read and write *and* do my numbers! I'm quite lit-
erate, as they say. That *is* the right word, I believe?'

She didn't dare look at Mackenzie, knowing she was
being rude, but then, this woman was being rude to her.
All the same, she sensed Mackenzie's amusement at the
little exchange. Mrs Hatherall simply ignored her again
and suggested they all take some food before the visitors
had to depart.

Half an hour later they were all seated round a big table in the homestead parlour, and Mrs Hatherall was dishing up a concoction of meat and vegetable stew that was swelteringly hot on such a day, but which nevertheless they all ate with determination.

'And how do you like Australia, Miss Baxter?' Sam Hatherall enquired with a friendly smile. 'Does it come up to your expectations?'

His wife intervened before Prissy could answer.

'How do you expect the child to answer that, Samuel? She's hardly been here five minutes. She can't possibly have formed an opinion yet.'

'Oh, but I have, Mrs Hatherall. I'm in the habit of making instant assessments of places—and people too.' Prissy spoke lightly, well aware that the woman's words were intended to be dismissive and disliking her more by the minute. 'I think Australia's a vast, beautiful country, and I'm sure there's far more to it than I've already seen. It's far hotter than I'm used to, of course, but I'm sure I'll get accustomed to that in time.'

'You intend to stay, then?' Edna put in. 'Most young women who come here alone can't wait to go back to England when they've discovered the flies and the monotony, and that not every man here is seeking a wife.'

Her meaning was perfectly clear to Prissy, who could have told her that James Mackenzie had already made her an offer. She bit back the tempting words and smiled sweetly at the other girl, refusing to let her see how riled she was by the condescension of these Hatherall women.

'But I didn't come here seeking a husband, Miss Hatherall. I came to work—and to find alternative employment from my stage career...'

She knew it was a mistake as soon as she'd said it. She had intended making it sound grand and important, but then she saw Mrs Hatherall's incredulous look.

'You're an *actress*?'

It couldn't have sounded more damning if Prissy had said she was courting one of the Aborigines, and she felt a sickly, unwarranted shame in the pit of her stomach at this reaction. Then, as her chin lifted in her defiant way, she heard Mackenzie give a low chuckle. For a second his hand pressed hers and was just as quickly removed.

'Prissy was a real find, Mrs Hatherall. She's just the type of girl to be cheerful and amusing for Robbie, with the added advantage of being able to sing to him and get him to act out little plays with her when he gets bored.'

Prissy was startled at this assured defence of her. Besides, she hadn't been aware that Mackenzie knew of her attempts to get Robbie to act out little pretences, especially when he became morose and was obviously aware that something was missing in his young life, without really knowing what it was.

'Won't you sing for us, Miss Baxter?' Sam Hatherall was saying enthusiastically. 'We don't have a pianoforte, but I'm a dab hand on the old squeeze-box, if you don't think it too gross an instrument to accompany a performer such as yourself.'

She looked at his smiling red face with gratitude. He was kind and generous, and, whether he was aware of the snide words of his womenfolk or not, he more than made up for them.

'I'm sure Miss Baxter would not want to do any such thing——' his wife began.

'Oh, but I would, if you'd like me to. It's a long while since I've sung in front of an audience, and it would be such fun to be accompanied on a squeeze-box.'

Again, she didn't look at Mackenzie. This was between herself and the Hatheralls, and she needed to prove herself. Sam went out of the room and returned with the instrument. It was less than tuneful, but it would serve the purpose.

The audience arranged itself on chairs around the room, the women faintly smiling and clearly expecting Miss Prissy Baxter to show herself in her true colours as a common playhouse actress. As for Mackenzie...Prissy couldn't fathom his expression now and decided not to try. She gave whispered instructions to Sam and he struck up the notes of the tune she requested.

If Mrs Hatherall had expected a raucous, risqué song, she was mistaken. Prissy sang the haunting notes of a child's lullaby, her voice soft and alluring. It was a song that had brought tears to the eyes of more than one audience at the old Alhambra. When it was over, there was silence for a few seconds, and then Mackenzie began to applaud, and the women reluctantly followed suit.

'That was beautiful, Prissy,' Mackenzie said without reservation.

'It certainly was. You have a rare talent, Miss Baxter,' Sam said with enthusiasm. 'How about singing something livelier now?'

She laughed. It had been a lovely experience to sing in front of a rapt audience again and, yes, she was tempted to sing a different kind of song, but there had been a certain expression in James Mackenzie's eyes as he listened to her that would disappear if she broke into a more satirical rendition. And she didn't want to break the spell. She wanted him to remember her singing the way she had done just now.

'I'd rather not, if you don't mind. My throat's a little sore, and I think I may be catching Robbie's cold.'

'Then you must take some of my excellent throat liniment back to Ballatree Station with you,' Sam said, at once the salesman.

Mackenzie stood up. 'Aye, and it's time I looked to my own needs, Sam. I've a list as long as my arm and by the time we get the supplies loaded on to the wagon it will be high time we thought about leaving.'

'And don't forget that we promised to take back some gifts for Robbie, to make up for his disappointment in not coming here,' Prissy added. The statement linked her and Mackenzie, and Prissy could see by the tightening of their mouths that the thought didn't please the Hatherall women one bit.

And then she forgot them as she spent delightful minutes browsing through the toy counter of White Junction and chose a spinning top for Robbie, while Mackenzie purchased a mechanical toy soldier that marched up and down after winding the key in his back.

It was another hour before the month's supplies were loaded on the wagon and paid for, and by then it was well into the afternoon. Time enough for them to be on their way if they were to be back at Ballatree Station before dark. Prissy thankfully said goodbye to the Hatherall women, and to Sam with a genuine liking, and added her thanks for accompanying her so delightfully.

'Any time, dear young lady,' he said gallantly. 'You must come again, and bring that young scamp with you next time. I always like to see him.'

'We will,' Mackenzie promised, and urged the horses into action, while Prissy let out a long sigh of relief.

It had been a prickly afternoon, but she was quite certain that, however much Miss Edna Hatherall might have designs on James Mackenzie, she would never be the right sort of wife for him. All the same, she couldn't resist finding out just what Mackenzie thought about that.

'Miss Hatherall seems a pleasant enough young lady,' she said innocently, as they left White Junction behind and headed north into what seemed like an endless horizon of bush and scrub.

Mackenzie snorted. 'Your falseness does you no credit, lassie. I'm more used to you saying what you think, so let's have it. The two of you disliked each other on sight, did you not?'

'I can't speak for Edna——'

'Then speak for yourself. I've not been aware of any lack of it in the past.'

She stuck her tongue in her cheek for a second. How could she say what she really felt? That Edna Hatherall was a colourless, spiteful-minded girl who would be totally wrong for James Mackenzie? What did she have to base such assertions on, anyway? A mere couple of hours in the girl's company, and that of her dreadful mother? Or perhaps it was jealousy, a more basic determination to find objectionable anyone who might capture Mackenzie's heart!

'I don't think you'd like to hear what I think. I'm probably prejudiced anyway, because I once knew a girl who was very like her in appearance,' she invented quickly. 'She was pale and thin and said hurtful things whenever she could—not that I'm suggesting Edna Hatherall is anything like as devious, of course! It's just that it's difficult to separate the characters of two people in your mind, when their outward appearance is so similar.'

'I see,' Mackenzie said, and from his tone she was perfectly sure he didn't believe a word of it.

'I'm sorry. Now I've offended you——'

'Not at all. I'm just wondering why you thought it necessary to concoct such a tale. Still, I've no objection to listening to you rambling on and entangling yourself in deeper and deeper water.'

'I don't consider I'm entangled at all. And I certainly thought Mr Hatherall was a very nice person, and his store a veritable Aladdin's Cave of goods. Why must you always put the wrong interpretation on what I say?' She got quickly away from the subject of the women, and managed to sound indignant.

'And how is your sore throat?' Mackenzie went off at a tangent, enquiring solicitously with a sideways glance at her. 'There doesn't seem to be much evidence of it now. In fact, I'd say you were in fine voice.'

She relaxed, leaning back against the hard wooden seat in the wagon and throwing back her head with a small laugh.

'All right, you've caught me out there. I just didn't want to sing any more, that's all. The atmosphere wasn't altogether right.'

'I thought your song was perfect, and the singer too. You give it something very special, lassie. The emotions run very true.'

It wasn't what she had expected to hear at all and, for once, she was tongue-tied.

'Don't tell me I've found a way to silence you at last?' Mackenzie said. 'I must remember to pay you more compliments.'

'I thought you might have paid some to Miss Hatherall,' Prissy blurted out.

He jerked on the reins and the horses stopped. Prissy was ready for it this time, and clung on tightly.

'Why the devil should you think that?'

His brown eyes flashed, and the angles of his jaw were hard and uncompromising. He had a very handsome face, even when it was angry, Prissy thought faintly, very strong and masculine, and it was even more handsome when it was gentled by laughter. She wondered how it looked when it was softened by love, and doubted that she would ever know.

'It was something Iona said,' she muttered. 'About Edna Hatherall crying because you wouldn't marry her.'

'Good God, I've never given any thought to the matter! Iona delights in making up fairy-tales to suit the moment, lassie, and you'd do well to ignore them.'

'It's not true then, that you and Edna——?' She stopped, suddenly embarrassed to be asking such things at all. It was none of her business what he did. Except that if Miss Edna Hatherall ever moved into Ballatree Station, Miss Prissy Baxter would assuredly move out! She suddenly realised that Mackenzie was laughing quietly and that the wagon was rolling again.

'You women get the daftest ideas. I've never had the slightest intention of asking Edna Hatherall to marry me. Iona thinks I'm in need of wifely comforts, and I dare say she dreamed all this up because Edna's the only eligible white woman around for miles.'

Except that now there was another one...

'Anyway, I've already asked somebody to marry me,' he finished.

'Look, Mackenzie, I know you didn't mean me to take that seriously, and I don't. You're still feeling the loss of your wife, and I understand that. Let's just go on as we are, shall we? I'm happy enough to have got this job, and I think that in time Robbie will accept me totally. But I haven't been here five minutes yet, and besides, I don't want to think about marrying anybody—not yet...'

She realised he hadn't said anything while she babbled on, getting more embarrassed by the minute.

'Have you quite finished analysing me?' he said shortly. 'Are you in the habit of doing that to everyone, or am I the only one to get the treatment?'

'I thought I was analysing myself, not you!'

'Then since you've decided that I wasn't serious when I asked you to marry me, and you don't want to marry anybody, I think we should leave it there for the time being. We both know where we stand now.'

'I suppose so,' Prissy said uncertainly, not at all sure what the last few minutes had accomplished. Was he agreeing with her about not being serious in asking her to marry him? Was this his easy way of getting out of an awkward situation he'd never meant to develop? She could only conclude that it was, and it plunged her into a deeper gloom than she'd have believed possible.

At the end of the afternoon on the fifth day of the following month, Iona carefully carried a birthday cake to the dining table, amid clapping from Robbie and much pleased surprise from Prissy. All the stockmen had been told it was her birthday and there had been good wishes all round that morning, and a few exuberant kisses, too. Now it was the family's turn, and Davy and Iona were included in the birthday tea.

'I've never celebrated my birthday in bright sunshine before,' she commented. 'It's usually gusty rain and wind, or else a good old London fog covering everything so you can't see a hand in front of your face.'

'Do you miss it so much?' Mackenzie asked.

She nodded, seeing no point in lying. 'But I'm getting used to it here now. I might as well, don't you think? I can hardly hop on the next boat and go home!'

'I've got a present for you,' he said abruptly, as if he didn't want to linger on her words.

She looked at him in astonishment, not expecting this. Robbie had brought a present to her room that morning, a small musical box that played a popular tune of the day. Mackenzie must have bought it at the supply depot, and she was touched by his thoughtfulness. And now this!

It was a long parcel whose slender shape she recognised at once. She took off the brown paper and gasped at the bolt of shimmering creamy silk fabric with a silvery thread running through it. It was the most lavishly beautiful material, and hardly one that she'd have expected to find in this wilderness. There was a little package attached, and inside it there were matching buttons and ribbons and thread. Already she could imagine the gown made up, hugging her waist and then billowing out in a flattering swirl of silk.

'It's—it's—oh, I don't know what to say,' she stammered, at which Mackenzie laughed out loud.

'I must remember to buy you a gift more often, then, if it stops your chatter!'

'But where did you get it? I saw nothing like this at White Junction!' She had made a point of looking through the bolts of sensible fabrics, wrinkling her nose at some of the dull shades and sighing wistfully for something pretty and dainty—and now there was this!

'Sam keeps his finer stuff wrapped away,' Mackenzie informed her. 'There's not much call for it but, as he says, it's best to be prepared, and he always brings back some kind of frippery from Sydney when he gets new supplies.'

'And I'll bet Mrs Hatherall disapproves,' she said, feeling a bit like a conspirator at the thought.

'That she does,' Mackenzie agreed with a dry smile.

'Are you going to kiss Pa?' Robbie shouted, in one of his better moods in honour of the day. 'You said you had to kiss people when they give you presents.'

'So I did, you little wretch,' Prissy grinned, remembering how he had fought to resist her that morning when she'd wanted to thank him properly for the musical box.

She glanced at Mackenzie, leaning back in his chair, hands behind his head, his eyes challenging her at his son's words.

'I can't kiss your pa properly when he's sitting down,' she said, suddenly nervous.

Mackenzie stood up slowly and held out his arms. As usual, he towered over everyone in the room. Before getting completely embarrassed at the way Davy and Iona were grinning, and Robbie was suddenly frowning, Prissy moved towards Mackenzie and wound her arms around his neck, unconsciously sensual. She pressed her warm lips to his—and tasted their instant response.

His arms had closed around her at once and they were locked together in an embrace that excluded everyone else in the room. She could feel his heartbeat merging with hers and it was an extraordinary, pulsating sensation. They stayed together for a long, endless moment that left her breathless, and to Prissy it was far more than a kiss. It was a promise of what her future could be, if she agreed to marry him.

Suddenly she felt small hands tearing at her skirts, and realised that Robbie had had enough of this kissing game. His face wore its more habitual scowl again and he clamoured to be picked up in his father's arms.

'Pa's got to kiss *me* now,' he said, his voice vibrating with a jealousy he didn't understand, but which told Prissy instantly that, whatever Mackenzie's plans for marriage, he had better take his son into consideration, or he'd be heading for even more trouble.

'All right, you wee burr, I'll kiss you.' Mackenzie said laughingly. 'Did you not want me to kiss Prissy after all, then?'

'*No,*' the boy said, suddenly shrill. 'She's not my new mother!'

'Dear God, we're not starting that nonsense again, are we?' Mackenzie put the boy down, his irritation all the sharper at knowing it was just what he had had in mind. 'Prissy's your nursemaid and this is her birthday, so don't go spoiling it with your fussing. You're the one who insisted that she kiss me!'

'Well, now I don't want her to,' Robbie said sulkily, glaring at Prissy like a small demon.

She sighed, beginning to know that one day's calm in this house usually heralded two days' tantrums. The boy had suffered one huge trauma in his young life already, and his father marrying again, too soon, would be another. Once she could talk sensibly to Mackenzie about it, she intended to tell him just that, whether it concerned herself or not. They rarely spoke of his wife, but Flora Mackenzie was still here, in this house and in his life.

'Prissy cut cake now,' Iona said encouragingly.

'And Robbie can have the first piece,' Prissy said generously. 'You've got to make a wish when you eat a piece of birthday cake, for good luck.'

He sat mutinously as the cake was put in front of him, and then he bit into it, glaring at her.

'I wish you'd go away,' he said.

'Robbie, you'll go to your room until you can learn some good manners,' Mackenzie thundered at him, at which the boy threw the cake across the room and rushed away.

Iona ran after him. 'I see to him, Mackenzie.'

Prissy chewed her lip in frustration. It should be herself soothing the boy and bringing the smile back to his face, but she'd be the very worst person to try and console him right now, she thought miserably. As a nursemaid, she was a complete failure.

'I'm sorry. That was all my fault,' she mumbled to Mackenzie.

'Don't be ridiculous,' he said shortly. 'The boy has to learn some manners, and I'll not have him speaking to you that way. He'll apologise——'

'Oh, please, don't force him,' she began, aware that Davy was calmly getting on with his tea as if nothing was happening. The way the Aborigines did that unnerved her, yet already she was beginning to accept it, to ignore them when occasion demanded it as they seemed able to ignore exterior happenings, without malice, without any thought of rudeness.

'He's got to learn,' Mackenzie went on relentlessly.

'Then let me teach him. It's what I'm here for, isn't it? And this little episode didn't mean anything. He was just unhappy at seeing somebody else kissing his pa, that's all. You can understand that, can't you?'

It was as far as she dared go right now. It wasn't the time, and Mackenzie wasn't in the mood for discussions about the rights and wrongs of marrying again.

'But the bairn suggested it!'

'He's a *child*, Mackenzie. I kissed him this morning for giving me the musical box, and he squirmed and protested so much that it all ended up as a bit of a game. No doubt he expected you to back away from me too, and . . . well, you didn't exactly react in the same way he did. It was all a bit of a shock to him.'

It was a bit of a shock to her, too, to realise how easily she had slipped into Mackenzie's arms, and how well she fitted there. To know she had been shiveringly anticipating how it would feel to be kissed by him once more, as if she had truly come home in this alien place...

'Aye, you're right,' Mackenzie said slowly. 'He's come to depend on me a lot these last months, and sometimes I forget that his mother's memory is still very dear to him, even though I suspect he no longer recalls her physical presence clearly now.'

But what about you? Prissy wanted to cry out. Is Flora Mackenzie's physical presence so dearly remembered that any other woman would only be a mechanical necessity to you? From the way he suddenly pushed back his chair and went out of the room, Prissy could only assume that time, after all, had not yet done its work.

CHAPTER NINE

PRISSY was saving the new frock to wear at the shearers' supper. She had stitched it lovingly all through the dusty heat of a burning midsummer, needing to work in the comparative cool of the evenings when Robbie had gone to bed. If the dust-storm had been wild and terrible, the motionless calm of the relentless summer heat sapped all her strength, and both she and Robbie were glad of an afternoon rest each day when the sun was at its strongest.

In the evenings, apart from the pleasure of working with the beautiful fabric, she was glad to have something to do to relieve her of the necessity of sitting with Mackenzie.

After the birthday tea, a new constraint had developed between them. It was as if Mackenzie knew all too well that he had moved too fast in suggesting marriage, and was studiously avoiding being in too close contact with her, especially when Robbie was around. She assumed that he'd realised at last the boy's need for time to get over his mother's death, before presenting him with a substitute parent.

Prissy had managed to convey her own thoughts to him a few days after her birthday tea. She was not one for putting off things that had to be said. Not when they were almost bursting out of her head...

She found the opportunity when Mackenzie was giving her another riding lesson, and pronouncing that she was making a good job of it at last. They had ridden quite a long way from the homestead into the bush, and Prissy slid off the mare's back thankfully.

'I'll never make a real horsewoman,' she said honestly. 'But I'm not quite so scared of the beast now.'

'I didn't think you were scared of anything,' Mackenzie commented. 'It took guts to travel to the other side of the world alone.'

'Your wife did it——'

'My wife had me,' Mackenzie said abruptly.

Prissy took a deep breath. Now was the time. 'I want to talk about her, Mackenzie——'

'Well, I don't.'

'Why not? I know that you don't forget her. I've seen the way you stand and look at her portrait sometimes. By the way, I was wondering who painted it?' She changed the subject slightly, seeing the fury in his eyes.

'A boundary rider with a talent for painting who stayed with us for a year,' he snapped. 'He was so grateful for finding work in the outback that he offered to do the painting as a parting gift. It's a good likeness of her and the bairn.'

'You miss her, don't you?'

He spoke angrily. 'What kind of a damn fool question is that? Of course I miss her. She shared my life for seven years. You can't brush all that aside.'

'Yet you were prepared to marry the first person who came to look after Robbie,' she said indignantly, putting all her own feelings to the back of her mind. 'You must see that it was a mistake to be so hasty, Mackenzie. Both for you and the boy.'

'Oh, aye, I see it well enough, now. I see that you were quite the wrong person to thrust on the bairn.'

'Oh!' Prissy said in a small voice. It wasn't what she meant at all.

'You're too young and too pretty and too—too everything,' he went on. 'You're like a young colt, when Robbie needs a...'

'An old grey mare?' She giggled, to cover the way her heart was beating more rapidly, because, whether Mackenzie knew it or not, he was looking at her in a certain way, and it was nothing like his derogatory words suggested. 'No, he doesn't, and you know it. He just needs time, to get used to everything. Some days I know he likes me quite a lot. I can sense it. Ma Jenkins used to say I had a rare gift for sensing things.'

She looked at him steadily, and he looked away. She put her hand on his arm, feeling the tension in it, and feeling, momentarily, so much older and wiser than he.

'You need time too—James,' she said daringly. 'You know the old saying that Rome wasn't built in a day, nor an Australian summer neither. Can't we just go on as we are, and just see what happens?'

'I can't see any other course,' he said in that brusque way of his that she was beginning to know hid his deeper feelings.

'But we can still be friends?' she persisted. 'I can't abide living in a bad atmosphere all the time. I used to have such happy times...'

She drew in her breath, remembering it all with a burst of nostalgia. The laughter, the nonsense, the screaming impromptu performances at Ma Jenkins's boarding house, kisses and tears, and the love and friendship they all shared.

'We'll have some happy times here,' Mackenzie said gruffly, seeing her face. 'I owe you that much. When the shearers move in, and everything's all hustle and bustle, you won't have time for feeling sad. And at the end of it, the shearing supper will put a smile on your face. You can perform for us, if you've a mind to it. The men will relish a bit of singing from a pretty girl.'

'I'd like that,' she said, cheering up at once. 'Can I practise on the pianoforte?' She hadn't dared use it when he was around, and not often when he wasn't, with that portrait of Flora Mackenzie staring down at her and making her feel like an interloper.

'If you like. Though I dare say one of the shearers will accompany you on a fiddle on the night, since we all eat out of doors. There are too many of us for sitting tidily round a table, and 'tis not our way.'

'That's all right,' Prissy smiled. 'I'm getting used to your ways now. And I'll wear my new frock in your honour.'

She shook out the soft folds of it now, admiring the way the silver threads glittered in the sunlight. It had a tight-fitting bodice, with a row of the tiny buttons all down the front as decoration, and the others at the back for fastening. She had sewn the ribbon into lovers' knots, and they decorated the edges of the puffed sleeves and looped up the flounced hem of the skirt.

It was as beautiful as a wedding gown, she thought lovingly, and immediately wished the thought hadn't entered her head, since she was quite sure now that Mackenzie was regretting his hasty proposal of marriage, and was more than relieved that she hadn't taken him seriously. She gave a dress rehearsal for Iona, twirling around in her room and revelling in the feel of the sensual silk against her skin.

'You look real beaut, Prissy. Better than nice white lady at White Junction.'

Prissy laughed out loud. Edna Hatherall's charms had clearly not been enough to tempt James Mackenzie into marriage, and, though he might be regretting his impulsive offer to Prissy Baxter after all, at least there were no other white women in the vicinity, and time was passing. It was a shock to Prissy to realise she had been here several months already, and the lingering tug of her old life was beginning to fade at last.

'You think I'll do, then, Iona?' she persisted.

'You'll melt boss's heart,' the woman said.

Robbie came into the room without knocking, and stopped, open-mouthed, at the sight of Prissy.

'Are you a princess, like the one in my picture-book?' he said at last.

She laughed, scooping him up in her arms, and for once he didn't protest. Not wanting to push her luck, she put him down again at once.

'Not a princess, love, just Prissy. How do you like my new frock?'

He reached out and touched the fabric. 'It's soft and nice, like you,' he said.

'Well that's the best thing anybody's ever said to me, Robbie. You can kiss me if you like.'

She waited, wondering if this was too much to ask. After the disastrous kisses on her birthday, she hadn't attempted any kind of affectionate embrace with anyone, but now she offered her face and, after a minute, she felt the briefest peck on her cheek.

'Now shoo,' she said, more moved than she had expected. 'I'm going to change back into my ordinary clothes, and then we'll sing some songs and I'll play the piano today.'

Iona took him out of the room and Prissy slid the cream silk over her head. In her underclothes, she grinned at her reflection in the looking-glass, seeing how ridiculously pleased she looked.

'One out of ten,' she murmured. 'You've still got a long way to go, but it's a beginning.'

And there was no other place to start.

The shearers moved in at the end of the month. By then, there had been more activity at Ballatree Station than Prissy had seen so far. As well as the regular stockhands who lived in the bunkhouse, drifters seemed to be appearing from nowhere, carrying bed-rolls and an assortment of eating and drinking equipment slung about their persons in a similar fashion to Badger, the rogue of the road.

They were soon informed of the role of Miss Prissy Baxter, where she had come from and in what circumstances. Mackenzie made sure of it, wanting no trouble.

The men bedded down in the open clearing near to the bunkhouse, keeping small contained fires going throughout the night, obviously well used to fending for themselves. In the morning and evenings, they tucked into huge breakfasts and dinners provided by Iona and Prissy.

The drifters were ready to assist with the annual round-up of the sheep into the huge shearing pens, bringing a constant haze of dust with them, so that the air was filled with it, and breathing became even more difficult. But their real purpose was the shearing, at which these men were experts, travelling around the remote outback stations to offer their services for a good rate of pay, and spending it just as hard in the gambling halls of Sydney.

Once the shearing began in earnest, there were endless amounts of tea to be brewed and taken to the sheds. By now, Prissy began to feel as if she had been doing these jobs for ever, and London and a theatrical life was something in the distant past that had nothing at all to do with her.

'Put the can down on the floor and the men can help themselves, lassie. They've got their own mugs,' Mackenzie called to her, when she looked around for somewhere to put the huge billy-can of tea on that first morning of shearing.

Along with half a dozen other men, Mackenzie was stripped to the waist in the steaming shearing shed. He held a captive sheep between his legs, the deft strokes of the knife skinning the fleece cleanly from the animal's back. Prissy watched, fascinated, as Mackenzie's bronzed muscles glistened with sweat that ran down in small rivulets and caught in the coppery covering of hair on his chest.

She had never seen him without his shirt before. She had always known he was powerfully built, but somehow this was like seeing him for the first time. She felt a sudden wild urge to put her hands on his skin, to feel the power in those knotted muscles and ease the tension out of them. She swallowed drily.

'Over here, Prissy, me darlin',' she heard another voice say, and dragged her gaze away from James Mackenzie to where a good-looking shearer was making no secret of his admiration. 'Sure and I'm fair parched for a sight of your sweet face, let alone a drink of that tea.'

'Get along with you, Mick O'Neil,' she laughed. He was Irish and thoroughly wicked, she'd decided at once, with that audacious twinkle in his blue eyes and the gift of the gab, as they called it. Already he'd set his eyes on Prissy, and she admitted to herself that she was flattered by the attention.

The man finished fleecing his sheep and gave the animal a push on the rump as he gathered up the wool and threw it on the pile in the corner of the shed. At the same time, he caught Prissy around the waist and whisked her around the shed in a quick two-step that left her breathless and laughing.

'You'll be sure and give me a dance or two on the night of the supper, won't you? Sure and 'tis all I'm living for——' he said mournfully.

'You'll be out on your ear if you don't stop wasting time, O'Neil,' Mackenzie shouted from the far end of the shed. 'Leave the girl to get on with her work, and you attend to yours.'

'Yes, boss!' O'Neil winked hard at Prissy and dug his knees into the next animal dragged in for him by a willing lad.

'Do you think our boss is feeling a mite jealous, me boys?' O'Neil said jokingly to the rest of the men. 'I'm thinking he wants to keep the lovely colleen all to himself! No wonder he put in a bid for her at Sydney Town.'

Prissy was already backing out of the shed, not wanting to get caught up in any trouble that might develop, when she saw Mackenzie leap up from his crouching position and go for the Irishman. It hadn't taken her long to realise there was no love lost between them, and she gave a small scream now as she saw the gleam of Mackenzie's knife near the man's throat.

'Look, you scum, I pay you to do a job of work and nothing else. If you want to make insinuating remarks, go and make them elsewhere.'

'For the love of God, I meant no harm,' O'Neil gasped. 'Sure and nobody would blame you if you did take a fancy to the girl now you've got no woman of your own, and sorry we all were to hear it. Who'd blame you for bringing a new woman to this Godforsaken place!'

Prissy heard the taunts with something like horror. Mackenzie would hate to have his private business bandied about by a bloke like this, true or not. And it was evident that the other shearers in the shed were of the same opinion, that O'Neil had opened his mouth and blabbed too much. Even as Mackenzie went for him again, the rest of them were down on O'Neil like a pile of stones and hauling him away. They dragged him outside and one of the men threw a bucket of water over him to cool him down.

She saw Davy Golightly struggle to put a restraining hand on Mackenzie's arm as he would have gone after him.

'Forget him, boss. O'Neil best shearer we got, 'cepting you. After this year, he no come back, heh?'

Prissy shrank against the side of the shed, seeing Mackenzie struggle with his own inclinations to thrash the man and send him packing. But what Davy said was true. Shearing time was the busiest time of the year, and they had a good team. And Prissy had heard the name Mick O'Neil mentioned many times. He'd be a loss this year. Next year could take care of itself...

'All right,' Mackenzie snapped to the man doused with water, his hair and clothes already steaming in the heat of the sun. 'Just do the job you're being paid for and don't cause any more trouble.'

Prissy sped away from the shed, acutely aware that she'd been the cause of this furore. And suddenly wondering if there could be any truth in what the Irishman said. It was highly unlikely... but all the same... could Mackenzie really have been jealous at the harmless flirtation between herself and Mick O'Neil?

She dismissed the thought just as quickly. It was more likely that Mackenzie got annoyed because he saw Prissy as his property, which she certainly was not. And neither did she see any reason why she shouldn't flirt with O'Neil if she felt like it. Not too much, of course, not enough to give *O'Neil* the wrong idea, but maybe just enough to annoy Mackenzie a little...

* * *

By the time the last of the fleeces had been piled high on the carts, catalogued and put ready for Mackenzie and one of the men to take the load to White Junction for Sam Hatherall to take on to Sydney in a few days' time, everyone was ready for a party.

The shearers were a transient bunch, moving from station to station and travelling many hundreds of miles during the course of the season. They worked hard and played hard, and made the most of what free time they had. They got their dues from James Mackenzie once the final day's work was done, and tomorrow morning they'd be heading west to a remote place called Redring Station.

Long trestle tables were set out in the clearing for the shearers' supper, and Iona and Prissy served up great dishes of cold meats and hot vegetables, and fresh fruits of every description to finish up. There was ale in plenty and tea for those who preferred it. And only after all the eating and drinking was done did Prissy go to her room and change her workaday frock for the shimmering cream silk.

She fastened the buttons with shaking fingers. Her face was flushed from the exertions of helping to prepare and serve the meal, and everybody was waiting now for the entertainment Mackenzie had announced so baldly.

'You won't find it as civilised an audience as you'd get at one of your London theatre gatherings,' he had told her.

'I'm not daft enough to expect it,' she'd retorted. 'It'll be reward enough if I can bring a smile or a tear to their eyes——'

'Then you expect too much, lassie! By the time they've sunk a few gallons of ale, they're more likely to be in a stupor than to make sense of what you're singing.'

'I'll have to make sure I keep them awake then, won't I?' she had snapped, mortified at the way he seemed to be undermining her talents. 'Will somebody be capable of playing a tune?'

'Oh, aye, there are one or two that bring fiddles along with 'em, and you'll have no lack of music—of a sort. And most of 'em will prance about in a semblance of dancing once the singing's done. Then they usually fall about and sleep it all off beneath the stars. I'll insist that they be still while you're performing, though.'

He hadn't exactly filled her with confidence, Prissy thought resentfully. He could have been more positive, more encouraging. But that wasn't Mackenzie's way. He was a plain-speaking man, and he said what he thought— the same as she did.

She'd sung to some rowdies in her time, but none that had gone staggering about in a drunken stupor while she was singing. She squared her shoulders. That might have been the way things happened around here in the past at the shearers' supper. But this year there was Prissy Baxter to sing to them...and she refused to admit that it was all making her more nervous than if she'd been singing to a theatreful of customers at the Alhambra. She wanted to do well, and she wanted to do well for James Mackenzie, if only to prove herself.

There was a knock on her door, and she opened it quickly to find him standing there.

'Can I come in for a minute?'

'Yes—of course,' she stammered, her face even more flushed because her head had been full of thoughts of him. She saw his gaze move over her in the tight-fitting bodice and flaring skirt of the new gown. His eyes lingered and then moved on, and her heartbeats were very fast. She knew she looked her best. Her dark hair was soft and loose and flowing, framing her face, and she knew without a doubt that if ever she had wanted to look beautiful, she wanted it now—for him.

'You're very lovely, girl,' he said at last. His hand reached out and caught at a tendril of her hair, capturing it in his fingers. She wanted to turn her head, to catch his fingers to her cheek, but somehow she couldn't move. She was held, mesmerised, by these precious moments when he seemed to be looking at her with all the longing inside her own soul.

From somewhere outside the house came the sound of men's laughter, raw and brash, and the spell was suddenly broken. And anyway, she was sure she had merely imagined those soft looks from James Mackenzie...

'I wanted to thank you for being such a splendid helper tonight,' he said briskly. 'And you may remember I promised you a small bonus.'

'I don't need anything.' *Only you*...

He was drawing something out of his pocket, something that gleamed richly and which looked vaguely familiar.

'I want you to have this, Prissy. It will look very well with your new gown. Let me fasten it for you.'

As if in a dream, she turned to face the looking-glass and watched their images as he placed the necklace around her throat, where it lay against her skin. It was a string of opaquely beautiful pearls with a larger pendant pearl at its base. It was the loveliest thing Prissy had ever seen. She touched it reverently.

'I can't accept this,' she gasped.

'Yes, you can. It's yours. Wear it for me tonight.'

He spoke roughly, and then, as if unable to resist the temptation, he bent and kissed the nape of her neck and went quickly out of the room.

Prissy stood quite still for several minutes after he had gone, and all the night sounds seemed to fade away. She was conscious only of the drumming of her heart, and the realisation of why the pearl necklace seemed so familiar to her. She saw it every time she looked at the portrait of Flora Mackenzie and the infant Robbie. It was Flora Mackenzie's necklace, and this time last year Flora would probably have worn it to the shearers' supper.

Prissy felt the sob in her throat, and with it a wild urge to fling the necklace away from her. It wasn't decent to do this. Why had he done it—to prove to her that his Flora was still very much a part of him—and break Prissy's heart in the meantime?

Vaguely, she heard the men calling her name, and the fiddlers begin striking up a merry tune. She heard Robbie's eager young voice screeching for her, and she lifted her head high and went out into the clearing, to curtsy low and smile the brilliant smile that only Miss Prissy Baxter, songstress, could smile at an audience.

She sang the plaintive songs that had them all sniffing for remembered homes far across the sea that few of them would ever see again. She sang the risqué ditties that had them slapping their thighs and shouting for more. She sang patriotic songs that reeked of sentiment and had some wallowing in their ale, and finally she said she was too exhausted to sing any more, but that if they wished she would give each man who wanted it one dance only before she retired to her bed.

And then she groaned aloud, knowing she shouldn't have been so generous, as they lined up one by one and she was jigged around energetically by clammy hands and clutching arms, and bodies that were none too clean and still smelled of sheep, and wanted to press tightly against her. There was none of the finesse of the courtly dances of London society in the exuberance of these men, but they were all hard-working, eager to be rewarded in a dance with the shapely Miss Prissy Baxter, and she didn't have it in her heart to disappoint any one of them.

Then it was Mick O'Neil's turn. He'd waited until the end and clasped her to him in a proprietorial way she didn't care for very much.

'Will you give me room to breathe, for pity's sake, O'Neil?' she said laughingly. 'And stop treading on my toes. I'll be black and blue in the morning.'

'Ah, me darlin', you'll be in heaven long before that,' he said dramatically. She looked at him suspiciously. He'd been drinking hard all evening, and his speech was slurred and heavy.

'It'll certainly feel like heaven to get to my bed after being mauled around by you pack of dingoes all evening,' she muttered.

'Isn't that just what I've been saying to you, sweet thing?' He leered against her face and she turned away sharply at the rank smell of him. 'I'll come to your room once all these rednecks are sleeping the peace of the wicked, and we'll take the stairway to heaven together, you and me——'

'Don't be so daft, O'Neil——'

Before she could decide whether to treat this seriously or as a joke, the man was pulled roughly away from her, and Mackenzie had taken his place.

'Get off to your bed-roll, man, and sleep it off. You can be on your way at first light,' he said coldly. He looked at Prissy. 'My dance, I think. You did offer yourself to every man here.'

Her face burned. 'I trust you mean that to be taken in the proper way, sir!'

'What other way would I have meant it, unless you have other ideas?' He pulled her close and, amid cheers and guffaws, they did a silent shuffle around the clearing, in a way that would be called totally immodest in town, but seemed like a slow and lovely dream here in the outback.

And Prissy gave up being angry with him for treating her, at that moment, almost as blatantly as Mick O'Neil had. She gave up agonising that she was wearing his wife's pearls, and that it was perfectly possible that Mackenzie might be fantasising that he held Flora in his arms. For now, it was enough that he was holding *her*, as if he really meant it.

The night had finally settled into silence, and the darkness was already giving way to the first hint of a pearly dawn, when Prissy heard the small click of her door-handle. Too late, she remembered that, in the bustle of getting a dead-weight Robbie into bed long after he was asleep and then removing all her finery, she had tumbled into bed exhausted, and had forgotten to bolt her door.

'It's me, darlin'. Don't be afraid...'

She resisted the urge to scream and bring a score of men running. She sat bolt upright in bed, dragging the bedcovers up to her chin. Her hair fell about her shoulders and she could see O'Neil stumbling about in the half-light. She grabbed the first thing that came to hand, which happened to be the bright plaster model of St Paul's Cathedral she kept on the table by her bed.

'Don't you come a step nearer, Mick O'Neil, or I'll break your head,' she hissed.

He paused, his thinking befuddled from drinking too much ale last night, and trying hard to keep awake to carry out his promise to himself with this lovely prize of a colleen.

'I mean it,' Prissy snapped. 'You get out of here before I call Mackenzie——'

'And what d'you think the great boss man's going to do when he sees me in here? Do you think he'll believe you didn't ask me in, when you been enticing me all week, me darlin'?'

At his sneering voice, Prissy felt her senses swim. She hadn't enticed the lout, but she certainly hadn't done anything to stop him flirting with her. In his sober moments, O'Neil could be a charmer, and quite a gallant with that blarney of his. He was anything but that now, and she saw to her shame that this was partly her fault. Too late, she knew it.

'Look, O'Neil, it seems we've both made a mistake,' she whispered frantically, not wanting to wake the entire homestead, and wishing he'd stop weaving about and knocking into furniture. 'Just get out of here and we'll say no more about it, all right?'

He gave a laugh that was loud enough to waken the folk at White Junction.

'You ain't getting rid of me that easily, darlin'! Not until I've had meself some kisses from those sweet lips of yours. I'll wager Mackenzie's had quite a few since you moved in, ain't he?'

He lurched forward and tripped, sprawling across the bed. Prissy screamed, and crashed the plaster model down on his head, where it shattered into a thousand pieces. O'Neil groaned, shaking his head like a half drowned puppy and scattering bits of plaster around the room as he struggled to stand up.

Within seconds, Prissy's door had burst open and Mackenzie stood there. Iona and Davy Golightly were close behind. Dimly, she could hear Robbie crying, and she saw Iona slip away to calm the boy. Prissy felt shame sweep over her like a tide as Mackenzie hauled the Irishman to his feet.

'He—he came in here—he frightened me—I had to hit him—I thought I'd killed him——' she blubbered.

'It would take more than a bash on the head to kill this one,' Mackenzie said savagely. 'Think yourself lucky he was too drunk to do what he obviously intended, lassie. Now perhaps you'll see where your simpering glances can lead. Help me get him out of here, Davy, and see him off my property once and for all.'

Prissy shivered from head to toe as the two men hauled the loudly protesting O'Neil out of her room. The rest of the men must surely have heard the rumpus, and word would soon spread that Mick O'Neil had been to Prissy Baxter's room, whatever the truth of it. The Irishman himself would assuredly boast of it, Prissy thought sickly.

But she was more numbed by Mackenzie's accusation. He'd spoken as if he thought she'd *invited* O'Neil to her room, or at the very least wanted him there. When all the time she had been repulsed by the man, and it wasn't *O'Neil* that she wanted... The shame of what had happened wasn't hers, yet she felt it as keenly as if it was, all the more so because of Mackenzie's harsh words.

The weak tears she couldn't stop suddenly became a torrent. She had never felt so young and vulnerable and alone, and she turned her head into her pillow, wishing she'd never come to Australia in the first place, and most of all that she'd never set eyes on James Mackenzie.

Mackenzie didn't appear at breakfast with the men, and, though the shearers made a good attempt at normal conversation, Prissy guessed most of them were aware of what had happened. They were eager to get away from here and on their way to Redring Station for the next job. It was a long way west of Ballatree, and would take more than two days' riding to get there. Nobody mentioned Mick O'Neil, until one of the fiddlers, an older man than the rest, gave Prissy's hand a small squeeze before he left.

'Don't you go fretting over what happened with that Irishman, dearie. He were always a troublemaker, and, good shearer or not, we'll be glad to see the back of him.'

'But you'll catch up with him at Redring Station, won't you? I don't want to be the cause of breaking up your team,' she said unhappily.

The man shook his head. 'I doubt that we'll see him at Redring, and good riddance to him. He was heading in the wrong direction the last we saw of him, and there's nothing that way except for the supply depot and the south road to Sydney. I dare say he'll be trying his luck with some of the ladies there—begging your pardon, miss,' he added.

She smiled faintly, not taking offence. All she could think of at that moment was that if Mick O'Neil thought to try his luck with Miss Edna Hatherall at White Junction he'd be fortunate not to get her mother's umbrella beaten about his head.

CHAPTER TEN

A COUPLE of days later, Prissy awoke with the uneasy feeling that something definitely wasn't right.

'It's unnaturally quiet, isn't it?' she said, as she walked into the kitchen.

There had been a welcome calm over the place ever since the shearers had moved on, but this was different. She took stock quickly. There was no fire burning on the stove and no welcome kettle singing to greet her. Mackenzie was desperately trying to calm his son who was snivelling into his sleeve.

'Can you do something with him?' he said at once, ignoring Prissy's question. 'He's been a thorn in my side ever since he awoke this morning.'

'What's wrong with him?'

'Iona's gone,' Robbie shrieked, jumping away from his father and pulling Prissy's arm up and down as she tried to shush him. At his words she felt her heart jump.

'For pity's sake, laddie, I've told you it won't be for long. It never is.'

'What do you mean—*it never is*?' Prissy said at once. 'Where has she gone?'

Mackenzie turned away from her and threw some sticks into the stove, coaxing the fire into life and placing the kettle firmly over it.

'She's gone walkabout with Davy,' he said curtly. 'It happens from time to time—as I've mentioned before. They go off into the bush, living the way their people did before the white men came and so-say civilised them. They live off anything they can find, fruit and berries

and any animals they can kill, and whenever they find
them they'll shin up the eucalyptus trees for the wild
bees' honey. It may last for three or four days, maybe
more, but I guess not this time. They'll not want to leave
you in the lurch——'

'*Me!* What do you mean—leave *me* in the lurch?'

Mackenzie spoke shortly. 'I'd have thought it was obvious. While Iona's gone walkabout, you'll have to take
over the running of the house. Milk the goats, feed the
chickens and bring in the eggs, collect the water from
the creek, see to the cleaning and washing——'

Her mouth had dropped open at the list of essen-
tials—now she spluttered with anger.

'I'm not employed to do all those things. I'm here as
a house helper, but my duties mainly apply to caring for
Robbie——'

'You'll do what's required of you, lassie,' Mackenzie
said grimly. 'And right now, we're all needing breakfast.'

'And what if I refuse?' she said hotly.

'Then we'll go hungry—you, me *and* the boy. The men
will fend for themselves as usual.'

She looked at him scornfully. 'Stop funning with me,
Mackenzie. You wouldn't let your boy go hungry, and
you can see to yourself well enough. I know that from
the journey from Sydney to here——'

'But I shan't be here all day. You know that Fred and
myself are away to the supply depot with the fleeces.
We'll not be back until nightfall, so if you care for the
bairn at all you'll see to his needs and not make such a
flounce about it.'

She glared at him furiously. It *was* true that today he
had planned to take the fleeces to White Junction. But
surely if the Aborigines had gone walkabout it could have
waited another day...but apparently there was no
knowing how long they'd be gone, and Mackenzie would

want to get his wool to Sydney while it was in prime
condition to fetch the best price...

'Aren't you angry that your chief stockman chooses
this time to leave you?' she demanded, finding it amazing
that Davy Golightly could do such a thing.

Mackenzie shrugged. 'We have an understanding. As
long as he's always here at lambing time and for the
shearing, I make no demands on him when his past life
claims him more than I do. What right does any man
have to deny a man his ancestral birthright? We're the
interlopers in this country, not the likes of Davy
Golightly.'

Prissy was silenced by the simple logic and fair-
mindedness of the man, even if she privately thought it
sounded completely daft. She wondered if all bosses
would be so tolerant. But it was enough to make her
stop making any further retort. And she really had no
choice but to do as Mackenzie said.

'All right, I'll do the best I can. But you'll get back
as soon as you can tonight, won't you? There'll only be
me and the boy in the homestead——'

'You needn't let that trouble you, lassie. Hans and the
other men will be in the bunkhouse, and if you start
getting fretful when it gets dark, ask one or two of them
to jaw with you in the clearing outside the house. You
needn't feel lonely and I doubt that it'll be much after
sundown when Fred and I get back. You'll manage just
fine.'

He was more certain of her competence than Prissy
was. The unknown number of days without Iona
stretched ahead, filled with doing all the tasks that had
never been hers before, but which were allotted women's
tasks. Flora Mackenzie would have done them uncom-
plainingly as the wife of the homesteader, and as the

thought came into her head Prissy knew that she'd darned well do them too.

She wasn't so positive a couple of hours later. By then, she'd seen Mackenzie and Fred go off on the loaded wagon, after she'd produced a miserable looking breakfast of half-cooked porridge and bread and dripping. The men from the bunkhouse had gone about their business, and she and Robbie looked at one another.

'Are we going to collect the water from the creek?' the boy said.

'I suppose we'd better do that first,' Prissy agreed reluctantly. The bush was always kept well cleared from the edges of the creek, and there was no real need to fear, but she still couldn't forget the way that Flora Mackenzie had died there. She could never think of it without a shudder.

'Come on then, and you can sit on the cans,' Prissy said, knowing she couldn't dither all day, and that the sooner she got it over with, the better. The cart was pony-drawn and the metal cans all fitted with lids to prevent the precious water slopping on the ride back to the homestead.

It wasn't a long way to the creek, but the task of filling the cans and lifting them on to the cart, taking them back to the house and lifting them down again to put them in the cool of the larder was enough to make her arms ache appallingly. The sun was high and bakingly hot, suffusing the waving grasses of the bush in a shimmering dusty haze, and the day's work had barely begun yet.

'Iona keeps kettles on the stove all day,' Robbie said importantly. Prissy groaned, because keeping a fire going was the last thing she wanted to do in this heat, but it was essential for cooking and heating water.

'I *know*!' Prissy said. Except that, of course, she hadn't thought to keep the fire topped up with wood and there were only the faintest embers showing now. Furiously she encouraged it into life with the bellows, coughing and spluttering as black smuts flew about the room.

'There's something in my eye,' Robbie howled. 'It hurts, and it's all your fault——'

'Stand still, you little ninny, and I'll get it out,' she instructed, while he squirmed and flinched and generally made a song and dance about the whole thing.

Robbie's bad temper and her own to match it continued all day long. She hated having to milk the goats, to lean her head against their restless bodies and gingerly pinch their udders to squirt the thin stream of milk into a pail that one of them immediately knocked over, to Robbie's screaming delight.

She hated having to search in the dirt for the hens' eggs, when the nasty squawking things moved threateningly near to her as she invaded their territory. She discovered she was hopeless at baking bread, turning out heavy lumps of dough in place of Iona's shining crusty loaves.

She served up a meal for herself and Robbie of half-cooked potatoes and sliced meat that the child said tasted awful, and he refused to eat it. By the end of the day she got him kicking and protesting to bed because he wanted to see his pa, and his pa hadn't come home yet, and when she sank down exhausted in Flora Mackenzie's old rocking-chair in the parlour she looked up at her portrait with something like mutiny in her heart.

'All right, so I'm no outback woman,' she muttered to the silently mocking features of the other woman. 'I never professed to be, did I? I'll never be any good out here, and I wish to blazes I'd never come! How does that please your ladyship?'

'I'm sure if my wife could answer back, she'd say you weren't doing so badly for a town lass,' Mackenzie's dry voice said from the doorway.

Prissy's heart jumped. She'd been so concerned with herself she hadn't heard the wagon return, and for Mackenzie to find her here—like the lady of the manor—after all she'd been through today, was just too much. She burst into noisy, angry tears.

'I'm not doing well at all! I'm a total failure and you know it, so don't patronise me!'

She found herself wrapped in his arms and his hands were in her hair, smoothing it down from its unruly state. She hadn't had any time to attend to her own toilet that day, and she felt a complete hoyden—dirty and dishevelled.

'Prissy, do you think I expected you to find today easy? I did not, but the fact that you've come through it unscathed is good enough for me. Tomorrow will be better, I promise you.'

Tomorrow? She gave a watery smile, not wanting to remove her head from his chest, where it felt so good. She supposed that she should get him something to eat. It was what a good wife would do, or a good house-keeper... but she was neither, and there were only the remnants of a badly cooked meal and that leaden bread...

'I've brought back some provisions from White Junction,' Mackenzie said briskly, moving away from her sniffling body. 'Mrs Hatherall insisted on sending a cake for us when she knew Iona had gone walkabout, and there's a fresh-baked loaf as well. I thought you'd be glad of it.'

'That's very kind of her,' Prissy sniffed, even more aware of her own inadequacies, but feeling treacherously hungry at the thought.

And there was some goat's cheese in the larder that she'd completely forgotten and some pickles that Iona had made from root vegetables and vinegar. They could have a cold feast if nothing else, and she began to feel slightly less miserable at the thought of it.

'By the way, you needn't bother about seeing that Irish rogue next year,' Mackenzie said casually. 'He called at White Junction on his way south and said he's giving up the shearing trek and striking out for Van Diemen's Land with his dues to set up a place of his own.'

'Oh.' Prissy was so surprised and thankful to hear this that she didn't even bother to comment that it was highly unlikely she'd be around this time next year anyway. She didn't know where she'd be, and it had just come into her head as a muddled thought.

But it was a thought that was becoming clearer. She couldn't stay here for ever, not once she'd paid her passage money back. Definitely not with the fond feelings she had for James Mackenzie, who didn't even know she was alive except as a house helper. She dismissed the marriage proposal he'd made to her as no more than one of those impulsive remarks a man made to a girl and just as quickly regretted. She'd heard enough of those at the old Alhambra to put them in their proper place in her mind.

'So what are we having for supper? The kettle's coming up to the boil, so a nice cup of tea will be very welcome— but no, you sit there while I do that. You can make the supper in a little while, if there's anything to eat in the place.'

'Cheese and pickle, and Mrs Hatherall's fresh-baked bread?' She said it all in a rush, praying he wouldn't think it meagre fare to offer a man who'd been travelling all day.

'That sounds just right. Hans and I ate full to bursting at White Junction at midday. Mrs Hatherall's a fine cook, even if she does tend to stuff a man overfull with meat and mouth-watering pastry.'

It was a cheerful remark which didn't help to restore Prissy Baxter's peace of mind one little bit. But later, when they'd both eaten and Prissy was feeling slightly more human again, she was aware of the cosiness of the night. Robbie was asleep, the men attending to their own amusements, and Iona and Davy had gone walkabout.

That left just herself and James Mackenzie in the house, sitting either side of the fireplace as if they were matching pieces on a chessboard. The futility of it didn't escape her, and the more she thought about it, the more conscious she was of Flora Mackenzie's portrait between them.

'You seem very restless tonight, lassie. I thought you'd have been tired out, and I reckon you did a good job today.'

It was praise, coming from him. And she *was* restless, but not in the way he meant it. She had a restlessness inside her soul that came from loving a man who didn't love her, and there was no antidote for that. She jumped up from her chair and wandered to the window.

'I was just wondering what drove people like Iona and Davy to go off into the bush. It's something I could never imagine doing, certainly not in the dark.'

She gave a small shudder, trying very hard *not* to imagine it. Mackenzie laughed.

'It's as natural for them to be free of the white man's so-called civilised trappings as it is for you to sing to an audience, Prissy.'

'Well, I didn't find it so difficult to give that up, professionally, anyway.'

'You still enjoy it though, don't you? And a bit of relaxation would be very welcome tonight. Why don't you play the piano and sing for a while? I'd like to listen to you.'

'Sing for my supper, you mean,' she said lightly, because the thought of playing and singing for James Mackenzie alone was as enchanting as it was poignant.

'No. For me,' he said softly, and she caught an unguarded look that said he was missing the softness of a woman's voice, and the gentleness of a woman's company here in this room where they rarely sat together in such companionship, and which she had always thought of as Flora's domain.

Part of her wanted to refuse him, but a far greater part knew she could refuse him nothing. She moved to the instrument and lifted the lid, running her fingers swiftly over the keys. She had been extraordinarily tired, but somehow the tiredness left her as she played the gentle songs that matched her voice, and finally the haunting words of a love song filled the room.

'That was beautiful. You've a rare talent for catching a man's heart with your voice, Prissy.'

She closed the lid quickly. If she sang one more song, he must surely know she was singing the words only for him, and it wasn't just her voice that was reaching out to him.

'I don't want to sing any more. I'm tired, and I need my sleep. I suppose I have to do the same things tomorrow that I did today?'

The very thought of it reminded her that her muscles still ached, and that the endless rituals of milking and baking, fetching and carrying, had to be done for their survival in this land.

'Oh, aye, 'tis your task now until Iona comes back, but it's no bad thing to know the way of things in the outback. Some day you'll be wanting to wed, even if not to myself, and a young girl should know the basics of housewifery.'

He came across to where she was still sitting at the piano and held out his hand to her. She put her fingers inside his, and wished she dared put them to her lips. She wished she dared say there was only one man she wanted to marry in all the world, and it was on the tip of her tongue to throw her pride to the four winds and say that if he still wanted her, she'd be willing...

'By the way, you know I said we'd not be seeing the Irishman around here again?' he said casually, clearing all such daft thoughts from her head, and obviously still making an effort to be sociable. 'I didn't tell you he'd spent half a day at White Junction penning some letter or other for Sam Hatherall to take down to Sydney. Probably putting in a complaint that he was run off my station, but much good it will do him. These ticket-of-leavers think they own the world.'

'He's a ticket-of-leaver?' Prissy said, wide-eyed. 'But doesn't that mean he's a—he was a——'

'Aye, a convict,' he finished for her. 'But you've no need to let that worry you. As I told you once before, there's all sorts in this country, and once a man's served his term he's as good as the next.'

She didn't feel half as magnanimous about it as Mackenzie did! Not when Mick O'Neil had come to her room and frightened her half to death by his loutish ways.

'Well, you might have told me what he was,' she said indignantly.

Mackenzie looked at her out of lazy brown eyes.

'Why? You seemed to have taken a fair liking to the man, so why should I intervene and break up your little amusements?'

'You know very well there was nothing like that,' Prissy snapped. 'I never meant to encourage him, and I can hardly help it if men who haven't seen a white woman for some time go a little crazy in the head when they do! Some even make offers of marriage without giving any thought to the woman's feelings or whether the match would be suitable or not!'

She said the last words without thinking, and saw how his face darkened.

'Am I included in this scathing opinion of men? You think that, because I hadn't seen a white woman for some time, I made an offer to the first one to come into my clutches, do you?'

'I'm not in your clutches. And no, I didn't mean it the way it sounded. Your situation is quite different.'

She was horribly embarrassed, remembering that he was alone because his wife had died, and that if she hadn't there would be a lovely little family living here at Ballatree Station now, and Prissy Baxter would be very much in her proper place.

'I'm truly sorry,' she rushed on when he didn't say anything. 'I didn't mean to imply that you were a man of Mick O'Neil's sort.'

'I should damn well hope not,' Mackenzie snapped. 'I've no wish to force my way into a woman's bedroom, particularly one who's as prickly as a burr when she wants to be.'

'Perhaps we'd make a good match after all, then! Because you're undoubtedly the prickliest man I ever met!' Prissy said hotly.

Then she saw that his mouth was beginning to twitch, and she saw how daft it all was. The two of them were standing here wrangling over nothing; she with her hands on her hips like a fishwife, and he the epitome of the tall dark handsome hero of some fantasy tale, trying to force his will on the cringing heroine. Except that Prissy Baxter was no cringing heroine ready to give in to any man, and never would be.

'Prissy, I think we should both get to our beds and stop this senseless arguing.' The smile in his voice took the sting out of his words. 'Morning will come all too soon, and you'll be bemoaning the lack of beauty sleep. Not that you need it at your age, but I do.'

'You make yourself sound like old Father Time,' she muttered, because Mackenzie's lightning changes of mood always set her heart beating faster. She wondered if he was always like this, or if bereavement had changed him so much. Did he ever laugh and sing and behave like a young man in love with no cares save that of the daily round?

And after coming all the way to Australia, obviously prosperous enough to start this sheep station and make a success of his new life, it was doubly cruel that his wife should have died so tragically. She'd never really given much thought to what private torment he must have gone through these last months.

As she passed him, she reached up and kissed his cheek contritely.

'Goodnight, Mackenzie, and I'm sorry I'm such an irritation to you. I'll try to behave, really I will.'

She sped to the door, wondering how she'd had the temerity to kiss him like that, and couldn't resist a quick glance back before she closed the door behind her. But it was long enough to see him staring after her with an odd expression on his face, a mixture of tenderness and bewilderment, as if he, too, had felt something like a minor shock.

*   *   *

Robbie was banging on her door early the next morning, and she groaned, realising the aches and pains of yesterday hadn't gone away after all. Muscles she hadn't known she had screamed out in protest that yesterday's exertions had to start all over again, and she soon found that Robbie was still in a foul mood because Iona hadn't come back.

'I don't like your porridge. Why the blue blazes do I have to eat it?' He scowled when she slapped the dish down in front of him.

'Robbie, I'll have none of that kind of talk from you,' Mackenzie thundered, while Prissy clapped her hand over her mouth. It was the first time she'd heard Robbie mimic one of her occasional expressions, and he'd obviously been saving it up to suit the moment.

She ignored the temptation to shout that Robbie heard far worse expletives from the stockmen, and rounded on the boy instead.

'For pity's sake, I'm doing the best I can. Try it with more sugar on it,' she snapped, sprinkling sugar more lavishly on her own gruel to prove a point. Mackenzie frowned at the extravagance, but she didn't care. It was her digestion, and she saw no reason why she should be obliged to eat the salty, savoury dish the Scotsman preferred. Besides, she hated the taste of it intensely.

'Can't you understand that the bairn hasn't been brought up to eat in your soft southern ways? The stuff's too runny. He doesn't need pap, he needs a good solid lining to his stomach.'

Silently, Prissy stood up, took the child's dish from him and tipped it into the slop bucket. She banged a plate of bread and dripping in front of him.

'Right. You can get on with that, then, because I'm not making any more, and you'll get nothing else until midday.'

On the other side of the table, Mackenzie stood up slowly.

'Are you undermining my authority, lassie?'

She looked at him coolly without blinking. She'd discovered that when he got his dander up it was the only way to counter those black-browed stares of his.

'I am not. I'm merely safeguarding my own position in this household. If I'm the child's nursemaid and house helper, *and* chief cook and water-carrier and farmworker at the present time, then I insist on doing things my way!'

She paused for breath and saw him place his knuckles on the scrubbed table. It probably helped him to resist hitting her, she thought angrily. But she knew she was right. Robbie ate his porridge perfectly well when Mackenzie wasn't around. If she didn't take charge now and stop this eternal game of playing one of them off against the other, the child was never going to learn discipline. And that was what she was supposed to be here for.

For several minutes the man eyed the girl across the table and then he gave a brief nod. He looked at his son sternly.

'You'll do as Prissy says. If you don't want your porridge you'll say so beforehand and you'll get something else. Otherwise, you'll eat what's put in front of you.'

There was silence for a few minutes and then Robbie spoke sulkily. 'Why can't Iona come back? I like Iona best.'

'I like Iona better than you too, you nasty little boy,' Prissy said calmly.

Robbie stared at her in astonishment.

Mackenzie turned to the door. 'I'll leave you two dunderheads to sort out your own differences. Mebbe we can have a bit of peace and quiet by the time I see you next.'

Prissy looked at the boy after his father had gone. The brows were drawn together just like Mackenzie's, the brown eyes just as sparky.

'Which of us is going to throw the bread at the door after him?' Prissy said, picking up a piece of the loaf.

'Can we do that?' he said in awe after a startled silence.

''Course we can if we want to. We can be two proper pigs if we want to. As long as we eat it all afterwards, of course. We mustn't waste good food. Do you want to eat bread that's been all over the floor where the dogs have been sleeping?'

He shook his head vigorously, not quite sure if this was all a game or not.

'Well, neither do I. I'd much rather eat it off my plate, wouldn't you? It's too good to waste.'

Her eyes challenged his for a minute as she pushed her own porridge aside and bit into a piece of bread and dripping. Robbie gave a lop-sided smile and then picked up his own bread and demolished the lot. It was a small kind of victory, but one that filled Prissy with a feeling of hope at last.

'Are we going to fetch the water?' he asked when they'd finally finished eating.

'I suppose so,' she said with a sigh. 'And milk the goats and collect the eggs...' She couldn't resist a groan. If only Iona was here to do these things...

'I'll show you how Iona talks to the goats if you like, so they don't move about when she milks them.'

'Are you teasing me?' Prissy asked suspiciously.

'No. Iona says goats need talking to, then they be friends and stand still. You didn't talk to them yesterday.'

And you didn't tell me Iona's secret, Prissy thought caustically. But if he was ready to do so today, that must be something else in her favour.

'Come on, then, let's get started,' she said. Without thinking, she held out her hand to him, and just as unconsciously he put his own small hand in hers.

At the end of four days, the Aborigines finally came back, and Robbie threw himself into Iona's arms with obvious adoration. Prissy wondered at once if he was going to revert to his old aggressive manner but, to her relief, he seemed more content than at any time since her arrival. There had been a definite change in their relationship.

'I think I can safely say that Robbie's finally mellowed towards me,' she said jubilantly after a blissfully quiet breakfast the following morning, while Iona and Davy were showing the boy the brilliantly hued birds' feathers they'd brought back for him from the bush. They'd already held him entranced with their tales of living off the earth the way nature intended, colourful tales that Mackenzie listened to more sceptically than his gullible son.

'Didn't I tell you he would, given time?' Mackenzie said tersely in answer to her question.

'Aren't you pleased? I thought you'd be pleased, but you don't look it! What the blue blazes have I done that's wrong now?'

'For one thing, you could stop using that ridiculous expression. You heard how Robbie picked it up——'

'Well, talk about the pot calling the kettle black! I've heard you say far worse, and I seem to remember you telling me once that he'd have to get used to bad language from the men. I don't consider my bit of nonsense is corrupting him——'

'His mother never found it necessary to use such talk,' Mackenzie snapped.

Prissy felt a cold shiver of anger run through her. 'Oh, I see. I'm sorry I don't come up to her high standards, but we all have our own little ways, don't we? Some of your words aren't exactly up to the King's English!'

'Mebbe that's because I'm of a superior race,' he taunted.

'You—you're certainly the most arrogant man I ever met!' she spluttered. 'If that's the way you all behave north of the border, I'm glad I've never met any more of you.'

'And you're such a connoisseur of men, of course,' he said sarcastically.

She felt her cheeks burn. 'I don't even know what the word means, but I can tell from the way you said it that it's not complimentary. Well, if that's the way you think of me, you can stew in your own juice, James Mackenzie. I obviously don't come up to your lofty standards at all, so now that Iona's here to do your bidding, I'm off.'

She stormed out of the kitchen, ignoring Robbie's astonished face as he came in from the clearing with his arms full of birds' feathers. Her eyes were streaming with hurt, and she marched straight for the stables and threw herself over the back of the grey mare. She didn't know where she was going. All she knew was that she had to get away, from Mackenzie, from Ballatree Station, from everything that she loved and hated in equal measure.

She rode and rode, head down, until she could ride no more. She had no idea how far she had come, but she saw that she was near the tree-fringed shade of a water-hole. She slid off the animal's back and scooped some water into her parched mouth, and splashed some of it over her heated face. She lay down in the shade of a spreading tree and tried to think haphazardly about her future.

And finally, when the sun had dropped lower in the sky and begun to leave long shadows, she knew she had to go back, because there was simply nowhere else to go. She was all too conscious of the screeching of the cicadas, and the frequent unidentified rustle in the bush. She had heard the threatening call of the wild dingo from time to time, and knew that, out here, there was only the alien night in front of her. While at Ballatree Station, for all its frustrations, there was safety—and James Mackenzie.

CHAPTER ELEVEN

IT WAS dark by the time she returned to the homestead. Robbie had been in bed a long while, and Mackenzie had plenty to say to her.

'Do you realise the boy thought you'd run away? Do you have any idea of what that meant to him, after the way he lost his mother?'

She couldn't believe he was saying these things to her. 'What about Iona going away!'

'That's different! He understands about walkabout.'

'Well, it's more than I do,' she snapped. 'I think you're all mad, the lot of you.'

She was unbelievably tired. If she'd ached before, doing all Iona's chores as well as her own, she ached a hundred times more now. She was still a novice at horse riding, and she was almost dropping with sleep.

'You have no consideration for other people,' Mackenzie went on relentlessly. 'Did you no remember that I'm responsible for you?'

'Oh, so that's what this is all about, is it? You didn't want to get in hot water with the Ladies' Committee for losing one of their girls! You didn't care about *me* at all!' Angry tears stung her eyes at the thought.

'Don't be stupid. Of course I cared about you. I was worried sick, once I realised how the time was going on, and you hadn't returned.'

'Really?' she said sarcastically.

'Really. Now get something to eat and get to bed. You look done in.'

'I am. And I couldn't eat a thing. I had some wild fruit and berries. You'd have been proud of me for going native——'

'God give me patience! You might have poisoned yourself!' Mackenzie exclaimed.

'Oh—*damn* you, Mackenzie!' Prissy said, tiredness and frustration overcoming her in sweeping waves. She whirled about and rushed straight off to her own room. He was impossible, she raged. He was simply and infuriatingly impossible. She undressed in the dark, stumbling into her bed and falling asleep immediately.

She awoke to the sounds of frantic activity, realising with a groan that it was morning already. It felt as if she'd hardly put her head on the pillow before Iona was rushing into her room without knocking.

'Is Robbie here?' she gasped.

'No, I haven't seen him. What's going on?'

She couldn't collect her thoughts together as Iona ran out of the room again, shouting something back that Prissy couldn't follow. But there was a sense of urgency in the woman's manner that had Prissy fully awake now. She struggled into her clothes, aware of shouting outside the house and a peculiar noise she couldn't quickly identify. Although it was daylight, she saw that the sky was unusually overcast as she threw back her curtains and peered outside.

At the same instant she recoiled in startled surprise. Lashing rain was beating against the house, turning the tinder-dry clearing into an instant quagmire. The wind was in full force, a hot, surging wind that moaned through the bush and bent the branches of the pliant eucalyptus trees in supplication. She felt her heart thump at this savage explosion of the first flash flood she had experienced since coming to Australia.

She ran out of her room and into the kitchen, which seemed to be full of people. Mackenzie was there, Iona and Davy, Hans and Fred, the regular stockhands and the stable-lad, scared and young as the man railed into him.

'Are you sure you never saw the bairn this morning, laddie? *Think*, for God's sake! And you're saying you didn't think the pony's state was anything unusual?'

'No, I didn't, boss,' the boy snivelled. 'The pony was settled down last night, and this morning it came limping back to the stable as if it had been out all night, dirty and exhausted. I just thought it had got out. I never thought anything else was amiss.'

'You never thought to report to me as soon as you saw the animal?' Mackenzie snapped. 'You never thought my wee son might have gone joy riding on it and fallen off somewhere?'

Prissy gasped, trying to make sense of all this, and unwilling to believe what her mind was telling her was true.

'Why should I?' the boy howled. 'The little 'un's been told often enough not to go out on his own. I just thought the animal had broken free and come back of its own accord. 'Tis not my fault!'

He stopped abruptly as Mackenzie made a move towards him, and Davy put a restraining hand on his arm.

'The boy speaks true, boss. It's not his blame,' the stockman said.

Prissy couldn't keep silent a second longer.

'What's happened?' she burst out. 'Where's Robbie?'

Mackenzie turned on her at once. She had never known such despair and hate mingled in one face.

'It looks as if he's gone wandering. Iona here says he heard us arguing yesterday and was upset by it all day.

He wouldn't eat or settle at all, especially when you didn't come back by his bedtime——'

'Oh, dear God, no. Oh Mackenzie, I'm so sorry!' she cried, her mind in a turmoil at the thought of Robbie wandering about in the bush. And in this sudden torrent of bad weather...

She felt a real fear ripple through her, remembering her own terror last night when it began to get dark. How would young Robbie be feeling now...?

'So you should be,' Mackenzie snapped. 'You've a duty here and, whatever your own feelings, you should put the child's needs first. But we'll deal with that later. Right now, we've search parties to organise. We'll spread out in all directions, two to a party. The first group to spot the bairn will fire two shots in the air. Have you all got that? *Two shots.* The women will remain in the house in the hope that he returns on his own, and Iona will fire two shots if that happens.'

It was clear that he didn't think it would happen that way. He simply ignored Prissy as he gave his orders, and she and the Aborigine woman spoke simultaneously.

'Iona track with one of the men. Iona find trail.'

'I'm coming too! I can't just stay here and twiddle my thumbs when you're obviously blaming me for all this!'

The stable-boy looked uncomfortably at Mackenzie. 'I'll stay back if the women want to go, boss. Iona would be more use than me.'

Mackenzie nodded. 'Aye, I'll not deny that. All right. But Prissy will remain here——'

'*No!* If you won't let me go with you, I'll follow on my own. Do you think I'll be able to rest, knowing Robbie's somewhere out there——'

'We waste time, boss. Let the woman come,' Davy said practically, already pulling on heavy outer clothes to keep out the worst of the weather.

Mackenzie was curt. 'Then she comes with me. I won't have her suggesting any mad schemes to put anyone else in danger.'

Prissy bit back a furious retort. He was clearly distraught at the thought of Robbie going off alone into the bush, and she couldn't blame him. The child was so little, and there were so many untold dangers. It was totally impractical and quite impossible to clear all the land within the boundaries of the property, and the innocent grazing pastures were interspersed with great tracts of encroaching wilderness outback that could swallow up a child in an instant.

Mackenzie threw a heavy cape towards her.

'Put this on. You'll be hot inside it, but at least it'll keep you fairly dry.'

It was an understatement. As they went outside and got the horses from the stables, Prissy felt the rush of humid air on her face that no amount of rain could cool. Almost as soon as it fell, the rain steamed on the hot earth, and her feet splashed in sudden pools of water that hadn't existed before, and would vanish just as quickly when the storm ended.

'How long will this go on?' she stuttered at Mackenzie, as she grappled with the mechanics of getting on to her mare.

'Since I'm no clairvoyant, I've no way of knowing,' he said coldly. 'But usually only for a few hours. I pray to God that we're in time.'

She didn't need to ask what he meant. A swollen creek could become a dangerous overflowing river instead of providing life-saving water. A previously innocent waterhole could become a deep pool of death that could easily drown a man or a child...

She no longer felt affronted at the way Mackenzie was treating her. His fear for his son was transmitted to Prissy. Stubborn, frustrating and aggressive as both the man and the boy were, she loved them both. And it was clear to her that Mackenzie's genuine love for his son was pushing him, both in his manner and in the superhuman way he forced his horse on, calling endlessly for Robbie, through tangled bush and across the great plains.

By the time they had been searching for a couple of hours, Prissy was exhausted. They were soaked to the skin, and she was beginning to shiver violently. She could hardly see through the driving rain, and her hair was constantly being blown into her eyes and her mouth, and stinging her face. She wanted to beg him to stop, to rest, but she dared not. It would have been useless, anyway. Mackenzie wouldn't rest until he had found his son, and why should he? Robbie was all he had left.

Once, she thought she heard a shot, and felt a surge of hope, bellowing to Mackenzie to stop and listen. He shook his head decisively.

'It was only one shot,' he shouted back. 'Somebody's probably got a dingo. 'Twas nothing to do with us.'

So now she knew why he'd insisted on two shots when they found Robbie. A single shot merely signified the killing of some wild thing, and the thought terrified her even more. They were moving at a snail's pace through a tangle of bush themselves now, and every small crackling noise in the undergrowth set her nerves jumping.

Then, as suddenly as the rain had begun, it stopped, and within minutes the clouds had scudded across the sky and disappeared, just as if they had evaporated. And with the end of the rain and the appearance of the sun

the blistering heat and steaming began in earnest. Prissy
was stunned and unnerved by the unearthly noises as the
ground beneath their feet and the foliage all around them
reacted almost violently to this new state.

'I can't keep this thing on a minute longer,' she gasped.
She slid off the back of the mare and ripped the sodden
cape from her shoulders.

She looked down at herself. The frock she'd quickly
donned that morning was a muddy mess of fabric that
clung to her body. At any other time, and with any other
man, she might have expected some lewd remark at the
way her shape was revealed, but this was James
Mackenzie, who was an honourable man and suffering
in dire misery at the fate of his son.

Impulsively, she reached up and put a hand on his
arm. He too had got down from his horse, wearied
beyond measure, but still tense and alert, still listening
for the longed for sound of Robbie's voice that never
came.

'Mackenzie, I know we'll find him safe. Don't lose
faith, please don't.'

He looked at her, this irritating young woman whom
he saw as the cause of all these new problems, and felt
an unmanly burst of emotion well up inside him because
of the compassion in her beautiful blue eyes.

'You ask an impossibility, lassie. I've little faith inside
me any more. What man could have, when I've already
lost the dearest thing I had? And now——'

Prissy swallowed, pushing aside her own feelings at
Mackenzie's oblique reference to his wife.

'You haven't lost Robbie, nor will you. He's a true-
born child of the outback, isn't he? You've said yourself
how well he's grown with this land. He belongs here more
than we do—in the same way as Iona and Davy. He'll
be all right, I know he will.'

'How do you know? You're just a slip of a lass. Do you have second sight or something?'

'I just feel it inside me.' She refused to be angry with him, knowing what he was going through. 'Oh, I know I'm not clever like you. I'm no use at being an outback woman and I admit it willingly. But I've a great fondness for Robbie, whatever you think, and I can't believe that anything's happened to him. Call it instinct or what you like, but I just know he'll be all right, James.'

She used his name nervously, unsure of his reaction. But to her he was a man lost within himself, needing to have his identity restored the way a wife would have given it to him. Prissy couldn't fill that role at this moment, if ever, but he wouldn't have been Mackenzie to *Flora*—that single, remote name that gave him status, but set him apart from involvement in a close and loving relationship. The only one who held any kind of key to his heart was Robbie, who called him 'Pa'...

For a second, Prissy wondered if she was dreaming. She lifted her head, heard the rustling of the leaves and the struggling of the earth to absorb the last vestiges of rain for the foreseeable future. But surely she hadn't been mistaken—surely there was a different, faintly familiar sound coming from somewhere ahead of them. She turned to Mackenzie, hardly daring to ask, but he had heard it too and was already leaping back on to his horse.

'Robbie! Stay right where you are and don't move!'

Mackenzie yelled out the boy's name, digging his heels into the horse's flanks with a force that made the animal squeal in protest. Prissy struggled on to her mare's back, knowing the man had forgotten her instantly. She tried desperately to keep him in sight as he tore off through the bush, guided by the pounding thud of horse's hoofs until she saw his sweating animal stopping ahead of her.

By the time she reached him, Mackenzie had thrown himself off the horse and was crouching over something very small and frightened and dirty that was crying uncontrollably.

'Stop your noise now, my bairn,' Mackenzie was saying roughly as he rocked the boy in his arms. 'Everything's going to be all right. You're safe now, and we'll soon get you home again. Hush now, my wee one.'

Prissy felt her eyes prickle, feeling that she shouldn't be intruding on these private moments. James Mackenzie might be a dour man at the best of times, unable to express his deepest feelings. But right now, his feelings were raw and exposed, and she wasn't completely sure that all the tears were the boy's. It was something Mackenzie wouldn't want witnessed, and she had half turned away when she heard Robbie sobbing out her name.

'I didn't want Prissy to go 'way, Pa. I went to find her——'

She heard Mackenzie give a smothered oath, but Robbie was rushing on, not heeding any thought of chastisement.

'Then Charger slipped and threw me off his back and I fell into the bush and got all scratched, and he fell on top of me. He hurt me bad.'

'Where did he hurt you, Robbie?'

'My leg.' The boy started crying pitifully now. 'It hurts when I move it, Pa.'

Prissy moved forward now. She knelt beside the man and the boy, seeing the weariness and relief in one, and the cuts and bruises and frightened small face of the other. She longed to gather Robbie up in her arms, but he was not her child, and he was still held too fiercely in his father's embrace for there to be any room for her.

'Show me where your leg hurts, Robbie,' she said huskily. The bond might not be there, but she still felt as deeply for these two as if this really was her child, her man, and she knew the feeling was a dangerous one.

'Prissy, I thought you'd gone 'way,' he shrieked at the sight of her. 'I didn't want you to go. I'll be good if you stay...' He struggled to reach her and gave a little cry as he clutched at his ankle.

'Keep still, love,' she said, feeling his leg with gentle hands.

The ankle was very angry—red and black and swollen—but it didn't appear broken, and was probably just badly sprained when he had fallen with the pony on top of him.

'You'll be all right,' she said with relief. 'A few days in bed is what you need, and a promise to me and your Pa that you never do such a daft thing again.'

'I won't,' he said in a small voice. 'I promise.'

'Then let's get you home,' Mackenzie said briskly. 'You just cover your ears for a moment while I fire off two shots to let the others know we've found you safe.'

Prissy did the same as the two shots blasted into the air, and then came the task of getting Robbie on to the back of Mackenzie's horse. He cried out constantly every time he was moved. Prissy spoke quickly.

'He can't be moved without giving some support to that ankle. He'll be in agony by the time we get back to the homestead if we don't.'

'Aye, you're right,' Mackenzie agreed. 'I could make a splint from a couple of branches, and bind it with twine, but it'll only chafe the leg and make it sore.'

'Will this do?' Prissy bent down and ripped the limp fabric of her frock, tearing a long circular strip from all around the hem. She handed it to Mackenzie, and saw the spark of approval in his eyes at her ingenuity.

It was no less than his own, she thought later, as he fashioned the rough splint out of branches and bound them together with twine from his saddlebag. Prissy wound a thick pad of fabric gently around the boy's painful ankle to keep the branches from touching his leg, and then Mackenzie saw to the rest. Finally the ankle was as rigid as they could make it for the journey back to the house.

It was very slow progress. Time and again they paused to make Robbie more comfortable or to give him a drink of water. The sun was high and dehydrating, and they all felt slightly light-headed by the time they got out of the bush and began the careful ride across the plain towards the homestead. By then, other riders were racing towards them in answer to their signal that Robbie was safe, and beyond them was the wagon, with Davy Golightly in the driving seat.

'Is the boy all right?' Fred shouted.

'Aye, he'll live. Just a sore ankle, but 'twill mebbe serve to remind him of his foolishness,' Mackenzie shouted back, reverting to his usual manner.

He caught Prissy's glance, and a slight smile touched the corners of his mouth, and she knew how much all his brusqueness was a façade. Underneath, she was discovering that there were times when this hard man could be surprisingly soft-centred after all.

Davy brought the wagon to a halt beside them, and between them the men lifted the boy carefully on to the blanket in the back.

'My woman waiting with hot water and warm bed, boss,' Davy said. 'We take him in?'

'Aye, I'll be along right behind you,' Mackenzie said gruffly. 'He'll not be running off again for a wee while yet.'

As Mackenzie let his son go off with Davy and the men, Prissy saw that he visibly wilted a little in the saddle.

'You look as though you need hot water as well, and something stronger than tea to revive you,' she said.

'I'm no doubting that.'

As he glanced her way, she saw the grin that had faded from his lips return again. His gaze went over her, and she was suddenly conscious of what a sketch she must look. She hadn't had time to pin up her hair that morning, and even if she had, the rain and wind would soon have reduced its styling to the way it must look now, wild and flyaway and more like a scarecrow's thatch than the sleek hair of a young lady.

She looked down at her tattered frock that had once been pale blue. It was now a dirty slate-grey, soaked through, and at least nine inches above her ankle where she had torn off the hem. She sat astride the mare in a totally undignified way, and she hadn't even noticed that she had lost a shoe somewhere. She couldn't even guess what a guy she must look...

'Well, why don't you say it?' she burst out. 'Now that it's all over and Robbie's safe, why don't you yell at me that this was all my fault? We both know it! Why don't you tell me how wicked I was for leading him astray? Why don't you say exactly what you think of me? You've never been slow at doing it before!'

She felt the tears welling up in her eyes. This day had been an ordeal for all of them, and she couldn't bear it if Mackenzie ordered her to go now. That hadn't been her intention yesterday at all...

'I was just thinking that you look magnificent at this moment,' Mackenzie said. 'I wish you could see yourself. You remind me of the picture I once saw of an Indian squaw, who looked wild and beautiful and as if she'd brave the whole world to do what she thought was right.'

Her mouth had dropped open long before he had finished speaking. If this was a joke she didn't appreciate it, and, if it was his idea of flattery, she still didn't know whether to be pleased or not.

'Are you making fun of me?' she asked suspiciously.

'I am not! I wouldn't dare, when those eyes are flashing at me like blue darts.'

'Well, then—thank you—I think.'

Mackenzie laughed, relief at his son's safety making him as reckless as if he'd drunk champagne as they cantered on towards the homestead now. His words were grudgingly sincere.

'You can be the most delightful young woman as well as the most irritating one I've ever known. And I'll tell you another thing. You'll never be more of an outback woman than you were today.'

He dug his heels in his horse again as one of the stockmen called to him, and she followed more leisurely, feeling absurdly pleased at his words. She treasured them as if they were jewels, knowing that it was the finest compliment a woman could expect to get from Mackenzie, and one that he wouldn't give lightly.

The rest of the day passed hazily. Robbie needed a lot of settling down after a good scrub, with plenty of food and drinks, and piles of picture-books and toys around him on his bed. By then, his ankle had been bandaged properly, with a compress of vinegar to help take down the swelling.

Nobody had eaten any food all day, and they were ravenously hungry. They had all had a very necessary token wash and change of clothes on their return to the house, but long before bedtime Prissy decided that a hot bath was the only way to help her taut nerves. Mackenzie's good mood had already vanished, and he was morose and snappy with everyone, and she was glad to escape from him.

Iona helped her lift the heavy cauldron of hot water off the hook by the fire. They ladled out several buckets of water and took it to Prissy's room, where the hip-bath stood ready. She eased herself wearily out of her clothes, and lowered herself gently into the water with a sigh of relief. There was no need for pushing home the bolt on her door now that the likes of Mick O'Neil were gone.

She lathered herself all over with Iona's homemade soap, revelling in the clean scent of it, and the way the softness of the water was beginning to make her feel human again. She let her hair trail in the water until it floated around her shoulders like a dryad, and she was lying drowsily against the headrest when her door opened without warning, and a small figure came limping in.

'I can't sleep, Prissy. My leg hurts too bad. Can I come in with you?' Robbie said plaintively.

The boy was halfway across the room when she jerked upright at this intrusion into her privacy, her wet hair flying about her face. She was thankful that the soapy water covered her body adequately enough, even though she slopped half of it over the floor with her sudden movement.

'For pity's sake, Robbie, shut the door. I'm not decent!' she yelled.

The boy stood uncertainly, his eyes filling, and seconds later James Mackenzie was in the room behind him, angry and embarrassed on Prissy's account.

'Robbie, will you get out of here this minute before I lock you up? I'm sorry, lassie, I'll see that he doesn't bother you again,' he said roughly.

But not before he'd taken stock of the scene in the bedroom and seen the unusual vision that was Prissy Baxter.

He hustled Robbie away as fast as the child's injured ankle would let him, but at the same time he was caught by the sight of soft white shoulders glistening with soapsuds, by long trailing dark hair that curled enticingly around her flushed cheeks, by brilliant, startled eyes the colour of a summer sky; by the hint of womanly curves hidden by the sudden clutching of arms around knees at these intruders, curves that were undeniably those of a sensual woman, and no troublesome chit of a girl...and there was also the scent of her, wreathed in youth and freshness, tantalising all his male instincts as provocatively as a morning breeze in the highlands. Sweet tantalising memories that never failed to tug at his heart...

He turned away abruptly and got Robbie protestingly to the door. He spoke again without turning round.

'When you're dressed, come to the parlour and take a dram with me. We've things to discuss.'

She wanted to shout at him that she had no intention of sitting cosily in the parlour with him, with Flora's portrait between them, drinking sociably as if tonight was a special occasion. Then she remembered that of course it was a special occasion to Mackenzie, because he had got his son back safely...

Prissy was too weary to think straight, wanting to resist, yet knowing all the time she would do as he said, just because the looks Mackenzie had given her were enough to start up all the turbulent, helpless feelings inside her again, whether he was aware of them or not.

She stepped out of the hip-bath and rubbed herself dry with the scratchy towel. And finally decided that if he was going to propose some idiotic form of marriage again, she still had enough pride to tell him no.

She hadn't come to Australia like some of those ninnies on the emigration boat, prepared to grovel to any man who'd take them into a marriage of convenience. It was crystal-clear to her that James Mackenzie still belonged in spirit to his Flora, and if Priscilla Baxter married anyone at all, it was going to be for love.

She put on a high-necked frock and tied her still damp hair up in a twist on top of her head. She looked serviceable enough, the way a child's nursemaid should look when facing her employer. It was the way she intended to look from now on, showing none of that treacherous feeling of wanting to look feminine for him...

'Come in, and don't hover by the door like a servant,' he said tetchily, immediately scattering her suspicions that this was to be some kind of intimate tête-à-tête. She closed the door and leaned against it. He handed her a glass of golden-brown liquid.

'Drink this and stop looking as if I'm about to ravish you. I'm not Mick O'Neil.'

She stared at him defiantly. What was this now? Was he telling her he didn't find her attractive at all? His own darkened eyes when he'd come into her room had told her differently, however much he denied it.

'If you were, I'd have screamed the place down when you interrupted my bath,' she said stiffly.

He smiled faintly. 'Well, I don't flatter myself you're implying that you'd welcome my attentions, lassie. You've already made that perfectly clear.'

She drank the fiery liquid quickly, feeling her head spin as she did so. People can change, she wanted to shriek. People can fall in love without warning, against their better judgement... people like Prissy Baxter, but obviously not like James Mackenzie...

She realised he'd drunk more than one glass of spirit and seemed disinclined to leave the bottle alone. In the murky alleyways of London, she'd seen the pathetic dregs of men who buried their troubles in the bottle, and she'd never thought Mackenzie was one of them. Normally he was a good example to his men, but this wasn't any normal day, and he was drinking steadily, though he was far from insensible.

He threw himself into a chair now, his long legs sprawling out in front of him.

'Why the devil can't you sit down? My head aches abominably, and I've no intention of ricking my neck to look up at you all the time.'

'I'm not surprised your head aches. It'll be worse tomorrow if you don't stop drinking that stuff——'

'Concerned about me, are you?' he mocked her.

'Only as much as I'd be concerned for anybody who thinks the solution to his troubles is in a bottle,' she was goaded into saying.

She saw Mackenzie's hands grip the glass tightly and then he thrust it away from him, clenching his hands together. He gave a bitter laugh.

'Aye, it can't help a man's soul to come to terms with things. But you don't know the meaning of trouble. You don't know how it feels to bury someone who meant all the world to you, and then go through the same agony again—wondering if fate will strike you for a second time.'

The raw anguish in his voice stilled every other thought in her head. She swallowed convulsively. Fate had taken Flora from him, and today it might have taken Robbie too... and she saw just how terrible today must have been for him. The pain went far deeper than condemning Prissy's own stupidity in riding off in a huff yesterday. It was more poignant than the petty arguments between a spirited young upstart Englishwoman and the arrogant boss of Ballatree Station. Her warm heart reacted to his needs at once.

Without thinking, she ran to him, kneeling on the floor beside him, desperate to ease that cold, lost look in his eyes. She put her arms around him, uncaring that she had no right, and that he wouldn't want this reaction from her. But he was so steeped in drink now, he'd probably remember none of it in the morning anyway.

'I'm so sorry,' she whispered. 'I didn't think...'

From somewhere deep in his chest she felt the racking of sobs he couldn't release, and her own ready tears flooded her cheeks at his incapacity to weep. Women were so much more blessed in that way than men, after all...

'You didn't stop to think that my wee bairn is all I have left now, is that it? But it's no matter. You have no notion of life yet, lassie.' It was a condemnation she felt all the more keenly because it was said entirely without emotion, as if he had none left inside him.

'Why did you ask me in here tonight?' she queried huskily. 'You look so tired...' Then the usual platitudes, about a good night's rest doing wonders, simply stuck in her throat, because it obviously needed more than that to cure James Mackenzie's ills.

He hardly seemed to know she was there, crouching on the floor with her arms around him, so close in body she could have counted every pore on his skin, so far in spirit she might have been on another planet. His voice was still ragged, somewhere in a different life that she couldn't enter.

'Just to say thanks for helping with the bairn, and for a bit of company to stop my thoughts. But it'll take more than a soft woman's company to do that tonight—so away to your bed now and sleep safely.'

He didn't push her away, but he might as well have done, Prissy thought, stricken by the realisation that he didn't need her, after all. Right now, he had all that he needed in his memories.

CHAPTER TWELVE

PRISSY discovered that Mackenzie remembered more of the previous evening than she had expected. She took Robbie his breakfast in bed, insisting that he should stay there for the morning, and Mackenzie came to see the boy before he went off with Davy.

'Are you still cross with Prissy, Pa?' Robbie said straight away.

'I'm not cross with anybody, just relieved that you're both all right.' He looked at Prissy. 'I mean that. And I owe you my thanks for your indulgence in a man's weakness. I suggest we forget all about the last few days. I'm sure we're all feeling better this morning.'

'I thought you'd have a gigantic headache,' she said awkwardly. She was a little nonplussed at his comments, not sure whether his reference to a man's weakness meant his emotional state or resorting to the whisky bottle.

'None that a good day's work in the open air won't cure. I'll see the two of you later.'

He bent and kissed the top of Robbie's head, running his hand gently around the boy's cheek for a moment. There was no doubt in Prissy's mind that he was a man capable of great tenderness, but he certainly kept it all for his son, and only that when the occasion demanded it. Mackenzie wasn't one for showing tender feelings too freely.

But she was relieved that the alarming incidents of the past few days were to be overlooked, if not completely forgotten! He'd apparently forgiven her for riding off in a show of temperament and starting off the chain reaction that had led to the hunt for Robbie. She shivered, remembering how awful yesterday had been, and resolving to make every day a better one from now on.

'Do I have to stay in bed?' Robbie complained. 'Can't I go outside?'

'This afternoon,' she promised. 'I've got some mending to do and I'll bring it to your room while you play with your puzzles, and then we'll learn some new rhymes to recite to your pa this evening. Would you like that?'

'About London?' he asked, perking up.

'If that's what you want——'

'Tell me what it's like.' His interest caught, Robbie began to eat his breakfast, only wincing now and then when he moved his leg too fast and the pain in his ankle reminded him that he was hurt.

'Oh, it's a very large place with hundreds and hundreds of people who are always in a hurry. The streets are so narrow and some of the houses so tall that if you look up between them you can hardly see the daylight. And on the ground there are nasty cobblestones that hurt your feet if you don't have stout shoes to wear...'

She became aware of Robbie's astonished face.

'What's cobble—things?' he said.

'Of course, you wouldn't know, would you?' She hadn't thought about that until now. 'I don't suppose you even know what a town looks like. Have you ever been to one? To Sydney, for instance?'

'I've been to White Junction,' he said uncertainly.

'Yes, well, half a dozen buildings in the outback doesn't exactly add up to a town,' she grinned. 'Some day you must get your pa to take you to a proper one.'

'I don't want to go there if it will hurt my feet,' he said positively. 'Do they have sheep in a town?'

'No, you goose!' Prissy laughed. 'They have theatres and fine streets, as well as narrow ones, and people with lovely manners and servants who take them about in carriages...' And Prissy, who had been quite sure she would secretly yearn for such things for a long while after she had turned her back on them, realised that she hardly missed them at all right now. And how odd it was that it all sounded so false compared with the life here.

'Pa's got a wagon, and he don't need servants to take him anywhere,' Robbie said with unconscious pride.

'Ah, but your pa's a very special man, isn't he?' Prissy said, knowing that for once she and Robbie were in perfect agreement.

In fact, they were growing closer together as the days went by. As the friction between them lessened, she hardly noticed how time was passing, one month, then two, then three months, since she'd first arrived at Ballatree Station, hardly knowing the back end of a horse from the front. And now she could milk goats if she had to, ride tolerably well, feed chickens and do many tasks that Miss Priscilla Baxter, songstress, would never have dreamed of doing.

She had also fallen in love, but that was something she kept well under control, now, thankful enough that Mackenzie, too, seemed to be mellowing with time, and the clashes were no longer so frequent between them. Time changed everything, she realised, softening bad memories as well as happy ones.

She had even had a letter from Ma Jenkins via the White Junction mail service, brought back to her by Mackenzie on one of his monthly visits. She read some of it out to Mackenzie and Robbie, seeing the boy's incredulous face as she did so.

'Just listen to this, will you? Ma's got a new lodger in the house—called Marvello the Marvellous—who reckons he can saw a lady in half in front of your very eyes, only he keeps losing his partners before he gets around to doing the act! Can you blame them?' She burst out laughing, imagining the hazards of being a magician's assistant.

'Does he really saw a lady in half?' Robbie squealed.

'Of course not. It's all a trick,' Mackenzie said quickly. 'It's what they call an illusion.'

'Your pa's right,' Prissy said, hoping the boy wouldn't have nightmares over her thoughtless words. 'And I expect Marvello does all sorts of other tricks, like pulling rabbits out of hats——'

'Rabbits live in the bush,' Robbie said scornfully, dismissing the idea of magic. 'Everybody knows that.'

Prissy smiled at Mackenzie over the boy's head.

'Of course they do, love,' she replied.

She folded up the letter, to read the rest in private. And to laugh and weep a little over some of the antics Ma described...but it was as if she were seeing it all now from a distance greater than the many miles between England and Australia, and the letter described other times that were lovely to read about, but had nothing to do with her any more. Incredible as it seemed to her, she knew she had moved on...

And then, one fine morning, a bit of the more recent past caught up with her in a way that threatened to shatter all her newfound peace of mind in an instant. She and Robbie were drawing pictures in the front clearing, and she shielded her eyes from the sun at a sudden clatter of wheels. The sun wasn't quite as strength-sapping now that it was autumn, but it was still invigoratingly warm.

A wagon was approaching that certainly wasn't Mackenzie's, and Prissy felt a stirring of excitement at the thought of visitors, praying at the same time that it wasn't going to be the Hatherall women from White Junction. She could see two women in dark bonnets and formal clothes seated beside a man in similarly sombre attire, and soon realised that they were strangers.

'Robbie, go and fetch your pa,' she said quickly. 'I think he's in the shearing sheds with Davy.'

The boy ran off, his ankle back to normal now, and Prissy stood up, brushing the husks of grass and bits of dirt from her skirt. She felt less than presentable, but if people descended on them without warning they had to take them as they found them. By now, she was in agreement with Mackenzie in that respect, and the niceties of correct little tea parties that might once have seemed so alluring to her were a million miles away from her thoughts now.

'Good afternoon,' she said with a polite smile as the man jumped down, the well-dressed ladies alighting stiffly behind him. 'I assume you'll be wanting to see Mr Mackenzie, and I've just sent the child to fetch him. My name is——'

'We know what your name is, Miss Baxter,' one of the ladies said in a cold strident voice straight out of an English country estate. 'And it's not Mr Mackenzie we've come to see, it's you. Although the two of you together have certainly got some serious explaining to do.'

Prissy gaped at the woman, thrown completely off balance at such an attack. She had never seen this woman or her companions before, and the way the three of them were looking her up and down and making snide remarks she didn't yet understand, she considered they were treating herself and Mackenzie like—like *crim-*

inals, she thought in astonishment. And for whatever reason, she had no idea.

While she was still grappling with a suitable retort to make to this stranger, Robbie came running back to Prissy's side, and Mackenzie came striding across the clearing behind him. From the iron set of his jaw it was clear that he'd heard every word.

'I don't know you are, madam, but I'd be pleased if you would explain those remarks,' he snapped. 'This is my property, and strangers are always welcome providing they don't abuse my hospitality.'

His meaning was clear. He hadn't invited these people here, and already they had been unnecessarily rude. Unconsciously, Prissy drew nearer to Mackenzie, her arms tight around Robbie's small shoulders. They presented a small, complete unit, and the three strangers exchanged glances before the man spoke up harshly.

'You are Mr James Mackenzie, sir?'

'I think you know full well who I am. Will you please get to the point, man?'

Prissy knew Mackenzie's temper was shortening by the second, and intervened hastily, whether it was her place to or not.

'Won't you all come inside and take a cold drink? I'm sure you've travelled a long distance and you must be thirsty.'

The trio looked at one another again, and Prissy began to get exasperated. The second lady spoke up, her voice similar in accent and style to the other.

'You seem to be acting very much the lady of the house, Miss Baxter. May I enquire as to the whereabouts of Mrs Mackenzie?'

Prissy felt her cheeks go crimson with shock, and she heard Mackenzie utter an oath.

'My wife is dead,' he said harshly. 'And you people will either give me a satisfactory explanation why you think you have the right to question me about my family, or remove yourselves from my property at once before I have you forcibly removed.'

Out of the corner of her eye, Prissy could see the swarthy figure of Davy Golightly, and several of the stockmen who had recently been in the shearing shed with Mackenzie. If she thought their silently waiting presence would intimidate the strangers, she was mistaken. The man spoke smoothly.

'We have every right, Mr Mackenzie, and I'll thank you not to take that tone with me. My name is Thomas Vine and this is my wife,' he indicated the first of the women. 'This other lady is Miss Pringle and we represent the Ladies' Committee in Sydney. This would normally be no more than a routine visit to see how Miss Baxter is faring and to collect an instalment on her five pounds' passage money from you as her employer. However, because of certain information received just before we left Sydney several weeks ago, it's now at our discretion whether or not we consider this a suitable place of employment for Miss Baxter.'

Prissy gasped, while Mackenzie looked murderous.

'What exactly do you mean by that remark?'

Mrs Vine spoke quickly.

'Mr Mackenzie, do you think we might avail ourselves of the cold drink Miss Baxter offered? And it might be less public if we were to continue this discussion inside the house.'

It was obvious that the men were taking more than an interest in what was going on, and Mackenzie turned abruptly, telling them to follow. Prissy went numbly, her thoughts whirling in her head. *Certain information re-*

ceived? What in the blue blazes could they be getting at!

'Iona, bring cold drinks if you please, and then make yourself scarce,' Mackenzie bellowed as soon as they were indoors. 'Take Robbie to the stables and let the lad take him riding while we entertain our visitors.'

His tone implied that he would as soon entertain a pack of wild dingoes, and the visitors were very much aware of it. Thomas Vine's mouth compressed.

'I'm sorry to observe your attitude, Mr Mackenzie,' he said coldly. 'I assure you that the Ladies' Committee do very worthy work regarding the welfare of the young women who arrive in Australia completely unaware of what's ahead of them——'

'Don't you mean in following up their passage money?' Mackenzie spoke just as coldly. He refused to say anything more until Iona had brought a jug of lemon cordial and a tray of glasses and had taken Robbie out of hearing. Silently, Prissy poured the glasses of cordial and handed them round.

'All right, now let's have it,' Mackenzie ordered.

Thomas Vine cleared his throat.

'Mr Mackenzie, did you not state on your original application form that Mrs Mackenzie wanted someone to help in the house and with your son?'

'I did.'

'And is it not a fact that when you came to Sydney and took Miss Baxter into your employ, your wife was— forgive me—already dead?'

'It is a fact,' Mackenzie said, his eyes steely.

Miss Pringle leaned forward, pushing her pince-nez farther back on her thin nose.

'But surely, sir, you must have realised that in not advising us of this situation you were then applying under false pretences?'

'Why? I still needed someone to help in the house, and even more so to care for my son——'

'But it was not your *wife* who wanted these things,' Mrs Vine interrupted.

'Oh, I see. You think I should have given up running my sheep station to attend to doing women's work and rearing my bairn myself, is that it?' he said, heavy with sarcasm.

'We do not, sir,' Vine said sternly. 'Nor do we think it savoury that, knowing your wife was dead, you brought a young and single female into this house, and are spending nights alone with her——'

'*Savoury?*' Prissy almost screamed the word. 'Just what are you implying by that, you nasty-minded creatures?'

'Prissy, be quiet,' Mackenzie snapped. 'May I ask where you got this information, Mr Vine? On what do you base your statement that I spend nights alone with Miss Baxter, which, incidentally, is totally untrue as my son and my stockman and his wife live in the house——'

He stopped abruptly as Thomas Vine took a letter from his coat pocket. Prissy could hardly believe this was happening. They were putting an evil interpretation on a situation that was completely innocent, despite the fact that Prissy might have wished for it to be different...

'This letter was sent to us from White Junction by a Mr Michael O'Neil.' He heard Prissy's indrawn breath and glanced at her with satisfaction. 'I see by your expression that you're acquainted with the gentleman, miss.'

'I'd hardly call him a gentleman,' she said savagely, 'and I can guarantee that whatever he chooses to tell you is undoubtedly all lies!'

'Mr O'Neil states that you and Mr Mackenzie are amorously disposed. He also suggests that the fact of a young woman being alone in the house with an unmarried man should be investigated, which the Ladies' Committee heartily endorses. Such an immoral situation undermines all the good work done so far on behalf of the Government——'

'But what about the child and the Aborigines!'

The man brushed Prissy's protest aside.

'The presence of the young child can be disregarded. O'Neil further states that it's a well-known fact that after shearing time every year the Aborigines in the house go walkabout, which would certainly have occurred just after he himself left Ballatree Station after a night of drunken revelry.'

Prissy sensed keenly that these superior white people disregarded the presence of the Aborigines, too, and felt a rush of shame on behalf of Iona and Davy, whom she considered her friends. Mackenzie was shouting angrily at the strangers now.

'For God's sake, have you never been to a sheep station on the night the shearing's finished? Of course there's revelry. A good boss always provides an outdoor supper with food and drink——'

'But on this station there was also a certain kind of entertainment, was there not?' Mrs Vine put in meaningly. 'I understand there was a seductive kind of singing by this young woman, dressed in the flimsiest of clothes in front of several dozen men, in the manner in which she used to entertain in some dubious theatres, I dare say. And then followed a dance with every man present, which was conducted in the lewdest manner.'

Prissy gasped, furious tears starting in her eyes.

'It was nothing like that at all! The man is a vicious liar. If you must know, it was Mick O'Neil himself who was the worst drunkard of the lot, trying to force himself on me in my room that night, and this is his way of getting revenge! You must see that!'

She saw that, far from vindicating herself, she was digging herself in deeper. O'Neil had come to her room that night. In their eyes, she could see that he would not have done so without an invitation. And they were so wrong—so very wrong!

'I'm surprised you even bothered to check up on me,' she said, her voice scratchy. 'Do you do this for everyone who comes to Australia, hounding them like criminals?'

'We take our duties seriously, miss,' Miss Pringle said stiffly. 'And no, we do not follow up every story, but occasionally one comes to our notice that offends us greatly, and then we see to it that no scandal attaches itself to our purpose. The British Government has been generous enough in providing your passage money, and we consider it our duty to see that you're in a good situation and able to repay it.'

'You'll get your money,' Mackenzie snapped.

'We also want the assurance of this young woman's well-being, and we feel we should insist on her accompanying us back to Sydney to find some alternative employment. If Mrs Mackenzie were still alive, things would be different, but as it is——'

'I've no intention of going back to Sydney with you,' Prissy said at once.

'You can go if you wish,' Mackenzie said. 'I won't try to stop you.'

She stared at him. 'Is that what you want?'

Again, there was that feeling of being alone in this room with him. The others didn't exist. There was only herself and James Mackenzie, and the portrait of Flora staring down between them. It was as if Flora was telling her to go... telling her that Prissy Baxter had arrived on the scene too soon—an intruder who hadn't given Mackenzie time to mourn, to grieve... Prissy felt a strange sensation of disorientation—she couldn't read Mackenzie's expression at all...

'It's your decision, not mine,' he said. 'But if it helps you to make up your mind, I'll pay off your passage money and then you'll be free. You won't be beholden to these people or anyone else if you don't want to be.'

She gasped. 'But you don't owe me that! I've only worked for a fraction of the five pounds so far——'

'Don't argue with me, lassie. I've no wish to crush that free spirit of yours. I've said the money will be paid and there's an end to it.'

He might think he was doing her a great favour, but she could see only too well what these people were thinking. A man like James Mackenzie, without a woman of his own on this remote sheep station, wouldn't be merely paying her passage money. He'd obviously be paying for other services—and her cheeks burned with the shame of it. She lifted her chin.

'Then I'll return to Sydney with these people and find employment of my own. I don't need to be dependent on anybody. I had a career before I came here, and I can continue with it in Australia as well as anywhere else.'

'There's always employment to be found for a certain type of entertainer,' Mrs Vine commented.

Prissy couldn't even begin to argue with her any more. She felt drained of all emotion. It had all happened so quickly, and she still wasn't sure how she'd come to accept Mackenzie's offer of her passage money, nor why he'd offered it. Except that the arrival of these people had presented a simple way of ridding himself of a troublesome individual. Next time, she had no doubt he'd find some motherly woman to care for Robbie...

She felt the beginning of a sob in her throat.

'You'll explain everything to Robbie so that he doesn't fret too much?' She heard the crack in her voice and tried desperately not to let him see how anguished she felt. 'I couldn't bear to think of him going off into the bush to try to find me again——'

'I'll explain everything.' Mackenzie was tense and unyielding.

'Then I'll get my things,' she said blindly. 'There's no point in delaying.'

Please, please, stop me from doing this, she pleaded silently to Mackenzie. Say it's all a mistake, and you really do love me and intend to marry me...

'I'll get the money for you,' he said to Thomas Vine. 'You'll see that the girl gets safely to Sydney?'

'Of course,' Vine said. 'And she may still avail herself of our list of suitable employers if she wishes. We can always place a hard worker with a respectable family.'

She saw Mackenzie nod briefly, and wondered if he got the implication that his own employ wasn't considered 'respectable' by these narrow-minded bigots.

She fled to her own room and began bundling everything she owned into her travelling bags. Tears dazzled her eyes. She had awoken that morning without any inkling that this was to be her last day at Ballatree Station. Her last day with James... but it was very clear to her that he no longer wanted her, if he ever had, and perhaps in time the insipid Miss Edna Hatherall would become the next Mrs Mackenzie, after all.

The sobs threatened to stifle her and she pushed them down with an effort. When she had finished, she looked around the room that had been her own for all these months, gazing at it for the last time, as if she would absorb the essence of it to take with her into the unknown. This very homestead had been the unknown such a short while ago, and now it was the dearest place on earth.

There was one item she couldn't bear to take with her. She drew out the lovely pearl necklace James had given her on the night of the shearers' supper. She ran her fingers over every perfect pearl and finally pressed it to her lips. She scribbled a note to put beneath it.

'This never really belonged to me, anyway.'

She folded the note in half and wrote James's name on it prominently. And then she rammed her sun-bonnet on her head and went out of the room without a second glance.

'I'm ready,' she said to the group of people in the parlour. She saw Thomas Vine writing out a receipt and handing it to Mackenzie, and knew the five pounds' passage money had changed hands. She felt as if she had been bought and sold to the highest bidder. It was the worst feeling she had ever known, as bitter as wormwood.

'Take care of yourself, Prissy,' Mackenzie said after a moment, when no one seemed to know quite what to say.

'Kiss Robbie goodbye for me,' she choked, because it was the nearest she could get to flinging her arms around his neck and giving him all the kisses she possessed.

'We'll be on our way then,' Vine said briskly. 'We take the southern route back, Mr Mackenzie. It's longer, but less hazardous than directly over the mountains, and we still have several calls to make on the way.'

And more blood money to collect, Prissy thought caustically. If the man thought to make polite conversation with Mackenzie, he could have saved his breath. Mackenzie simply turned and walked back into the house and didn't even watch them go. If he had, he'd have realised that Prissy, too, sat bolt upright as if she were

carved out of stone, and didn't give one last look back
at the house she'd begun to think of as home.

They finally set up camp for the first night in a small
hollow somewhere east of White Junction, but well
beyond the boundaries of Ballatree Station. There was
a small water-hole in the hollow and a fringe of trees
surrounding it. These people might look stuffy and
citified, but she found that they were surprisingly resourceful when it came to temporary living in the
outback, and had obviously done this many times before.
Even the ladies had no qualms about using the small
tents that Thomas Vine rigged up quickly and efficiently.

'You'll sleep in Miss Pringle's tent,' the man ordered.
'We're well used to this kind of living because of our
commitment to our girls. We sleep light, so don't get
any ideas about running off, miss.'

'Where would I go?' she muttered. All this time she
had refused to speak to any of them, seething with resentment, and heartbroken because she was leaving
behind everything she loved in the world. But now she
bristled at his words.

'You've got it all wrong, you know,' she said more
loudly, when everything was ready for the night and the
camp fire was burning steadily in the small clearing with
a kettle beginning to boil for tea. 'Mr Mackenzie and I
are quite innocent of your charges, and I hope you know
you've ruined a good man's name by your accusations.'

'I don't recall hearing him deny it,' Thomas Vine said
flatly. 'And why else would a man part with five pounds
for a girl he hardly knew, unless there was some truth
in what Mr O'Neil said?'

Tears of frustration filled Prissy's eyes. Oh, *why* had
Mackenzie been so stupid as to pay over her passage
money? If he'd wanted to wash his hands of her so com-

pletely, he could have taken her straight back to Sydney at any time and demanded that the Ladies' Committee place her elsewhere, since she was such a bother to him. He didn't have to do this.

After a drink of tea that scalded her numb lips and a bite of seed cake, she crawled inside the small tent beside the stiff-necked Miss Pringle and tried to sleep on the rough blanket she'd been given. Neither woman undressed fully, merely removed their skirts and loosened buttons, and Prissy lay on her back, staring up at the glimmer of stars between the partitions of the tent, still unable to accept the way everything had changed so quickly.

She was sure she would never sleep. Her mind was too active, her heart too full. But the older woman's rhythmic snoring was enough to send her into a kind of stupor, and when she opened her eyes again it was morning and the sun was beating down on the coarse fabric of the tent.

Outside it wasn't so hot and cloying, and Prissy was glad to splash cold water over her face from the waterhole. She didn't like sharing a tent with the woman, and she resolved that the next time she would sleep in the open air. As long as a camp fire was kept burning, she'd brave whatever threatened her out in the night.

'We have a call to make at a place called Wooragee,' Thomas Vine told her. 'One of our girls has been there for six months and seems to be settling in well. It only needs a little self-discipline to come to terms with a new life, Miss Baxter. You'll do well to learn that.'

His wife added her piece as they climbed back into the wagon and prepared to continue their journey.

'I've been thinking what to do with you when we get you back to Sydney, and there's a Captain and Mrs Barlow who are looking for a housemaid. They're a God-fearing couple who will overlook any misdemeanours providing you give assurances to repent your ways. They're of a highly religious nature and will steer you well away from temptations of the flesh.'

Prissy listened with something like horror, seeing the austere Miss Pringle nod in agreement. So much for Mackenzie's comment that she was a free spirit and shouldn't be shackled down by anyone. These people were about to crush her—if she let them.

'But I don't have to take any employment if I don't want to, do I? I'm not beholden to you any more, now that my passage money is paid.'

Thomas Vine pulled the horses to a halt and looked at her keenly.

'What you say is true, but you don't know Sydney as we do. It's a city overrun with vices, and you'd do well to remain under our protection while we offer it. We don't dismiss our obligations lightly, and it's perilously easy for a young woman to slip into a life of debauchery.'

'Unless that's what you would prefer, of course,' Miss Pringle added slyly.

'No, it is not,' Prissy said angrily. 'Why must you twist everything I say? I lived a good life before coming here, and I've done nothing to feel ashamed of since.'

Vine jerked the horses' reins and they jolted on their way. And from the knowing, tight-lipped glances that passed between the two ladies, Prissy knew that none of them believed her. Because of Mick O'Neil's lies, she was as damned as if she'd come straight out of a bawdy house.

She felt utterly bereft. They had come too far for her to turn back alone, even if she had the nerve to do so over this inhospitable terrain. And even if she did, Mackenzie didn't want her, and she had never felt so steeped in misery in her life.

CHAPTER THIRTEEN

THEY reached the small homestead of Wooragee late in
the afternoon, when the sun was low in the sky, and
Prissy had begun to feel that she had been travelling
aimlessly for an eternity. It was all so different from when
she and Mackenzie had left Sydney and the goal ahead
of her was Ballatree Station and a new life, however
strange.

She felt now as if she were in some kind of no man's
land. Mackenzie had tossed her aside, and she was
wounded to her soul to realise that now she had nothing
and no one to call her own in this land so far from home.
But even in her misery, she never once thought of going
back to England. That would really be admitting failure.

She had no idea what lay ahead of her, only that she
had no intention of becoming a housemaid for the God-
fearing Captain and Mrs Barlow, whoever they were.
They sounded as insufferable as the three strangers with
whom she was forced to spend these days and nights.
The thought of spending the rest of her life with the
Barlow couple was enough to make her heart sink.
Compared with life in the outback, it sounded dull and
stifling.

'We'll be offered shelter here tonight,' Mrs Vine informed Prissy. 'You'll have to sleep on the floor in the
kitchen, but you'll be given a blanket and I dare say
you'll be comfortable enough.'

And much you care whether I am or not, Prissy
thought grimly.

The Wooragee homestead wasn't at all inviting. The couple who owned it were rough and ready, and the girl placed there by the Ladies' Committee looked at Prissy with suspicious eyes, as if she thought she might want to take over her job. Prissy thought that never in a million years would she want to stay here in this wilderness shack where the couple eked out a poor living with a few threadbare sheep and goats and a run of chickens.

The kitchen where she had to sleep was none too clean, and she was kept company by a watchful dog who growled every time she moved. She had no idea of the accommodation offered to her three companions; she was just mightily thankful when morning came and after a meagre breakfast they were on their way again, with a portion of the other girl's passage money jingling in Thomas Vine's money belt.

They had been plodding on for half a day, with the lower ranges of the mountains coming ever nearer, when Prissy spoke out in a low and vibrant voice.

'I want to go back.'

Mrs Vine gave a short laugh.

'What's this, then? Tired of the thought of reforming already, are we? And thinking to continue your seduction of a good man——'

'How dare you?' Prissy gasped in outrage at the slur. 'I want to go back because James Mackenzie is a better man than any I've ever known, and I was happier caring for his child than I've ever been in my life before, and there was nothing improper in our relationship at all. Even if there had been, it was *our* business!'

'Well, miss, you're certainly proving to be a hoity-toity young woman, obviously in need of guidance. It's a pity there's no place for wayward girls in this country yet, for you'd be an ideal candidate for it,' Miss Pringle said sanctimoniously.

'You're just not listening to me at all, are you?' Prissy raged. 'You'd rather believe the words of a ticket-of-leaver who was getting his own back because I wouldn't allow him to take liberties with me. I'm the innocent victim in all this, but your narrow little minds just won't see it, will they?'

'Do you ever stop talking?' Thomas Vine said, nettled at the way she refused to become docile and submissive as befitted her position. 'Being aggressive and insulting won't help your cause, Miss Baxter.'

She spluttered again. 'Don't you think I'm insulted? Look, I've said I want to go back. I'm not going to work for your Captain Barlow and his wife, nor anybody else you suggest. Take me back to Ballatree Station this minute!'

'We certainly will not. Do you think we can waste another two days there and back just to satisfy the whim of a flighty young woman?'

Prissy grabbed hold of the side of the wagon and flung herself off. She fell heavily, rolling over and over in the grass and winding herself. She was certain she'd be a mass of bruises by tomorrow, but it didn't matter. She was free of these hateful people who didn't understand the first thing about how it felt to be alone in a strange country.

'You can throw my things down. I'm going back to Ballatree Station,' she yelled, struggling to her feet as the wagon came to a sudden stop and the three people looked down at her disbelievingly.

'Miss Baxter, get back up here at once,' Vine said angrily. 'We haven't time to take you back, and it would be completely foolhardy for you to try and get there alone.'

She knew it, and her heart jumped at the very thought. But she knew that if she once got to Sydney with these people and submitted to their wishes she would be submerged in a world she didn't want. That free spirit of which Mackenzie had spoken so colourfully would be finally crushed for ever.

Thomas Vine jumped down from the wagon, the women alighting after him, glad of a breather if nothing else.

'Miss Baxter, I have to make a report about you, since we've followed up the letter from Mr O'Neil,' the man said. 'I beg you not to be so reckless.'

'Then take me back,' she said.

The ladies joined in the argument, but Prissy remained stubborn. She refused absolutely to go on to Sydney, and they refused just as adamantly to take her back to Ballatree Station.

Into her consciousness came a strange tinny sound, seemingly coming from nowhere, rising and falling, clanking like the unearthly sounds of some demon. But this was no spectre. She heard the two ladies utter small alarmed screams and saw Thomas Vine go for his rifle. Prissy might have felt alarmed too, except for the enormous surge of relief that overcame everything else.

Striding towards them, half hidden by the tall clumps of waving grasses, was a stocky figure she recognised. Unkempt, his greying hair a tangled mass of knots, his greatcoat hung about with pots and pans as he led his bedraggled nag nearer to them, was someone Prissy would never have considered in her wildest dreams to be a champion.

'Badger!' she choked out, pushing Thomas Vine's rifle away from him. 'Oh, Badger, I'm so glad to see you!'

She forgot all about the last and only time they had met, when Mackenzie pulled the stopper out of the bottle the rogue had given them, sure that it would be drugged, and that this fly-by-night would rob them while they slept. She forgot everything but the fact that here was her means to get back to Ballatree—if Badger could be persuaded to take her there. She stumbled towards him, seeing his eyes widen with astonishment at this unexpected greeting.

'Well now, if it ain't the little lady of the mountains,' he said expansively. 'Where's that good man o' yours then? Not left 'im, 'ave yer?'

'No—I—I——'

'Send him on his way, Thomas,' Mrs Vine said shrilly. 'Horrid, dirty little man——'

''Ere, missis, who are you calling dirty?' Badger said indignantly.

'Come on now, be off with you,' Vine said tersely. 'We're a respectable group of folk, and we want none of your sort around here.'

'The little lady here seems to think different,' Badger said, his eyes narrowing, as he saw Prissy suddenly move towards the wagon and pull her travelling bags out of the back. She came towards him.

'Will you take me to Ballatree Station, Badger?'

'Well now, I don't rightly know. I've me business to think about, see? I'd be losing trade if I made a detour out of me way——'

Prissy could see the way his thoughts were going. It might have angered her but for the way she heard the ladies tut-tutting at the thought of this oaf scratching a living in this wilderness with his pots and pans. Prissy refused to demean him further.

'Mackenzie will pay you handsomely for your trouble. You won't lose by it.'

Thomas Vine snorted. 'Don't be ridiculous, girl. The man's just paid your passage money to be rid of you. Why would he want you back?'

His words wounded her, and she lifted her chin defiantly.

'Because he's going to marry me, that's why.'

Miss Pringle tittered. 'Come now, Miss Baxter, what ever gives you the idea that Mr Mackenzie would entertain such an idea?'

Prissy gave her the full benefit of her wide blue eyes. Even standing knee deep in waving grasses, she looked a determined sight to the other woman, who moved visibly nearer to her companions.

'Because he asked me,' she said sweetly. 'Has any man ever asked you the same question, Miss Pringle?'

If it was hitting below the belt, she didn't care. The woman was a dried-up old spinster who would never know the touch of a man's hand on her skin, or the soaring, exquisite pleasure of a man's mouth on her own. But Prissy did. She had known it briefly and ached to know it again.

And one truth was suddenly singing in her veins, and sending new life surging through her. If he'd paid her passage money to set her free, he had also given her a certain status. She was no longer subservient to him, or anyone, and he had never retracted that offer of marriage. She would go to him on equal terms, telling him she had reconsidered his marriage proposal, and she would accept. There was never any question in her mind of the outcome.

And besides, and above all other considerations, there was the most important reason of all for marrying him. She loved him more than she had thought it possible to love anyone. Even if all the love was one-sided at present, with all the love spilling out of her, in time James would come to love her too, she was certain of it.

'You're a very cruel young woman,' Mrs Vine was saying now. 'I think in the circumstances we'd be well justified in washing our hands of you.'

'Then why don't you?' Prissy said. 'I absolve you of all responsibility in my future. Does that please your ladyship?'

Thomas Vine was not as easily moved.

'We can no more let you go off with this ruffian—if he agrees to take you back—than take you there ourselves, Miss Baxter.'

She turned to Badger. 'Will you take me?' she demanded.

''Course I will, if you say your man will pay for the privilege.'

'Then there's really nothing else to say, is there? Thank you for your trouble, and I hope we never meet again,' she said to the trio beside the wagon.

She threw her travelling bags over the nag's back and started to walk purposefully in the direction they had come, and Badger strode after her, whistling tunelessly while his motley baggage clanked noisily about his person.

'I hope you don't live to regret this,' Vine shouted after them, to which Prissy merely waved a hand without even looking round.

She was filled with sudden elation because she was going back where she belonged. And only later, when they had trudged for more than an hour through the bush and her legs were scratched through her torn skirt, did she begin to wonder about the sense of what she had done. Badger had offered to let her ride on the nag, and she did so for a time, but the beast was flea-ridden and she was a mass of bites before they had gone half a mile.

As the elation faded a little, she kept remembering the first time they had met Badger. According to Mackenzie, he was the worst kind of rogue, and she had willingly gone off with him. Because she was so mad to get back to Ballatree, she might have got herself into even more trouble.

Not that there would be much in her travelling bags for Badger to steal. She had very little, and not for the first time she was glad she had left Flora Mackenzie's pearls where they belonged. But Badger didn't know what she owned, and it made sense to get things straight between them as soon as possible.

When it began to get dark they stopped to make a meal and set up camp for the night. If the Ladies' Committee had disapproved of her before, how much more so would they do now, throwing in her lot with this disreputable person? Prissy thought fleetingly...

'We have to get a few things settled, Badger,' she said sharply, when they had shared the pot of kangaroo stew he'd heated over the fire. 'I'm not rich and I don't have anything of value with me, so don't even think of putting something in my drink to rob me while I'm insensible because you'd be wasting your time.'

He gave a wicked little laugh that made his face even more grotesque in the firelight. Somewhere an owl hooted in the night, and Prissy shivered.

'Now why would I go doing summat like that to a pretty maid like yourself?' He smirked. 'Any rightminded gennulman 'ould rather have his ladyfriend awake while he had his way wiv 'er.'

She felt her heart plummet and leapt to her feet.

'If I thought you were that kind of man I'd never have asked you to help me. And I'm *not* your ladyfriend——'

She stopped short as she saw that he was laughing silently again, holding his sides as if he thoroughly enjoyed making her squirm.

'No, ducks, that you ain't, and I'd say your man is well deserving of yer. I couldn't be doing wiv such a firecracker as yerself! An' Badger ain't no robber to 'is friends, neither.' He looked at her sorrowfully. 'I thought you wuz my friend, ducks, even if not my *lady*friend, if you gets my meaning.'

'Well, so I am, or I wouldn't be here at all. So you'll get me to Ballatree Station safely? Do I have your handshake on it?'

He stuck out a grimy hand, and Prissy tried not to shudder as she felt it clasp hers. She just managed to resist rubbing her palm on her skirt afterwards, knowing it would offend him greatly.

'Sure you do, providing you tell me where the place is,' he said cheerfully. Prissy felt a burst of frustration.

'You mean you don't know? But it's the biggest place for miles around here. I'd have thought everybody knew James Mackenzie's place.'

'I'm a travelling man, gel. Never stopping in one place long enough to know anybody—then nobody knows Badger.' He touched the side of his nose meaningly.

'Well, we go due north,' she said crossly, thinking this oaf of a man was going to be less than useless after all. 'I only travelled two days and nights with those people, so that should give us some guide, and I'm sure I know the way.'

Even as she said it, she knew it must take longer than before. There was no horse-drawn wagon to take her back to James. There was only the ancient nag which she could ride if she wished. She saw that there was really no choice. If she wanted to return to Ballatree, it was on Badger's terms. Take turns on the nag, or walk.

'You sort it out then, ducks. I'm turning in,' Badger said comfortably, rolling himself up into a ball inside his greatcoat, pots and pans spread all about him, and snoring in an instant.

Prissy reached for the blanket he'd offered her and gingerly spread it out. It smelled of something indefinable she didn't even want to identify. She was suddenly terrified. There were night sounds everywhere and the nag was restless, as if sensing danger in every movement of twig or branch.

She wept for Mackenzie's comforting company, instead of that of a wizened little man who was contained within himself and had no notion of a young woman's fears. She was quite sure she would never sleep...and only when she found herself blinking at beams of sunlight slanting at her through the branches of the trees overhead, did she realise with overwhelming relief that it was daylight again.

The crackling of the wood fire and the smell of something strong and succulent made her lift her head. Badger was cooking, and he suddenly caught sight of her as she threw off the blanket and headed for the seclusion of the bushes.

'Mind where you put yer feet and—er—other things,' she heard him call, and paid full attention to his warning. When she returned to the campsite he was putting some slices of meat on to two metal plates and a hunk of bread beside each.

'What is it?' she asked suspiciously.

'Eat!' he instructed. 'It's good.'

'Not until you tell me what I'm eating!' It might be something horrible, despite the fact that it was making her mouth water, and Badger was already eating heartily.

'It's only emu meat. It won't kill you. It's very tasty fried in its own fat.'

She almost gagged at the thought, remembering that strange, long-necked bird that had frightened her half out of her wits when she'd first seen it on the trek to Ballatree. Since then, she'd seen plenty at a distance, and thought them graceful, almost prehistoric creatures. She certainly didn't want to eat them. She put the plate down.

'You'll be starving hungry by the time we reach your man's place,' Badger said. 'But if you don't want it, I'll eat yours too. Can't afford to waste good food.'

She hesitated, then put a tiny morsel of the meat in her mouth. It was far more palatable than she'd expected, rather like a stronger-tasting goose. Closing her eyes, she ate a little more, and then she gave in and wiped round her plate with the bread, as Badger was doing.

'That's the way, ducks,' he said approvingly. 'You soon learn to live off whatever old Ma Nature provides when you ain't got no other option.'

Prissy supposed that you did. 'Can we get moving soon?' she said. 'I'm sure I can find which way to go once we're heading north again.'

It wasn't as easy as she had thought. She was sure the Vines' wagon hadn't come through so much bush, nor did she remember seeing a sluggish river when they had begun their journey. Before the end of the day she had to admit to Badger that she was hopelessly lost, and the bitter tears threatened all over again, as she wondered if she was destined to travel Australia with this unlikely companion for ever.

'Come on, gel, us cockneys don't let things get us down so easily, do we?' he said roughly. 'Besides, there's a place of sorts in the distance. Does that look like your sheep station?'

He was so stupid! Didn't he know that long before they reached the homestead, they'd have to go through the boundary gates and cross the great bush-scattered plains where the sheep roamed...? But obviously Badger knew nothing about sheep, any more than Prissy had a few months ago, and she craned her head to see where he was pointing.

'It looks like White Junction,' she exclaimed.

He frowned. 'I've heard o' that place, though I don't usually come this far on my travels. Maybe I could sell 'em a few pots and pans——'

'More likely they'll sell you a few,' Prissy said, overcome with relief at seeing a place she recognised.

'It's a supply depot, Badger, and it's only twenty miles south of Ballatree Station. I know the people, and I'm sure they'll lend me a horse to get back home.'

She saw his look and added quickly, 'I'll still need you to accompany me, of course. Mackenzie will want to pay you for your trouble.'

She crossed her fingers as she said it, praying that Mackenzie wouldn't turn all sour on her. She'd been so confident he'd agree to this—but all of a sudden she wasn't so sure. Why should he pay for her safe return, when he'd as good as turned her out?

Then she remembered Robbie, and, whatever Mackenzie might have told him about her departure, she relied on Robbie being happy to see her back. Right or wrong, she prayed she could use the boy's affection to blackmail Mackenzie into paying Badger off. And if he still wouldn't agree to that, then she'd pledge some of her future wages to pay him herself. Either way, she was going to be in Mackenzie's debt as much as before...but she refused to think about that at all.

'Good heavens, Miss Baxter, what on earth...?' she heard Sam Hatherall exclaim as she and Badger finally limped towards White Junction more than an hour later. By then her feet were so sore and every muscle in her body so ached, that it was all she could do not to throw herself into this kindly man's arms and weep with sheer fatigue.

'I'm so sorry to trouble you, Mr Hatherall, but we got lost and we've been travelling for ever, and if you could just lend me a horse to get back to Ballatree Station I'd be very much obliged...' and then everything swam alarmingly in front of her eyes and she felt herself sliding to the floor at Sam's feet, as if all her bones had turned to water.

She awoke to find herself lying in a bed between clean white sheets, her head cushioned by several pillows. Mrs Hatherall was sitting by the bed, her face a mixture of concern and disbelief.

'So you've come back to us, have you, my dear?' she said, but there was little real warmth in the endearment.

'How—how long have I been here? I don't remember very much...'

She twisted her head and realised how badly it hurt. She touched it carefully and winced.

'You'll be sore for a day or two, Prissy,' the woman said more kindly. 'You fainted and hit your head as you fell. You'll have a nice little egg there in a while.'

'And—Badger?' Prissy said weakly. The room seemed to swim alarmingly in front of her eyes, and she fought to remember everything that had happened, as if she were seeing it all through a smoke haze. She heard Mrs Hatherall give an undignified sniff.

'That awful little man! How could you associate yourself with him? And the things he's saying—including refusing to leave, because he says you're paying him to escort you to Ballatree Station. I don't believe a word of it, of course.'

'It's true. At least—Mackenzie will pay him when I get back safely. You don't know what's happened...' She brushed a shaking hand over her cold cheeks and wondered if she would ever feel warm again. The fall seemed to have drained all the life out of her.

'I know that this—Badger, as you call him—is telling some preposterous tale about you leaving Ballatree with some fine Sydney folk, and now you're going back to marry Mackenzie! The sooner you send him packing, the better. We don't want lying rogues of his sort around here.'

'Don't blame him, Mrs Hatherall. He's only repeating what I told him,' Prissy said wearily. She saw the woman sit up straighter.

'You told him you're going to marry James Mackenzie? I never heard anything so unlikely. And why would you have left the homestead if it were true?'

'It's a very long story——'

'A story is right! I'd say you and the traveller are tarred with the same brush,' Mrs Hatherall said severely. 'I don't know what James would say about all this. It's tantamount to compromising the dear man!'

Prissy was too weak to be angry with this insufferable snob of a woman.

'I'm sorry to disillusion you, ma'am, but Mackenzie asked me to marry him and that's what I'm going to do.'

'James has *proposed* to you?'

'Well, don't look so scandalised. I may come from a theatrical background and I know that offends your dignity, but I'm not a circus freak! And now I'm sure I've offended you again, and you're being very kind in letting me recover, but I'm better now, and Badger and me will be on our way.'

She threw back the bedcover and swung her legs over the edge of the bed. The minute she moved her head spun and she had to cling on tightly to the mattress. The woman pushed her gently back into the bed.

'You're not going anywhere, my dear, until you've had a night's sleep. We'll see how you are in the morning, and meanwhile I'll ask my husband to send someone to Ballatree Station to ask James to come and fetch you.'

'No, please don't do that. If Mr Hatherall will just lend me a horse I can get there perfectly well with Badger, and James will see that the animal is brought back safely. He really does know Badger, you know.'

The woman studied her for a moment and then shook her head slightly.

'I fear that James is not the man he used to be, consorting with all kinds of folk these days. Very well, then, but the man doesn't come inside the house. I'll see that he has food, but he stays outside.'

Prissy was exhausted when she had gone. She spent a long day in bed, feeling alternately better and so weak she felt she would never put one foot in front of the other again. The Hatheralls came and went, the daughter only staying a very brief time and obviously furious at the news that Prissy Baxter had announced she was going to marry James Mackenzie.

Prissy hardly cared. If James had wanted to pay court to Edna Hatherall, he'd have done so long before now. It wasn't Edna to whom he'd offered marriage, and it was a thought that sustained her all through the long day and night until she awoke the following morning, her head clear except for the large bump on it, and eager to be gone from White Junction.

'You're sure about this?' Sam Hatherall said time and again. 'I don't like it, Prissy, a young girl going off with——'

'I've come this far with Badger and I'm still in one piece,' she reminded him. 'Besides, why would he harm me? He'll get nothing from James if he does.'

She'd got into the habit of referring to him as James now. It emphasised her position to the Hatheralls, and made the thought of marrying Mackenzie less unlikely. She still had to cross the hurdle of declaring herself to him—and if he were in one of his prickly moods . . .

Nothing but obstacles to her plan came and went in her mind all the time they were riding back to Ballatree Station. The nearer they got to the boundary gates the more nervous Prissy became. It was one thing to be so certain everything was going to turn out the way she wanted it—it was quite another to face the man and say she'd changed her mind. She'd never stopped to think that maybe *he* had too.

'I'd like to stop and rest for a few minutes, Badger,' she said, when the familiar landscape was within sight, though still some distance away.

'All right, we'll have a brew-up,' he said, ever ready to light a fire and boil his billy-can. 'Getting cold feet, ducks?'

She was on the brink of denying it, of saying why on earth should she . . .? And then she caught the sympathetic look in his eyes. She gave a small nod.

'I suppose so. I went off with all my pride intact, and now I'm coming back, and I don't know how Mackenzie's going to take it.'

'You needn't worry about that! The first time I saw the pair of you, I knew the man thought you wuz a cracker!'

'Now you're being daft. We hardly knew each other then——'

'How long duz it take, fer Gawd's sake? You only have to look at somebody once to know if you're soulmates. You an' me now—we'd never be soulmates in a hundred years, but you and the sheepman, well, *anybody* could see the sparks flying between you.'

'And you think that makes us soulmates, do you?'

'Summat like that,' Badger grinned.

He was completely crazy, she decided, with a zany logic all his own. Perhaps it took a character like him to survive the life he had chosen. Whatever it was about him, he cheered her up, all the same. They drank the tea and stamped out the fire, and then they were on their way again. And this time there was no changing her mind. She was going home to Ballatree Station.

CHAPTER FOURTEEN

IONA was the first person at Ballatree Station to see her. She came running out of the house just as Prissy and Badger rode into the clearing, tears of joy in her dark eyes. Prissy jumped down from her horse and was immediately clasped in the black woman's arms. Iona hugged her tightly, babbling incoherently in her own tongue for a few seconds in her delight at seeing the English girl again.

Prissy hugged her in return. She was thankful but more than a little surprised that they had seen nobody on the way in. The property was large and scattered, but there were usually some of the stockmen about, or the boundary riders. It was well past midday and a meal break would be long over.

She realised uneasily that it was uncannily quiet around the homestead itself, yet she was aware of a distant noise she couldn't quite identify. It was the way an imminent storm gave certain signs and warnings of its approach, yet you still couldn't quite identify it.

'Prissy, you come back,' Iona gasped, finally able to speak intelligibly. 'Boy be glad and Iona glad, too. But why you go?'

Prissy flexed her stiffened muscles. Badger slid off his nag in his ungainly way, his pots clanking ludicrously around him as usual. Iona hardly looked at him, dismissing his uncouth figure as something beneath her attention.

'We'll talk about that later, Iona. But where is everybody? It's never usually so quiet. Is Robbie all

236

right? And Mackenzie? I must see him as soon as possible.'

And she had to say his name out loud because in some strange way it brought him near, even if his physical presence wasn't evident.

'Boy sleeping now. He wake later, see you. He stop crying then. Boss gone work. We got big, big trouble.' She waved her hands towards the area extending from the rear of the homestead. 'Davy, men all gone with him.'

The nagging thought that Robbie might have been crying inconsolably without her was quickly smothered as Iona gabbled on.

'What kind of big trouble? Tell me what's happened quickly, for pity's sake.'

There were times when Prissy was exasperated by the halting speech of the Abos, especially when she wanted to know everything at once.

'Wild dingoes come. Kill many sheep.'

'Oh, God, no,' Prissy whispered.

It didn't need more than the short staccato sentences of the woman to alert Prissy to what this meant. She'd been here long enough to recognise a catastrophe when she heard of it. If too many sheep were savaged that would be disaster enough for Mackenzie. But if the scent of blood became widespread, even their own dogs could be driven wild by the smell of it and turn sheep-killers.

Mackenzie had told her more than once how a sheepman had to be ever vigilant for the dingo attacks. For weeks, sometimes months, you thought you were safe, and then the attacks came with swift, bestial savagery.

'How long have the men been gone? When did they discover the dingoes were attacking?'

'Two hour. Or Three.' Iona spoke vaguely.

Time didn't have the same kind of meaning for her as for these fine white folk, and it had been their influence that had forced her into keeping to a timetable for food and sleep. Aborigines ate when they were hungry and slept when they were tired.

'Looks as if we have to sit tight until your man gets back then, don't it, gel? 'Tis no matter. Me time's me own and I've patience enough to wait for me money.' Badger smiled encouragingly at Iona. 'I wouldn't say no to a cup o' hot soup though, missis.'

Prissy started at the sound of Badger's voice. She'd practically forgotten his existence in those moments when her vivid imagination had soared away with her, but now he came within her focus again, and she knew very well he'd be staying put until he'd got his payment from Mackenzie for bringing Prissy back.

Iona looked him up and down with dislike sparkling in her eyes. Prissy could almost read her mind. *What made nice white missy travel with bad rubbish man?* After a few seconds, Iona simply turned her back on Badger, and it was clear that in her order of things, a travelling pot-man came very far down the list.

'Boss come back soon, he say. Boy sick, and boss not like to leave him too long.'

'You're not telling me Robbie's sick as well? What's wrong with him, Iona?'

Dear Lord, what else was she going to hear? By now her conscience was pricking her horribly at leaving them all in the lurch when everything seemed to be going wrong.

It was almost as if—as if *she* had brought all this on by leaving, and even as the thought came into her mind she knew how stupid it was. It was as much mumbo-jumbo as some of Iona's fanciful ideas, and right now she needed to keep her feet very much on the ground and not go imagining that demons were controlling her fate.

'Boy only sad-sick. He be well now Prissy back. Iona sure of that.'

Guiltily, Prissy heard the confident words, said without accusation, but cutting her like a knife all the same. Robbie was 'sad-sick' without her, and she'd gone off and left him without a word, leaving Mackenzie to explain why strangers from Sydney had come and taken her away.

Sydney was like London—a weird town she had described to Robbie, one that he had vowed never to visit, because it sounded horrible and hurt your feet . . . she felt a lump come into her throat. She had tried to make things interesting to him, to widen his horizons by telling him of other things. She had wanted him to accept her and had found a way of reaching him and brightening his days, and then she had gone away . . . and how could you logically explain your reasons for that to a child who had already lost his mother?

Robbie hadn't wanted Prissy at first, but deep in her soul she knew he would want her now. At least . . . she prayed that he would, if he hadn't felt too deeply betrayed for the second time in his young life.

'Badger's going to stay until Mackenzie comes back, Iona. He has business with him,' she said quickly, pushing her thoughts on to other things.

'Don't worry about me, ducks. I'll squat down here. Just a bit of food and drink for me and the nag from time to time will suit old Badger.' He suited the action to the words and sank down in a heap of pots and clothing exactly where he was, his arms folded in front of him.

Prissy could read his mind like an open book. All right, so he wouldn't defile the homestead and annoy this aggressively protective Abo woman, nor antagonise James Mackenzie. But neither would he move until he got the money Prissy had promised him for bringing her home.

'I'll see that Iona brings you something to eat and drink,' she said quickly. 'I want to see Robbie for myself. You can put Mr Hatherall's horse and yours in the stable for now, Badger. Tell the boy I said so.'

She rushed into the house and straight to Robbie's bedroom. The boy was fast asleep, one arm thrown above his head, one thumb firmly stuck in his mouth in his usual sleeping habit. Thankfully, she saw that he didn't look ill, and Prissy felt her eyes sting at the sight of him, more dear to her than she had ever expected another woman's child could be. He was so very much like his father, which might well have had something to do with her feelings...

She tip-toed out of the boy's room, not wanting to waken him until he'd had his afternoon sleep. She hesitated outside her own room and then went inside. It was a room she'd never expected to see again, and she'd half expected to see everything cleared out, even though it was less than a week since she'd left it. But nothing had been touched, except for the pearl necklace and the note she'd left for Mackenzie. There was no sign of either of them.

The sound of horse's hoofs made her run to the window but, before she could see who the rider was, footsteps were coming along the passage, and she didn't need to look to see their owner. She whirled around, her heart pounding as Mackenzie came into the room. His face was dark and uncompromising and showed strong evidence of tiredness and strain. His clothes were dusty and torn in places. She wished she dared run to him and hold him close, but she knew she didn't have the right.

'So, you decided to come back,' he greeted her caustically. 'Were the city folk too much for you, then?'

'No, of course not—well, in a way, but not in the way you mean!' She was stammering, feeling gauche and young and suddenly very silly to be chasing about the vast, perilous outback of Australia as if it were no more than a familiar London back alley. 'You sound almost as if you expected as much,' she added accusingly.

'It crossed my mind.' He spoke without expression of pleasure or annoyance. 'But I've no time for idle chatter just now. I'll just look in on Robbie, and then collect some more ammunition. You'll have heard about our trouble?'

'Iona told me. Is it bad?'

He gave a short laugh. 'It's never good when the dingoes move in packs and get the bloodlust, lassie.'

She shuddered, the words having a primeval sound to them that made what was happening all the more terrible.

'How many sheep have you lost already?'

'More than a score, mebbe far more. It's impossible to tell yet. You'll be staying, I take it?' He looked at her keenly, and she nodded.

'I'll be staying. And, Mackenzie—Badger brought me back. I said you'd pay him for his trouble——'

'The devil you did! Anyway, I've no time for such details now. I've more important matters to deal with.'

He turned on his heel and she heard him go into Robbie's room. For a second she wilted. This wasn't the kind of homecoming she had imagined. In her hazy half-formed dreams Mackenzie had welcomed her with open arms and kissed away all the misunderstandings between them. They had gone blissfully towards their happy-ever-after...

A sharp rapping on the window made her jump, and she saw Badger's gargoyle figure hovering there. Crossly, she went outside and told him everything would have to wait, and Mackenzie had no time to be listening to either of them at the moment.

'Makes no difference to me,' he shrugged. 'Just so long as I gets me money in the end.'

'You'll get it,' she muttered.

Suddenly the clearing seemed full of people and horses as Fred and Davy and three of the stockmen came galloping in, yelling for Mackenzie to make haste with that ammunition. Prissy rushed outside to hear what was going on.

'The entire mob's starting to panic,' Fred bellowed. 'Those that the dingoes don't savage will get tangled up in the fences and be smothered by the rest. We'll lose half of them if we're not quick about it.'

Mackenzie was already out of the house and handing out ammunition and extra guns as fast as he could.

'What can I do?' Prissy asked him quickly.

'Stay here and pray.' He picked up his own gun. 'The injured sheep will have to be slaughtered and buried with the rest to be rid of the stink of blood. There are pits ready dug to tip them in. Two of you men here come with me to take charge of that. Davy, carry on and join the others.'

'I'll help with the slaughtering,' Badger's lazy voice said. 'I've got the guts for it, man.'

Badger had removed his ludicrous greatcoat and his fingers were already twitching on the barrel of a rifle. Prissy turned away, nearly gagging at the thought of it all, but realising it must be absolutely necessary or Mackenzie would never sanction killing his own sheep.

'If you can handle a gun, you're hired,' Mackenzie said without pausing.

'The girl can help bury,' Badger said slyly.

'No, I couldn't!' Prissy cried, aghast.

'You only have to tip the bodies in the pits. Right, boss?' Badger asked, suddenly part of the team.

'It's not women's work,' Mackenzie snapped.

She looked at him, her heart beating very fast. 'But it would help, wouldn't it?'

'You're damn right it would.'

She was running towards the stables with Badger before she had time to think. They mounted quickly, galloping behind Mackenzie and the others, already far ahead of them in a cloud of dust. They were out of breath when they eventually reached the place where dead sheep had already been brought to a hollow, and injured ones were being fenced in nearby, kept well downwind of the others before they too were maddened by the hot, bittersweet smell of blood. It was a nightmare, Prissy thought, her own blood curdling, and it was something she never wanted to live through again...

She caught Mackenzie's look and gritted her teeth. If she ever wanted to be counted as an outback woman, now was the time, when she had volunteered for this task. Flora no doubt would have done it, and so would she.

The stench was everywhere. She worked like an automaton, trying to disassociate herself from the act she was performing. Time and again she flinched as the sound of a gun blasted out and she hauled a deadweight animal's body into the communal grave. In the distance, other guns were filling the air with their acrid smoke and shattering noise, hounding the predators off the property.

Time ceased to have any meaning, and after what seemed like an eternity Prissy began to feel light-headed and ill. She should never have come back, she thought wildly, then she would have been spared all this. Violent sobs she couldn't control raged through her entire body at the futility of it all, and she was hardly aware that someone was shaking her arm.

'Get back to the house, my wee lassie,' Mackenzie said harshly. 'Go and rest now. We're almost done here.'

She realised that no more dead or injured sheep had been brought to them for some time, and that the men were beginning to fill in the pits. The distant sounds of gunshots were lessening. Either the whole dingo pack had been destroyed, or they had been driven off the station. Either way, the thought of so much killing was sickening and horrific. If this was what outback living was really like, Prissy wondered how any woman could have the stomach for it.

She didn't wait for any more instruction. She threw herself over the back of her horse and lay with her head bowed against the beast's back, sobbing as if her heart would break.

Once she reached the house, she almost fell off the horse and went inside to find Iona, leaving the animal just where he was. She was too weary, too muddled in her mind, to care. Her head hurt appallingly, and when she touched it, she remembered her recent fall and the ugly lump that meant she should have been taking care.

'You come with Iona,' the Aborigine woman's motherly voice said gently, and Prissy wept quietly against her ample shoulders.

'It was terrible. I never expected it. Mackenzie was so strong, but I couldn't bear it——' She was speaking in short, jerky sentences now, because she had no breath for anything more.

'Iona soothe now. Bathe hands and face and bring hot drink.'

She led Prissy to her own room. There was hot water already waiting in a bowl and the black woman helped Prissy to wash herself as if she were a child.

Then, without warning, it seemed as if a tornado whirled into the room, and Robbie flung himself at Prissy.

'I prayed and prayed that you'd come back, and Pa told me you might if I believed hard enough.'

Prissy swallowed. 'Does this mean you're glad to see me, then?'

He wriggled against her, embarrassed at the question. 'Don't go 'way again, Prissy. I want you to stay for ever and ever.'

'For ever's a long time, Robbie, but we'll see.'

She couldn't commit herself. Today had changed everything. She had seen the cruelty of the land in all its enormity, and she wasn't sure if she could cope with it for ever, not even for Mackenzie, unless...

He didn't come back to the house for some time, and she guessed he'd be out riding with the boundary men to check on the fences and see that all was as secure as possible. It was already dark and Robbie had been put to bed long ago, serene with a child's supreme confidence that Prissy was back to stay.

She wished she felt as confident about Mackenzie's welcome. They'd hardly had time to exchange civil words with one another yet, and it was late in the evening before she had washed and changed out of her stained clothes into a clean frock. She tied her hair loosely into a ribbon at the nape of her neck and let the length of it lie about her shoulders. The day had seemed endless, and she was simply too weary to try and confine it in pins.

The smell of food cooking tempted her out of her room, and she went into the dining-room where Iona was setting out two places at the table. Prissy looked at them stupidly, and Iona answered her unspoken question.

'Boss say you eat with him. Me and Davy not hungry, and pot-man eat in bunk-house.'

'I see.'

This was to be some kind of ultimatum, then. It certainly wouldn't be a tête-à-tête, Prissy thought nervously. She was undoubtedly going to get clear instructions as to her future behaviour—*if* there was a future for her here at Ballatree Station.

Mackenzie came into the room, lean and dark in a black shirt and tidier breeches than his workaday ones, and considerably sweeter smelling than he'd been earlier.

But the day had had its effect on him. Prissy could see that by the deep furrows in his brow and the tension in his jaw. She already knew that despite the nature of the land and its privations, Mackenzie wasn't a man to whom killing came easily. It must have cost him dear to slaughter so many of his own sheep today.

'We'll eat first and talk later. You must be as ravenous as myself,' he said curtly.

They helped themselves to the dish of hot stew Iona had put ready on the table, and, despite her usual way of bursting out with everything at once, Prissy found herself tongue-tied for practically the first time since meeting this powerful, self-contained man.

She had the feeling that whatever she said right now she wouldn't be able to reach him at all. She ached to be close to him, physically and emotionally, but his hard, set face invited nothing from her until he was ready.

They picked at the meal in total silence and, for all her hunger, Prissy found she could hardly touch the nourishing food. After all that had happened earlier, she had no stomach for it, and the smell of cooked meat nauseated her. It seemed that Mackenzie had little appetite either, and finally he pushed his plate away.

'Since we're both just playing with the food, let's leave it and go into the parlour,' he said.

Where Flora's portrait would smile down at them...

He shut the door behind them, and Prissy had never felt so nervous beside this unsmiling man. Where was the love now, that she was sure he was capable of feeling? Where now, the tenderness she had glimpsed in him for his son?

'Now, tell me what you meant by saying I have to pay off your friend,' he said distantly. 'He'll get his dues for pulling his weight with the task today, but why should I feel obliged to him for bringing you back? And don't worry, he hasn't been sent packing. I've told him he can sleep in the bunk-house tonight, but he's to go in the morning. No doubt you'll be wanting to say goodbye to him.'

His tone rattled her. He obviously thought her a bigger fool than ever for trusting a man like Badger. But he'd been true to his word. He'd eventually got her to Ballatree Station.

'Of course I'll want to say goodbye to Badger. I owe him that much, and if the money's a bother to you I'm perfectly ready to pay it out of my wages. I'm in your debt for my passage money and I believe in paying my debts——'

'Is that why you came back?'

It would be so easy to say yes. To stick her nose in the air and say that she had never owed anyone anything in her life before, and didn't intend to start now. It would be easier still to play on his senses and say she'd felt guilty at leaving Robbie again without warning, or simply that she couldn't stand the stuffiness of the Sydney folk sent to fetch her. There were any number of reasons she could give for being compelled to come back to Ballatree Station.

'No,' she said flatly.

Mackenzie folded his arms. Neither of them made any attempt to sit down. The atmosphere in the parlour was as brittle as toffee, and Prissy was very conscious of her own heartbeats, sickening and loud. This should be the moment when Mackenzie strode across the room and took her in his arms, seductively demanding to know if there were other, more personal reasons...

He gave a short laugh, reading some of her thoughts— but not all of them. 'Then, why? Were you overcome with remorse at leaving Robbie for the second time? Or was the thought of working for me slightly more palatable than for some pious Sydney folk?'

'It was none of those reasons,' she said, colouring, because both had a hand in her decision. But neither of them touched the most important one of all, and if Mackenzie couldn't see it then he was the bigger fool...

She saw him stare at her, standing defiantly in front of him, tense as a spring, and for a second a look of uncertainty flashed across his face. It was gone just as quickly as they heard a cacophony of noise outside the parlour. The next minute Badger poked his head around the door and came inside, garbed as usual with his long coat strung about with pots and pans.

'Begging your pardon, folks, but I'll be off tonight. I don't like the confinements of the bunk-house with all them others, so if you'll just pay me, boss, I'll be on my way.'

He beamed at Prissy, revealing his crooked, discoloured teeth in a grimace of a smile.

'I've already paid you, man,' Mackenzie said abruptly.

'That was for the killing,' Badger said. ''Tis payment for bringing your intended home that's still owing.'

'My *what*?' Mackenzie snapped.

The man winked roguishly at Prissy, who immediately knew what it meant to wish the earth would open up and swallow her. It had always seemed such an affected term... but right now it was the only term that suited her feelings—she wished herself anywhere away from the dawning look on James Mackenzie's face.

'So you told him I was going to marry you, did you?'

'I did.' She stuck her nose in the air, knowing she'd have to brave it out now. There was no point in saying Badger had misunderstood. It would only lead to a humiliating argument between the three of them.

'But you needn't worry!' she added. 'I only said it because I knew it would ensure that he brought me back.

Everything can go on as before and you have my assurance that I'll see to Robbie and not bother you at all. You'll hardly know I'm here, and there's no obligation for you to concern yourself with any thoughts of marriage!'

'You're damn right there's not!' he snapped. 'If there's any talk of marriage, I'll be the one to do it, but I can promise you I've no intention right now of marrying any woman, knowing the trouble they can bring, and certainly not one who changes her opinion every five minutes.'

Prissy bit her lip hard. She hadn't changed her mind about loving him—not from the first instant of knowing she wanted to spend her life with James Mackenzie—he was everything she had ever wanted in a man. But seeing that iron-hard jaw and those inflexible muscles, and, hearing the dismissive way he spoke about her in front of Badger, she began to wonder why the blue blazes she had ever bothered.

'When you folks have sorted out yer differences, can I 'ave me money?' Badger said amicably as the two of them glowered at each other.

Mackenzie strode across to the desk in the corner and thrust some coins in Badger's hands.

'If it wasn't for what you did to help today, I'd throw you off my property right now. So take this and be on your way, man.'

Badger looked at Prissy and touched his finger to an imaginary hat.

'I'll wish you luck then, gel, and I reckon you'll be needing plenty to be hitchin' yerself to this one. Mebbe when the dust's settled I'll come back this way and see how yer gettin' on and sell yer a pot or two——'

'I think you'd better go now, Badger,' she said quickly, seeing Mackenzie clench his hands. 'And thanks for everything.'

At the door, the pot-man glanced back at Mackenzie.

'She did say it, guv. She said she wuz coming back to marry you. Ask the folks at White Junction if yer don't believe me. She told them an' all!'

Prissy stared at the door after he'd gone through it and the sound of his ironware faded away. She hardly dared look at Mackenzie.

'You shouldn't have come back,' he said abruptly. 'Once the break had been made, it was better to leave things as they were.'

Suddenly all her confidence seemed to crumble.

'I thought you needed me,' she said in a muffled voice. 'I thought Robbie would be missing me, and I knew there'd be no one else to take care of him for ages. What else could I do?'

'You could have gone away and forgotten us.'

'No, I couldn't, that was the trouble. And I know Robbie couldn't have forgotten me so quickly. Could you, Mackenzie?'

He gave a short laugh. 'Mebbe the bairn couldn't, but a man can learn to forget anything in time, and as long as he has his work——'

She felt the weak tears bubbling up. He was so hard, not allowing any emotion to slip through that rugged skin of his, and she was suddenly exhausted with all the travelling and the trauma of this day. Her head throbbed from her fall at White Junction and she sat down abruptly on the horsehair sofa, because if she didn't she knew she'd probably fall down.

'You don't need me, then. I made a mistake in coming to Ballatree Station in the first place and an even bigger one in coming back. What a fool I am!'

She leaned her head against the back of the sofa, knowing the foolish tears were trickling down her face and doing nothing to stop them. If he thought her a weak-minded city girl, then it didn't matter any more, because it was exactly what she was. She would never come up to his expectations. She *wasn't* a second Flora Mackenzie—the perfect partner for a man like him.

She felt the sudden touch of his finger on her cheek, gently wiping the tears away. The fact that his hands were roughened by outdoor work only made them the more caring as they moved against her skin. She opened her eyes. He had sat down beside her and he looked searchingly into her face. They were so close she could feel his warm breath on her cheek, and a feeling akin to breathlessness was building up in her breast.

'Answer me truthfully, Prissy. Why did you tell the pot-man and the Hatheralls that you were going to marry me?'

'Just so Badger would bring me back,' she said quickly. 'I knew he'd do it if there was payment in it for him. I told the Sydney folk too, and they thought I was completely mad until I said you'd already asked me. You *did* ask me, so I just said I'd agreed to it.'

'Aye, so I did.' His finger had left her cheek now, but his arm had slid around the back of her, absently caressing her soft dark hair that was slipping and sliding out of its ribbon. 'But it was said on impulse, lassie, without enough thought. I should have seen what you had sense enough to see. You're too young, and far too volatile for me——'

'Since when did you ever want to settle for a quiet life?' she demanded, twisting her body to look directly into his eyes. 'It's not your style, and the day that happens you'll be hanging up your bush-hat for good, if I know you.'

'That's just it, lassie. You don't know me at all.'

'Yes, I do. I know you had a terrible time when your wife died, and because you're a man in every sense of the word you found it hard to mourn, and everybody needs to express their grief when somebody dies. Even I know that, and I've had no great learning. But I've seen the way you care for Robbie, and the way he cares for you. Some things you know by instinct, and it's obvious that you're not as hard as you pretend to be.'

'That's what you think, is it?' he said, with half a smile. 'Mebbe you're wiser than you look after all, then.'

'Old enough and wise enough to make some man a good wife, I hope,' she said with great daring, not wanting to throw herself at him unless he made the first move. It had to be him wanting her—she already wanted him so much she couldn't think farther than that.

'Aye, well, if it's a husband you're wanting after all, there's a good many to choose from on Ballatree Station,' he said evenly, his eyes never leaving her face.

She felt her face flame and she moved away from him, leaping to her feet in a temper.

'Sometimes, James Mackenzie, you can be so *stupid*!' she raged, and he leapt up just as quickly, pulling her against him so fast it almost knocked the breath from her body.

'All right, let's both stop fencing. Tell me why you told people you were going to marry me. Was it for the bairn's sake, or because of the security here?'

'No, of course it wasn't——'

'So it must be for love,' he finished for her. 'And if that's so, then the offer still stands.'

She wasn't sure if he was patronising her or not, or even if she'd been trapped into revealing her feelings.

'I never said I loved you——' she began shakily.

'Then I'll say it for you. You love me or you'd never have come back. And if love is the reason for the irritation I feel whenever you're near, and the emptiness I feel when you're not, then I suppose that means I must love you too. It just took me a while to recognise it.'

She looked up into his face, dear and familiar and suddenly very aware of her in a new and different way. Before she could say anything more his mouth had closed over hers and as she swayed against him the sensation of coming home was overwhelming. It seemed to fill her senses, sending the blood coursing through her veins, and she was miraculously, vividly alive. Her arms held him close, and she knew with certainty that they would never part again.

When they finally broke away a fraction, Mackenzie spoke quietly, his mouth still touching hers as if he could no longer bear to keep away from it. His own voice was husky now, affected by the soft pliant warmth of her in his arms.

'Do we have a bargain then, my sweet lassie, or do you still think I'm only offering marriage for my son's needs? I promise you, it's not what I have in mind, and a man has certain needs of his own.'

'And you think that a woman does not?' Prissy whispered. She was still hardly able to believe that this was really happening, and yet in her heart it seemed that she had always known the sweet inevitability of it all...

'I think my woman talks too much,' Mackenzie said, 'when we have far more interesting things to do.'